The Voiceless Song

W. Todd Harra

PublishAmerica
Baltimore

ISBN: 1-4241-2353-4
PUBLISHED BY PUBLISHAMERICA, LLLP
www.publishamerica.com
Baltimore

Printed in the United States of America

Acknowledgments

A special thanks to my mother for always encouraging me to read, and my father for sharing his unique philosophy on life; Caroline Battista and Steve Wermus for their editing expertise; all my teachers and professors who helped me along the way; Sweet Melissa; my lunchbox heroes; it's-not-me-Chris Glen for the author photo; ABQ Sacks; Alpha Eta for their bread and butter; the fine people at the Gibson Guitar Co.; Albert, Ernest, and F. Scott; and brew masters everywhere.

Part I: The Spider and the Fly

Prologue:
Terror Reigns Supreme

The game was in full swing by now. Several bottles of whiskey adorned the rickety wooden table, befitting seeing as how all the men seated at the table were from the Emerald Coast. It was a few minutes after midnight, and, as usual, Jack Savage's night crew was sloppy drunk and playing cards to pass another dull night. The small guardroom's only illumination came from the flickering candlelight as it played off the mildewed, white marble walls. The air was fetid with the stink of unwashed bodies and sour-mash-infused breath. Occasionally, squabbles broke out, which drunken card playing tends to breed, but the guards' shouts and boisterous arguing didn't wake the prisoners: most of them sleeping soundly after another hard day's work—others sitting in a thick soup of black silence. It was status quo in Sing Sing.

Adjacent to the guardroom, in the main cellblock, the silent eyes of the awake reflected off the few burning kerosene lamps suspended from the walls. The cheap government fuel caused thick oily smoke to belch from the tin lamps and from there it coagulated into a thick cloud that hung suspended from the rafters. Silence. The blinking of the prisoners' eyes was the only sound on the row. The strict enforcement of the no noise rule prevented any of the eyes' owners from making sounds that would draw negative attention their way. The numerous pairs of eyes stared silently into the murky darkness waiting for the tempest that surely was to come. It always came. Who would it be tonight? The cold winter air howled through the iron bars, fresh off the Hudson River, sounding like the voices of the ghosts of previous inmates.

"Bollocks! Ya'r cheatin', ya' lousy Protestant bast'ard!" Jack Savage shouted as he threw down his cards in disgust, then slogged down three fingers of amber liquid from a dirty glass tumbler. The newest guard, Brian, a shiny faced young Irishman from the county Cork just shrugged and smiled drunkenly as he raked the coins from the middle of the table to a spot in front of him. With the quickness of a thunderclap, Jack's demeanor suddenly changed. His stormy face melted into a huge grin as he threw back his head and brayed with laughter. Slapping the wool fabric of his pants, he grabbed for the whiskey bottle and took a healthy pull. "Ah, deal 'em up again; we still got a few hours to kill, and I'm gonna win back my money. I sure as hell ain't gonna let anoth'arh lad from Cor-gaih nick it now." The game resumed in relative peace, the five men alternately shouting as the pot changed hands.

Two o'clock found the five guards much drunker and nearing the end of their nightly ritual. "We gonna go after that fuckin' Chinaman. He's been given me these eyes all day. I swear he's using some of that Orient magic on me," Jepatha Bambury, Jack's second in command, loudly proclaimed, his face flush with the amber liquid that had been fortifying him on this particular evening.

"Aw, fo'ck off then. Ya' got to choose last night, and since I took all the lad's money tonight, I'm gonna let him choose," Jack interjected before Jepatha could continue his monologue. "And kid, while you're up grab us another bottle that we can finish our game on." Grinning from ear to ear for being included as one of the gang, Brian hopped up and scurried the couple hundred feet down the darkened cellblock, 476 feet to be precise. While Brian fetched the shine, Jack produced a small silver snuffbox from his coat pocket. It was the size of a matchbox with a soaring eagle embossed on the lid. He opened the lid to reveal it filled halfway with finely ground white powder. Jack shook a small amount out into the small impression located on the posterior portion of his hand, between the index finger and thumb. With a guttural snort the powder disappeared. "Want a pinch 'o blurney t'ah take the chill off?" he asked passing the box around.

Each man obliged and took a pinch of powder, "For my health," one guard eloquently put it as he wiped at his bleeding nose with his blue wool sleeve.

Meanwhile, from as far up as four tiers, silent eyes followed young Brian's progress down the cellblock, noting his swaying gait in silent fear. Upon reaching the end of the corridor, Brian produced a large iron key from his wide, brown leather belt and unlocked the door. Stepping out into the chilly February night air he shivered and buttoned up his wool coat against the fierce wind blowing in off the river. *Hope it warms up soon*, Brian thought to himself as he navigated to the storage shed located behind the prison. Brian lit the lantern that hung on a peg outside of the shed before entering. Under an old musty tarp, way in the back, lay the night crew's stash. Brian flipped up the tarp and retrieved a clear bottle of the amber liquid from the wooden box. The booze was brought to the prison once a week by a Westchester County farmer that lived only a few miles from the prison. The farmer, like so many of his brethren, had found it easier to distill the corn in a still in his backyard than to hawk his wares in town. People, as the farmer has learned, can't always find money to eat, but they can always find money to get drunk.

Blowing out the lantern, Brian hurriedly walked back to the main block, clutching the booze in one hand and holding the collar of his coat closed with the other. "Good boy," roared a red-faced Jack upon Brian's return. With a flash of steel, Jack pulled a knife out of his blouse and popped the bottle's cork off. Before returning the concealed knife to its home, Jack tipped back the bottle and let the fiery liquid run into his belly. With an audible sigh of contentment, Jack relinquished the bottle to the guard to his left and wiped his mouth with his sleeve. "Now let's finish this game," he said roaring with laughter and pounding the rickety wooden table. The candles burned much lower before the Irishmen finished their game.

Chapter 1

Brian voiced his desired target, and the men retrieved their wooden clubs that had been resting in a dark corner. The guards trooped up to the second tier and move to their desired cell. An order is given and the cell door clangs open. The man inside, although lying inert on his bed, is awake, knowing they would come for him eventually. The cell is only seven feet long and three feet, three inches wide, so the man is dragged out into the tier's corridor by his hair. The man makes no sound as he is pulled over the end of his wooden cot onto the hard marble floor. The guards stand over his possum-like body, and without warning begin to pummel him viciously, raining wooden blows down upon his head and torso. "You piece of shit, you're too good to beg?" screams Jepatha panting and red faced in a booze-induced rage. "We'll make you scream! Hold him down boys," he quietly says, eyes gleaming. A malicious smile slowly takes shape on his face. The beating stops, and the air is so heavy with silence it almost has the consistency of thick cream. Labored breathing sounds from the guards as they secure the man's appendages without him struggling, their liquor-laced breath filling the surrounding marble cells. Jepatha slips out a 12 oz. ball-peen hammer from his pocket, a new acquisition as of today. He had bought it from a roadside vendor on his walk to work this evening because he thought it would make a nice addition to his torture devices. Maneuvering the man's foot so it was flat on the floor Jepatha Bambury proceeds to break every one of the man's toes on his right foot. The men watching cringe, this is bad—even for them. Sweat from Bambury's face pools on the floor; he is incredulous: the man has hardly squirmed. He is almost too sickened himself to go on, but raises the hammer again and again. Thwack! Thwack! THWACK!

The man begins to emit a noise generated from the primordial portion of the brain; low and animal it sounds across the cellblock. This is what Jepatha has been waiting for. In a rage of ecstasy, he begins swinging the hammer at the ankle and foot, iron hitting soft flesh and bone. With each bone-crunching thwack that echoed throughout the long corridor, the prisoner's screams could be heard echoing off the walls mixed with the maniacal laughter of the guards, a symphony wrought from hell. The silent eyes water in anticipation of their eventual night; their torture time would come, too.

After all metatarsals are smashed, Brain spits on the inert prisoner, "Ya' fo'ck…ya' scar faced freak! Aye've shit out better men than ya'! Mar'k my words, we'll be back another night soon." With that, he spins and walks down the length of the tier running his club down the bars of the cells on the way to the stairs making a loud repetitive clanging sound that causes most of the population to jump.

"Leave me for a minute," Jack tells the remaining three while crouching over the inert prisoner. "He's mine." The three remaining guards exit the tier silently and retreat to the guard quarters. The prisoner lying on the ground, close to unconsciousness, knew what was coming; it's what always came. Savage grabs the man under his arms and heaves him back into the cell. All the violence having made his aroused, Jack adjusts his crotch with a grimy hand and grins, showing his yellowed, crooked teeth. Slapping the prone man, "Ain't ya' even gonna foi-ght chicken shit? Makes for ma'rh fun." Savage ripped the man's pants down and began to gratify himself. The inert man could only moan in pain, pain so great he slips into sweet oblivion before Savage climaxes. Thank the Lord for small favors.

Chapter 2

The cell doors crash. The usual yelling of the guards plays in the background like some ethereal dream. "Opfer! Opfer, you shit, get the fuck outta your cell!" In the back of my mind I can hear the heavy pounding of the morning guards' feet on the metal stairs. "Opfer…Aw fuck, not again…Someone call the doctor! Now!" he shouts before yelling down the line, "Opfer won't be making it this morning; line clear!" The cell door crash and the tramping sound of 800 pairs of boots marching in lockstep echoes through the block. Darkness again.

"Hey there lad, can you hear me?" a congenial voice asks while gently shaking me. I open my eyes for the first time since my beating, intense pain shooting through my body. It's a kind of pain I've never experienced before, a debilitating agony. Birds pecking at my eyes couldn't bring more pain. The coppery taste of blood fills my mouth. I kind of turn over on my cot and see through my blurred vision the winter sun filtering in through the high iron bars. I squint at the sun and turn and vomit a stream of blood and bile off my cot, head spinning from the pain. I try to focus my eyes and can make out the waifish Dr. Warren standing over me. The man, the charlatan, the legend himself, my head falls into the cheap mattress and I vomit into it, too weak to pick my head out of the vomit, I just turn my head. "Feelin' sick? Eh?" Warren states the obvious, slightly chuckling to himself and not bothering to pick my head out of my vomit. Not like I expect him to.

The sonofabitch cares nothing for the inmates; he just makes sure inmates stay fit enough to work and are not faking illnesses. Inspecting my mangled feet while I lie in agony he comments, "Someone did a number on these. I'll be back with something for those later, but for now," he opens the black leather grip he left on the marble walkway and produces an amber vial with some liquid in it, "we'll give you a little laudanum for the pain. What's your name, son?"

Through a thick tongue I manage to get out, "Gregor...Gregor Opfer." I gaze up into the narrow face, framed by a shock of white hair, a neatly trimmed van dyke beard, small sunken black eyes, complete with wire-rim specs. Ever the prodigal grandfather figure. We have something we call people like you in my country, I think through the waves of pain racking my body, *Stück Scheisse.*

"Where you from, Opfer?" the good doctor asks absentmindedly as he fills a dropper with the opaque liquid. I look up at him by just moving my eyes from my position on the cot and spit out one of my canines onto the floor in a shower of blood. Laughing, the good doctor says cheerfully, "Open up there, Opfer, that's a good lad. I'll be back later." He drops the liquid down my throat. I gag as a wave of nausea washes over me but manage to get the tiny amount of liquid down. The doctor closes his grip and lights a cheroot before walking down the tier whistling. I sink into blissful oblivion as the opiate takes affect.

The next few days are like a horrific dream. I have visions of men and demons visiting me. Holding me down, as I fight and scream while they try to take my feet, trying to force their demonic poisons down my throat. They cannot fit enough men into the tiny cell to properly hold me down and must drag me onto the tier. My shouts and screams echo through my brain over and over: almost like shouting from the top of a mountain and listening to the sound of your own voice repeated as it grows softer. My brain roils and froths like the sea during a storm, but my body can't respond. I see my step-father's murdered body lying languidly in the cold Prussian dawn with flies collecting on the burned corpse...the bodies of all the men and women I have killed...the women I have raped...the graves I have dug in the forest. Then I saw nothing.

Chapter 3

The silent eyes of the prisoners listened for four nights straight as the European immigrant screamed again and again all night long; his sweating hands could sometimes be seen by adjacent cells reaching out between the bars, his voice pleading in strange tongues. The guards, hearing his distant infractions of the noise code, paid no heed on orders from the good doctor's instructions, "Some of the medications I gave the Prussian fellow will most likely cause hallucinations."

Chapter 4

Time has no bearing on one locked in a cage such as this; only the changing seasons seen through a tiny cell window alert me to the passage of time. I have no idea how long I chased the dragon. I awoke on *a* morning, this morning of whenever to an empty cellblock; most of the inmates are out for the day doing the slave labor the state seems to think will aid in our rehabilitation. I discover upon my awakening that Dr. Warren has put these bulky wooden splints on my feet and lower legs. I notice blood has seeped through the small screw holes holding the wooden pieces onto my lower legs and trickled down my leg where it has dried, like a crimson trail leading to my shattered feet. The wood is stained and dark from my blood. From the operation or from leakage I cannot tell. Either way, it hurts like Hades, and I fiend for more laudanum. The pain is unbearable, but manageable in a way that the initial pain was not. I can't stand up on my poor legs, for the pain is too great, not that the wooden splints are conducive to walking even if I could get onto my feet. Sitting up, I scoot my back against the wall and very gently dangle my legs over the edge of my cot, my knees almost touching the opposite wall. The cell is very tiny, only seven feet long, about the length of the cot, a little over three feet wide, and about six and a half feet high. Any leftover room is taken up by my slop bucket that sits at the end of the cell, my tiny window above it. Three iron bars separate me from freedom.

Shifting my weight on the thin mattress made of cornhusks and cheap fabric, I groan audibly in pain and from the stench of the damn thing. After my beating, sodomization, and subsequent illness, my mattress and thin woolen blanket are soaked with urine, feces, sweat: a stink worse than these foul little cells are usually infested with. The mattress is suspended on a wooden frame made of rough-hewn pine, fresh from the forests of New York's own Westchester County. I know because I can hear some of my fellow inmates as they fell trees during my quarrying duty; their shouts usually interrupt my thought processes, followed by the inevitable boom as the said tree comes crashing to the forest floor. Under my bed is the only allowed piece of literature, the Holy Bible. I groan and unbutton my black and white striped suit, stained and foul smelling, down to the waist and shuck it off gingerly. I notice with disgust that my chest has black and blue welts adorning it. *Those fiendish guards*...I let out a suppressed audible groan and reach under my bed to retrieve my beloved Bible. Dusting it off, I carefully set it in my lap. In the past two years of my incarceration, I have kept my mind sharp by memorizing passages from the Bible; I'm up to about seven hundred now. Apparently, there are some whisperings of an inmate memorizing nearly fifteen hundred, although I can't confirm it due to the strict no-talking rule. I run my hand lovingly over the dusty and worn leather cover, feeling the gilded parchment pages. The smell of the paper and ink, a breath of freedom...ah, freedom.

Being devoted to almighty God, I used to know a great deal of scripture in my native tongue. But, since emigrating from Prussia, I have made an effort to re-learn it all in my newly adopted tongue. It is not hard to learn this much scripture in a new language; the work I left behind required me to be somewhat of a linguist. These dull-witted guards can't even write their own names, much less memorize a few passages of scripture, and yet they have the power to beat a man like me who has done absolutely nothing to infringe upon the rules. The anger wells up in me as I clench the Bible with white knuckles. Gritting my teeth, I place the Bible gently back under my bed and study the black-stained marble walls. *I must escape this inferno.* I stare at the wall the rest of the day in deep concentration. Before too long, the rhythmic sound of the inmates marching back to their cells in lockstep can be heard, snapping me out of my trance. I get up and support most of my weight with my hands, face pressed to the bars, watching the blank faces file by me, heading to their respective cells. *The fools, they are broken men. I have seen that look on men before as they crouched on their knees before me, knowing pleading will do nothing to restore their life...right before I plunged my saber through their throats; the men's blood then spilling onto the Germanic forest floor of antiquity...the lifeless eyes staring up at me...accusing me. These men here in Sing Sing are the living dead. I refuse to lie down and die like a dog,* I think with resolve, gripping the rough iron bars so hard my knuckles turn white and blood seeps between my cold fingers.

Chapter 5

The warden, Elam Lynds, believes that physical labor deters inmates from committing future crimes, therefore effectively rehabilitating the inmate. Work? Yes, maybe a little work would be good to rehabilitate us *sinners*, but the backbreaking slave labor we are subjected to is above and beyond mere work. It's inhumane. I hear what we endure is similar to what the Negro people are subjected to in the southern states. Except I have heard that the masters of those southern slaves feed them, clothe them, and keep them in good health. And why wouldn't they? You want your "equipment" in prime condition for optimal yield. Lynds should take a lesson from the southern masters on how to maintain equipment. I wouldn't subject a mule to the atrocities Lynds subjects us inmates to. I guess his tiny mind can't grasp the simple farming concept—you reap what you sow. Sow the seeds of hatred and well…when his crop comes in he'll surely choke on it.

The captain, Lynds, is man of medium stature with a wide puffy face and a great shock of white hair, slicked back with little curls on the back of his head. His most notable features are his small, beady black eyes, sunk into his face, that always bear a look of unfettered malice. He could out stare a serpent. Lynds always wears black suits with a white collar underneath, although he is about as far removed from the clergy as any man that has walked the face of this earth. He's the Puritan from hell; even *they* would've kicked him out of their society. His rules, regulations, and work ethic are not fit for a prison but rather, fit for purgatory. That hogshead of shit makes us work ten-hour shifts straight with no food or water breaks. We are fed once a day, and only get new clothes when our old striped uniforms are threadbare. Sometimes in the winter the cold becomes almost unbearable in the flimsy uniform and cheap down jacket issued to us from November to February.

The only thing that keeps his system together is fear: the fear of punishment if we don't work as hard as we can, because it's certainly not the food. Our diet consists mainly of gruel, mush, and porridge, and stew: all semisolids. For a treat, we may get some coarse bread, moldy vegetables, and twice a year, we get an egg. Egg day is a big deal, and even though there is no talking, I can feel the excitement coursing through the cellblock on each of the four total egg days I have experienced. It's *something* to break the monotony, something to break the boredom of work and the hours of solitary contemplation that an inmate finds himself with at night.

Lynds subcontracts out with private contractors, and everybody comes out ahead, except for the inmates, of course, and the citizens of New York State. Essentially, the contractors get next to free labor, which increases their profit margin because they can keep their product dirt-cheap. Consequently, these contractors are able to competitively bid, and win, substantial federal contracts that generate more revenue for their company. Their company can then undersell competition, run them out of business, and then dictate market price. The state of New York receives money from the contractors as compensation for the inmate labor, and Warden Lynds gets kickbacks from the ones he chooses to deal with, and has subsequently become a very wealthy man. The gem in this operation is that I am New York State property, and private contractors are getting "free" use of me to manufacture goods that will then be eventually *sold* to the citizens of New York. So, instead of inmate labor benefitting them, it is actually *costing* them. And even though this system ends up costing the good citizens, it still manages to reinforce itself.

Upon my official processing into the New York penal system, I was assigned to work for the Stone Guild Corporation because of my prodigious size. I filed into the prison yard on a balmy April day along with twenty-three other inmates wearing whatever we had been sentenced in weeks or months ago. The other men and I were stripped down and forced to march under a small water tower and be subjected to a torrent of freezing water to effectively sanitize us while a dozen blue-uniformed guards swung their clubs idly and looked on. Once bathed, we were each dusted with talcum powder and pronounced by the prison doctor, "Effectively sanitized." As we stood naked and manacled together, the warden walked down the line ordering a guard to chalk us on the back, coding us for what kind of work we would do. Taking one look at my six foot, four inch frame, rippling with sinewy muscles, he immediately had me chalked with 'O', the code to signify outdoor manual labor, not that that didn't suit me. I'd rather be outside than sitting in a dusty prison shop making barrels or mattresses. But before deciding my work fate, he puffed his reasonable five-foot-eight- or nine-inch frame up to try to look me in the eye. "What happened to your face, boy?"

His breath was warm against my naked neck as I sort of tilted my head down to address him without really moving it, "Fell, sir."

Giving me a queer look he replied sharply, "I hope so, boy; you lie to me and you'll be sorry, really sorry. My men," he said motioning with his hand to the men behind him, "here will add another scar to that ugly mug." He smartly stepped away and continued down the line, popping open a gold pocket watch to consult. We stood nude, shivering, until the warden was finished before being marched into the cellblock for the very first time. And that was that for my first day; work didn't begin until my second official day as an inmate.

By luck of the draw, I happened to be assigned to the Stone Guild Corporation, a company that quarries white marble from the area. The marble is known to the rest of the area as Sing Sing marble for obvious reasons, and is highly sought for state houses and by the wealthy for the trimmings in their mansions. The entire prison, built about twenty-five years ago, was constructed entirely from prison labor using marble quarried from this site, and the quarry continues to be a rich source of marble for the greater New York area.

After being issued my uniform and Bible, I was marched to my assigned cell, feces and blood covered the moldy walls from its last inhabitant. I had nothing to clean them up with and scraped at the stains best I could with a small stone. Darkness fell quickly that night, and I was left to my thoughts in deafening silence, not touching the watery horsemeat stew and crusty black bread with a tin cup of tepid water. I sat up all night long. It was that first night that I quickly learned about the nightly beatings. A new inmate, Earl Jenning, that traveled up in the train car with me that afternoon was dragged out of his cell and beaten. I could see him from my vantage point on the second tier as he lay on the first floor begging and pleading as Savage and his crew pummeled him with their truncheons. Bloody and crying, he tugged at their trouser legs and writhed about in cataclysmic spasms. The man's right arm never was the same after that night and soon it withered and kind of died off. It shrank and became utterly useless, and he was transferred to indoor labor, I guess, because I never saw him with the outdoor crews. His pathetic screams echoed through my mind all night on that first night, as did the screams of past victims, until the ebony framed in my cell window turned steely and my first day of forced labor commenced.

Chapter 6

The days here up the river are long, but could be longer if I was stuck in my cell for the duration of the day like I am on Sundays. Sometimes I almost look forward to the workweek after sitting in my cell all day on the "Sabbath." Sick. These muckwashers have nearly managed to brainwash me. I 'enjoy' their tyrannical labor! And if I didn't keep my mind limber reading the Good Book, I probably would be no better than a drooling minion of the warden and his sadistic guards.

My workday starts at seven o'clock and ends at five o'clock. At six, when the sun is just starting to replace the moon, we are roused and marched lockstep to waiting wagons. Lockstep is a form of discipline invented by Warden Lynds. Every man must march in perfect unison as close to the man in front of him. A *clomp, clomp, clomp* resonates through the cellblock in perfect time when the men are marching to and fro their cells; it's the sound of my insanity, our insanity. In addition to the stepping in time, one's face must be wiped free of all expression and contain the distant look an idiot has—or a man that has stood too close to an exploding shell. I learned the hard way what expression to acquire my first full day at Sing Sing. "Hey, you filthy European, stop looking my way," yelled a guard, his breath rank with liquor as he swung his club at my knees bringing me to the floor in pain and halting the entire procession of men. "I'll be seeing you later, and maybe we'll work on how you ought to look when walkin' 'round here, you fuckin' piece of foreign scum." That was my introduction to Jepatha Bambury, and later that night to *the bath*. I pushed myself to my feet, not giving that bastard the satisfaction of seeing me grovel. "All right scum, get movin'," screams Bambury, shitty little wisp of a mustache jumping about in drunken excitement. I started lockstepping again in immense pain, but gritting my teeth, I managed to make it to the end of the block and out into the dusty, weed-choked yard. Great cupola topped guard towers, located where the outer walls intersect, are loaded with blue-clad men that keep a wary eye on us as we are halted before being loaded into the buckboard wagons. The metal on their muskets glinted in the early morning light, *I bet those bastards would love an excuse to take a potshot at us*, I mused before being roughly thrown onto the wagon by a blue-clad figure. The guard then ran a chain through the iron ring on the manacle of the right leg of each prisoners before padlocking it to the ring bolted to the wagon floor.

"He-yah!" the driver yelled, whipping the horses.

We are driven in the bouncing buckboard about two miles to the quarry and are quarrying by seven o'clock. The dusty, rutted road winds through the New York countryside, and we head in a southeasterly direction from the prison. Three guards on horseback as well as a guard accompanying each of the drivers of the ten wagons are all armed to the teeth with muskets, revolvers and sabers, like any of the twenty men in each of the bucking wagons, all manacled together, pose a threat. The wagons pulled into a clearing, dotted only with scrub pine, and before me lay a gaping hole in the earth. A civilian contractor, one of the overseers, assigned all the new inmates jobs. Sizing me up he said, "Ye'r a biggin'. I reckon you'll do fine diggin' an' loadin'." Without further instruction, he unceremoniously handed me a pick, and thus began my career as a Sing Sing slave.

The foreman of my site, Leland Gifford, is a downright sadistic man, which makes him such a valuable man to his company. Gifford is a rail-thin, tall man, skin leathery and wrinkled from years of managing men out in the elements. He always wears a fedora no matter what the weather, and chews tobacco with almost a manic fervor. Gifford's output is greater than any other site Stone Guild owns, and yet he has the fewest men. His method is simple really, if he thinks for even a second one of his men isn't working to maximum capacity he tells the Warden Lynds and that inmate is tortured with one of the prison's in-house discipline devices, or he will simply use a little motivational tool of his own. Gifford is a very *hands-on* foreman, meaning he isn't above jumping down into the pit with that bullwhip of his and lashing inmates. The trick, I have found, is not to stop while receiving the whipping; it'll stop faster. "Let's go, you Goddamn piece of Eur-peen trash," he screamed at me my first day in the pit, tobacco juice raining down my neck and staining the back of my striped uniform. "I've watched you slack all day. Don't think I'd notice did-ja? Think 'cause this is your first day ya' can slack off? Hell, them niggers over there been quarrying more stone than you, and they ain't got half the bulk you got." I dared sneak a peak at the coloreds he was referred to only to have the whipping commence. There is almost lack of air as the whip travels back, then the whistling as it flies forward, and the ensuing snap and wave of pain. I bit my tongue until blood flowed freely from it as Gifford whipped me, but refusing to make a sound, which only infuriated him more. Eventually he tired and left me alone. The pain was a welcome penance for the sins of my past, though I could hardly swing that pick the rest of the day. I still have the scars to this day, and occasionally new ones are added. But I learned on that first day, it is literally a life-and-death struggle in the pit.

I swing a pick for ten hours a day, and have for the past two years, six days a week. Some of the muscle I lost in the past years while I have been in America has been rapidly replaced…my reflexes never faded. I have been trained to kill in the king's most elite force, Die Sonneleute, and if the prison officials knew this, they probably wouldn't let me out to work; hell they wouldn't come within six feet of my cage. The policemen that arrested me found that out. I killed three before they could subdue me.

Chapter 7

The moonlight filtered in through the high window as I reclined on my bed the second night of my incarceration in Sing Sing. The place breathed an unhealthy silence at all times, almost like a slumbering bear in wintertime. Normally in "silent" places like churches and wakes, one would hear the clatter of objects being moved and dropped, feet shuffling, and even the occasional forbidden whisper. Not so much here, the inmates are scared to make even the slightest noise, lest the guard's wrath be directed toward them. Occasionally, I'll come to find, if the circumstances are dire, a note is floated down the cells. This is hard to do because paper is contraband, and once received, the note must be destroyed lest the guards find it. Last night, the night my fellow 'incarceree' was maimed, a note was floated to try to find out if he was still alive. Since most of the inmates are illiterate, I doubt many of them even have use for floating notes. When the scrap of parchment paper, ripped from the Bible, reached me, I read the shaky handwriting: Es he elive. It was written in blood. I ate the bit of paper. Hell, I had no idea if he was alive or not.

Even though the chilly April air swirled and howled outside the cellblock, the temperature inside must have been eighty degrees, with humidity to boot, or so it seemed. Sweating, I kicked off the wool blanket and stared unblinking at the ceiling. A rustling sound on the floor attracted my attention, and shifting my attention to the floor, a rat the size of my fist wove through the bars and headed farther on down the tier. Sighing, I laced my hands behind my head and reviewed the day. Finally, I was able to drift off to sleep with the boisterous laughter and yelling of the guards somewhere way down the block, barely audible. At some point in the night, they came for me.

I never had a chance to fight. The cell door crashed open, and two guards were holding me down before I became fully conscious. An all-too-familiar face from earlier was in my face. "Ya' foreign sonofabitch. Maybe a little slow? That's okay; you have a good teacher now. Believe you me, by the mornin' ole' Bambury here will have taught ya' to walk in proper formation. Eh?" His whiskey laced breath washed over me in waves. Grinning, Bambury revealed his crooked yellow teeth, and I was close enough to discern a dusting of white powder in the wispy little semblance of facial hair he tried pawning off as a mustache. His pimply red chin quivered in excitement, sweat beading on his narrow face. Swiveling my head, I could see two more guards out on the catwalk along with Bambury; fighting was a very viable option, but Sing Sing was my cross to bear. "Be a good lad and don't make this any harder on yourself. If I letcha go you gonna fight?" I shook my head. "That's a good lad." Bambury said soothingly with a pleased grin on his face, "Lets get on with it then." He motioned with his hand to follow, turned on heel and strolled off like we were going for a walk in the park.

They led me down the walkway to the steps and down to the bottom tier, and then marched me all the way to the end of the cellblock, blue-clad guards flanking me the whole time, truncheons polished and ready. Upon reaching the metal door at the end of the cellblock, Bambury produced a large iron key ring and flipped through them until he found the desired key. With a vaudeville flourish, he unlocked the door and swung it open and announced loudly enough for all 800 inmates to hear, "Welcome to your first bath!" His voice echoed off the white marble walls and reverberated in my ears, which were suddenly filled with the sound of my own pumping blood; *thump, thump*. The contraption that faced me was unlike anything I had ever seen before, and something I will never forget until the day I die. *Thump, thump!*

The bath is a wooden box stood up on end, the opening facing the doorway. A chair sits in the middle and a little lip at the bottom of the open side to catch any stray water. Over the chair, a pipe extends from the wall to over the top of the box with a chain hanging off to the side of the tiny room. A hole is cut in the top of the box to allow water from the pipe to flow directly into the box, and onto the person sitting in the chair. It is in essence, a water closet device; it's dimensions being roughly seven foot high by three feet wide by my quick calculations. "Well, what are *you* waitin' for? Sit the fuck down!" Bambury commanded, interrupting my incredulity. The guards behind me snickered; *I'd have you boys for supper*, I thought but then stepped forward and took a seat with growing trepidation. I tried to steady my mind as I have been trained to do as the guards tied me to the chair using leather straps. A metal collar is fastened around my neck to complete the contraption. "Now the fun part," Bambury proclaimed giggling, stepping to the side and grabbing the chain while the two guards that could fit into the tiny room backed out. A cold rush of water hit my body, electrifying every nerve in my body. Ice-cold water, pumped directly from the Hudson, filled the collar, past my chin and over my mouth. I shook the water out to keep breathing. Bambury and his minions laughed hysterically like gypsy children who've just pilfered a loaf of bread from a kiosk. My body started to convulse with racking shivers. My jawbone clanged against the metal collar, as Bambury adjusted the height of the pipe to allow the water to fall from an even greater height.

I bathed nearly all night. The guards took turns once Bambury got tired, and upon leaving, he ordered the remaining four, "Keep this up until it's time for morning roll call. I'm going to get some shut-eye, if ya' have any problems, fuckin' figure 'em out." While walking away he spun on heel and grabbed his chin as if in thought, "And one more thing," he said addressing a particular guard, "he doesn't get a dry uniform before going to work detail later this morning." Turning to me, Bambury said, voice dripping with sarcasm, "Hopefully we won't have to repeat this little lesson, but if you refuse to learn how to do things properly here at Sing Sing, then we can make this a nightly occurrence until you do." He whistled a cheerful little tune as he walked away. The freezing water flowed and I struggled to remain breathing the rest of the night.

Chapter 8

"Opfer!" A voice calls out. Startled, I snap out of my reminiscent daydream only to be greeted by the excruciating pain from my bound feet.

"Yeah," I reply, voice thick with pain, but not wanting to betray it.

"How you feeling?" The voice revealed itself: Dr. Warren.

"Well enough sir," I say with obvious disrespect, my Prussian accent purposely coming back and making my w's sound like v's.

"Good, good. We wouldn't want you to be bored now would we?" he says while pulling a tobacco pouch from his vest and starting to roll a cigarette.

"Will I be able to go back to work?" I ask with obvious discomfort, torquing my body to face him.

Laughing and looking up from his paper skin filled with finely ground brown leaves, "Good heaven's no, you shan't walk normally again. They did a real number on those feet of yours." Carefully rolling his prize up and licking the end, staring at it and apparently satisfied, the charlatan continues, "I've talked it over with Warden Lynds and have gotten your work detail changed to the shoe factory. You'll be able to sit all day, because you'll obviously only be working with your hands." The *Scheisse* beams as if he is doing me a favor. Not waiting for a reply, he continues his monologue, "As you know, Warden Lynds says, and I must agree with him, 'Idle hands *are* the devil's workshop.' And we don't want any devils here, now do we? You'll be a better man if you ever get out of here." His face glowing like he actually believes the manure he's preaching; he takes a match from his pants pocket and strikes it on the bars to my cell then holds the flaming match his cigarette. "Mmm," he utters inhaling the rich smoke, "Blend of Arabic and Virginia tobaccos."

31

With his cane, he reaches in and pokes at the wooden framing around my feet. Pain shoots through my body, but I don't move a muscle. "How's this all holding up?"

Staring sullenly up at him I reply, "Well enough, a little bulky in these confines."

"Well, to be honest with you Opfer, I wasn't in the right frame of mind the other day when doing this, you know what I mean?"

I get a grin and wink then he cocks his head and makes a drinking motion—like we're sharing a secret! *You devil; you've probably crippled me!*

"Speaking of which," he says pulling out a flask, "think I will; want one for the pain?" The flask is offered in my direction. I shake my head. "Don't say I didn't offer." And with that, he tips the silver flask back and pulls it, then inserts the tiny white cigarette back between his thin bloodless lips. While screwing the cap back on his object of vice, he jovially continues, "I'll fix them right up for you if you're experiencing any discomfort, 'cause we need you back working."

Sullenly, I look up at him, "When do I start back?"

I am met with a furrowed brow, cocking his head to the ceiling, "I'd say the day after the morrow will do just fine; give you another day."

Like he's doing me a favor, the impetuous pig!

Changing the subject entirely, "You speak well for a foreigner. I'm impressed. How long have you been in the country?" he asks peering through the bars into the dim light of my cell.

"Four years," I answer in almost perfect English.

"Amazing, just amazing," he mutters scratching his chin.

"Pas vraiment quand vous parlez huit langues couramment," I say, telling him in French that I speak eight languages fluently.

"Oh, a smart one." He takes a drag of his cigarette pensively and muses under his breath, "Not just some piece of immigrant trash. Well then my boy, how's your Spanish? Porqué está adentro aquí?" When he asks me my reason for being here I immediately clam up. He notices and stops our little exchange puzzled.

Staring at him stoically, I utter, "Ik ben onschuldig." The ignorant sack of chaff has no idea how to speak Dutch. He stares right back at me; I can almost see the antagonistic seeds germinating. Dr. Warren is used to dealing with ignorant fools; he is the kind of man that *despises* when someone has more intelligence than him, especially a lowly immigrant inmate.

Puffing up he says, "By the way, I've been meaning to ask you, the other day when I was dressing your injuries I noticed some strange markings on your arm, almost like the ancient Chinese art of inking the skin: tattoo I believe it's called. What are those markings?" I sit and remain silent, hoping my impetuous behavior will go unreported to Warden Lynds. "Fine then," Warren hisses at me, his eyes mere slits, "but I have copied them down and sent the sketches to a colleague of mine at Oxford with whom I studied medicine." I instinctively rub at my upper right bicep and continue to stare at him. He takes a drag off his smoke, drops it, and grinds it out with his shoe in front of my cell, wipes his nose, pivots, and marches off. As he walks back to the stairs, he calls over his shoulder, "Oh, Opfer, don't forget to keep reading your scripture. As you know, God forgives all sins!"

Chapter 9

I have been incarcerated in Sing Sing for two years and ten months, my sentence beginning in 1850, and sometimes I believe these three years have been longer than the duration of my cumulative thirty-three years of age. The first few months were the hardest getting used to. I would almost swear sometimes that God simply doesn't *exist* in this den of inequity. Can he not penetrate these white marble walls? I have reached out to him time and time again, and he just doesn't seem to be there, and now he cripples me? What kind of God does that? I fear I may be losing faith! For the first time since being in Sing Sing, I hang my head and sob great, wracking sobs. Then I open my Bible and begin reading; maybe I can gain my salvation through the Good Book.

I used to pass my time in the first few months imagining what I would be doing if I were free and where I went wrong. The cell is much too small for pacing, so I would sit on my uncomfortable cot and think about the "what ifs." The inmate morale quickly set in; and by that I mean one either can go crazy thinking about the outside world or focus on doing his time. And, thus, I quit thinking about alternate destinies, and instead focused on doing my time, on my terms, though. I wasn't going to be a total slave to the system, I vowed. Sometimes though, I would daydream about my past, and let it unfold like the odyssey it was, savoring every colorful detail, or would be haunted by uninvited nightmares of unimaginable terror. I thought about my pseudo-happy childhood in St. Goar, located in the lush Rhine valley, with all my brothers and sisters, eating bratwurst and spicy sauerkraut, washing it down with great ornamental steins of black porter beer. Unfortunately, as the time line in my mind wore on, those pleasant memories turned to the bodies buried in the forest, the face of each victim haunting me. I'd wake up in the freezing cold soaked with sweat, dead tired from work, but unable to fall asleep due to voices of the dead keeping me awake.

I thought about Helga a lot at first; I would've thought about her regardless of my incarceration or not…The memories of her soft pale skin, radiant smile, chestnut hair, and ample bosom brought about hours and hours of solace, fighting the hours of the long, dark nights up the river with her radiance. As the months wore on, April turned to summer, and summer in turn gave way to autumn: my mind could only focus on the way Helga had been brutally snatched from my life, and was now my reason for being here. Helga was my angel, my savior, my temporary redeemer.

One day, I just shut it all out. All the pessimism, it was killing my soul. I couldn't think of anything because my whole life converged into one giant mess, my past too painful to think about, even my beloved Helga. I decided I was over and done with that; I needed to focus on repenting and redemption. I needed to get out of this cell on my own two legs before I got hauled out in a wooden box. So, I turned to the Bible. My qualifications for my previous service included the necessity for keen intellect, and having graduated at the top of my class from the university in Heidelberg, I possessed the ability to process and disseminate mass amounts of information as well remember details with an almost inhuman capacity. I turned my mind to memorizing the English Bible, having already read and memorized a large portion of it in my native tongue.

I stop daydreaming and lean forward and rest my forehead on the cool marble wall, the smell of dampness and musk filtering up into my nostrils. The injury has given me ample time to think and reflect. Memories I vowed to never think about again, my time in Sing Sing, my life. My legs hurt like the horses of Hades are pulling at them, with Gabriel himself at the reigns. Shifting, so I can lie down, I let out a groan of pain. As the pain subsides, I wipe the sweat from my brow and stare at the ceiling. I begin quietly reciting the book of Psalms; after awhile I tire and finish the tin cup of tepid water I saved from last night. A troubled sleep greets me.

Chapter 10

The prisoner on tier two silently rocked back and forth on his bed, occasionally fingering his left ear; the ear that had been chewed off by rats one night when he lay too sick to fend off the attack orchestrated by the rodents. The prisoner was tall and gaunt; a shadow of a beard played across his face, and long greasy hair dangled in his bloodshot eyes. Under his breath, he repeated frantically, "Oh, God, quiet now, quiet." The prisoner had been incarcerated in Sing Sing for the last 14 years, since '36, 14 long, hard years. The solitude, physical, and sexual violence had taken its toll and eroded this once-crafty criminal's brain to mush, but he did realize the new prisoner next to him was in dire trouble.

A foreigner had been assigned to the cell next to him about two months ago, when the weather was cooler and trees in blossom. Now it was hot and humid, the cell stifling, even in the middle of the night. The prisoner and the foreigner were on the same work detail, so the prisoner had gotten a good look at him. Tall, light-brown hair that was thinning on top, sky-blue eyes, and a very muscular build. A long scar that ran from his right ear to his chin marred his once-handsome face, and his nose was crooked, most likely the result of a broken nose. The man always carried himself in a very stoic, angry manner. Obviously, because of the silence rule, the prisoner had never spoken to him, but sometimes heard the man crying out in the night in a strange tongue. The prisoner nervously ran his index finger around the ragged hole on the side of his skull where his ear should've been. All the finger felt was scar tissue. He repeated his silent prayer faster now as he heard shouting and footsteps.

Last night, the man had been screaming in his sleep, and the guards had pulled him out of a cell for a beating. It wasn't a bad beating, but it was just enough to serve as a warning. Guard Savage had screamed and carried on, waking the entire population, and shoved the foreigner back into his cell. Tonight, after the sun set through the tiny window and only blackness could be seen through the porthole, the prisoner heard more screaming coming from the cell next to him. He tried to stop it; the violence scared him, even though he himself had been caught in his Manhattan tenement eating the flesh of a young boy, with the skulls of five more on his windowsill. The only reason his life had been spared was the fact he had chosen to dine on ethnic boys. If it had been white children, they would've strung him up long ago. My how he now longed for some of that tender flesh...

Rocking back and forth ever faster. "Oh, God, quiet now, quiet," the prisoner repeated faster and faster as the footsteps grew louder, and shouting intensified. The foreigner in the next cell was now pleading in his strange tongue, crying and weeping while yelling feverishly. The prisoner put his fingers in his good ear and the hole on the other side of his head and tried to shut out reality. He was crying now silently; tears flowed down his face through shut eyes as the calls stopped and only the muffled grunts and curses from the guards could be heard through muted ears.

Silence. The prisoner pulled his fingers from his ears and tried to peer onto the cellblock floor. The angle wasn't right. All of the sudden, a sharp crack startled the prisoner. The man jabbed his fingers back into his ears as the curses from the whipper could be heard with the repeated cracks of the whip. The man buried his head into his flimsy mattress as hard as he could and wept. Funny though: he doesn't hear screams of pain from the prisoner. After a few minutes, it all stopped and the cellblock grew silent again. The next morning, while being marched out of the cellblock, the prisoner saw fresh blood on the floor and some small pieces of pink flesh. His feet stuck to the floor after tracking through it.

Chapter 11

I awake with a start and sit up, sweating profusely. I must've slept through my compatriots' exit to work detail. Even their insistent lockstepping didn't wake me from my tormented, opiate slumber. Rubbing my eyes, I gaze to the floor; a tray of mushy food sits there, last night's dinner that I slept through. The boiled cabbage is covered with ants, and rats must've eaten the remainder, as there is hardly a morsel left. *Even the fucking rats won't eat that rubbish,* I think with derision while taking a sip from the battered tin cup. The liquid trickles down my throat, alleviating the scratchiness all the marble dust perpetually causes. Taking another sip of water, I tenderly swing my bound feet off the cot and manage to maneuver to the slop bucket to relieve myself. I rest against the wall with one hand out, bracing myself on the marble wall while urinating. A slight turn of my head towards the window allows me to catch a breath of the fresh morning air. The small strip of sky I can see through the window is azure, and morning birds chirp in the distance. That task accomplished, I have nothing to do but conquer the eventual boredom that will surely come if I let it. My last day of sitting in my cell recovering from my wounds passes slowly. I memorize more passages from the book of Psalms, watch the prisoners return from work, and dine on a meal of black bread, boiled potatoes, and rancid salt pork.

The next day, my cell door clangs open along with the rest of them. I am sitting at languid attention on my bunk on this chilly late February, early March day when the noise from the opening doors causes me to struggle to the standing position. The pain is intense, and I hold the bars for support at the entrance to my cell. "Hold," yells Jepatha from down the line and all the prisoners stand at attention, dressed and ready to exit their cells. Some banging and footsteps ensue in the distance. Dr. Warren appears in front of my cell.

He turns and motions to an unseen character: I'm guessing Bambury, because he yells, "In step!" And the prisoners step out of their cells, right face, and begin marching down to the bottom tier to get into formation.

Dr. Warren pushes me back into my cell and throws this black leather grip onto my cot. I fall down on the bed, my binds not able to move fast enough for my body. "Damn, it stinks in here," Warren comments, his nose upturned. I can't tell if he is referring to my ripe body odor or the smell from the yellow discharge coming from the binds, not that I give a shit either way about his fine olfactory sensibilities. He fishes around in his vest pocket, grumbling to himself. Finding his quarry, he pulls out his battered tobacco pouch. While the prisoners walk by the cell, he starts rolling himself one of his cigarettes, his thin fingers nimbly sprinkling the tobacco flakes into the paper.

Once the prisoners have all left the building and Warren has fired up his smoke, he calls down to one of the new guards, "Guard! Bring me a stool up here." He picks up his grip and walks back out onto the tier smoking furiously.

One of the new recruits brings up a wooden milking stool. "That be it, sir?" he asks Dr. Warren, his freshly scrubbed farm boy face glowing red.

"Well, my boy, why don't you stay here and help me remove these binds. I might need you to hold Opfer down. We don't want him moving around, now do we?"

With a malicious grin he looks at me. "Lie down on the floor!" he commands. Using no small amount of effort, I pull myself into a standing position and swing my body onto the tier's hall and collapse on the smooth marble floor. I lay panting in pain, but not too much, for I don't want Warren to know how intense my agony is. Taking his flask from his pocket he tosses it to me, "Drink that." I take a small sip. "More! For God's sake you're gonna need it!" I take a big swig and the laudanum-laced scotch flows down into my belly. My extremities tingle, and mind feels like it's enveloped in a soft pillow. The feeling grows as the fire spreads through my belly and the nagging pain from my legs melts away into blissful oblivion. The good doctor takes a swig himself, grimaces, and passes it to the guard. "Hold him, and put this in his mouth," he gruffly tells the guard handing him a small wooden dowel for my mouth. The boy takes a hesitant sip, sets the flask onto the floor and jams the piece of wood between my jaws. That is the signal for the good doctor. He commences with pliers and a hammer on the bandaged splints. The pain is bearable for a while, my grunts echoing off the marble walls of Sing Sing. As Dr. Warren's actions get more vigorous so does the pain. It builds exponentially. A great sweat breaks out on my forehead, and soon sweat is blinding me, rolling into my eyes. Soon, my grunts turn to muffled shrieks of agony through the dowel. I pass out from the pain when he starts removing the screws from my fibula bone that had held the binds in place.

The doctor is washing his bloody hands in a bucket when I come to. He gazes down at me from his position on the stool to my prone position with a leering, drunk opiate grin and says, "Finished; no big deal." He laughs a loud booming laugh; his blood-stained white shirt jiggling with his laughter. *What's that smell?* My hands come away from my uniform sticky. Craning my head up, my mind swimming with pain, I can see vomit covering my uniform. *That fucking guard puked on me when he saw what that monster was doing to me!* Bile rises in my throat, *oh dear Lord and savior!*

Chapter 12

The guard observes with horror, and Dr. Warren watches with gleeful pleasure as Gregor vomits on himself and passes back out, his head hitting the marble floor with a sickening thud. The guard, on his hands and knees behind Gregor, looking green around the gills, dry heaves over Opfer's inert body. "What? What in the fuck is your major malfunction boy? You're vomiting again? Have some self-respect! Stop that, get up and wash him off when he comes around! Then take him to his new work detail." With that, Dr. Warren wipes his dripping tools on Opfer's filthy pant leg and stows them back into his grip. Pleased at the outcome of his handiwork, he dusts his hands together and walks back down the tier to continue with the many pressing duties of a prison doctor. *I wonder if my friend from Oxford sent me a reply in regards to those tattoos,* Warren thinks as he whistles a little tune, still feeling good from that little snoot out of the flask. *One more can't hurt.* He brings out the flask and re-fortifies himself.

Chapter 13

I am awakened by the guard pouring the bucket of water Dr. Warren washed his hands in all over me. Uniform soaking wet and tinged pink where the white used to be I hack and cough, lying on the ground like a landed fish. "Here, chum, let me help you," the young guard offers shakily, his face a white mask, and specks of vomit around his mouth. Using an arm from a vomit-covered sleeve, he pulls me up into a sitting position where upon seeing my feet, I retch. My toes have been cut off to prevent the spreading of gangrene. A flap of skin is sewn roughly over the area; pus and coagulated blood crust along the rough hemp stitching. Generally, I'd say my mangled feet strongly resemble the feet of the Chinese women I've seen on the streets of New York City. Their parents bind their feet for beauty purposes and to attract a husband, or so I'm told, but all that really happens is they end up arched up and tiny. The poor women end up crippled for life...like me. What once were feet now only look like flesh hooves! Waves of rage wash through my brain, *those pricks Bambury and Savage are to blame for this. Their day of reckoning will come,* I think angrily, my rage causing me to shake. The young man interrupts my angered thoughts by timidly asking, "Can you stand?"

I look up at him and wipe some vomit off my chin with a filthy sleeve. "I'll try," I manage to spit out, my stomach in knots.

He puts his hands under my armpits and lifts as I struggle to get my legs under me and establish balance on my hooves. I immediately fall and catch myself on the iron railing. It resounds with a hollow boom. The pain is intense but somewhat bearable as I put more and more weight onto my hooves in an immobile position. Sweat rolls down my face in rivers as I cuss in Prussian. The guard, looking apprehensive, takes a step back and fingers the sap in his belt. I take a tentative step forward, falling against the rail again as the pain shoots up my legs. "Scheisse*!"* I scream. Wincing, I expel an audible gasp of pain. Blood oozes between the buttonhole stitches Dr. Warren closed the screw holes in my legs with. I manage another slow step while supporting most of my weight on the iron railing. The pain is intense now, almost unbearable. "Guard, run and tell Doctor Warren I am going to need some laudanum if I'm going to continue walking!" I scream at him. He looks apprehensively at me like he's undecided as if he should leave me alone when I'm not in my cell. "Now, you dullard!" I shriek in pain, "I'm not going anywhere like this. I can't even walk!" He makes haste.

A few minutes later he's back with a small brown bottle. I snatch it from his hands and greedily quaff a large amount. Instant opiate relief runs through my veins. Having done his task, the young guard must've gained some courage, "Come on let's get moving down to your new work detail. But first I'll get you a clean uniform," he adds thoughtfully. The pain has lessened significantly.

Though I am still soaked in sweat, I'm able to say without panting, "Hold on, we need to take this slow." I wipe my face for the hundredth time with my vomit-covered sleeve. White knuckled and through clenched teeth, I manage to make it to the end of the tier and down the steps. At the bottom, I must stop to catch my breath. Sweat runs torrentially down my face from the exertion.

After only a minute of rest the impatient guard, having newly grown a set of testicles, prods me, "'Nuf rest, let's go." Wiping sweaty palms on my damp uniform, I clench my jaw and continue my journey toward my new work detail.

The bouncy five-mile ride to the shoe factory in the buckboard along with the laudanum in my stomach has upset it, and I vomit violently outside the factory door before being ushered inside. The foreman of my new work detail, boot making, greets the young guard and me at the factory door, "I'll have to make some room to chain this here gimp up." While he talks, his bushy mustache dances up and down, I just stand there feeling like vomiting again, but not daring.

My young escort tells him, "This boy here won't give you no problems. Hell, he can't even walk proper! You might not even get any work outta him today."

Mustache dancing, he chortles, "Oh, we'll get some work outta him today!" He stares as me menacingly, eyes bright.

At this point, I just don't care, they've done every possible thing to me. *I really can't get much lower than I am right now. What can this foreman do to me that hasn't already been done?* These thoughts swirl through my head like snowflakes in a blizzard as the foreman finds me a workstation and begins explaining my task to me. *May God damn you, too, bushy-mustache man.* I never do get a fresh uniform.

Chapter 14

The good doctor whistled a shrill little tune, off key, as he gaily skipped out of the prison. It was the first of the month. What's there not to be happy about? At the entrance, he yelled for one of the guards to tell his driver to bring his calash to the entrance. While he waited, he thought about the large wad of currency notes tucked safely inside his soft black grip. The thought of the kickbacks from the companies that used the prison labor brought a smile to his face—Warden Lynds gave Warren a cut for his role in keeping the prisoners fit enough to work. For a moment, he even entertained the thought of giving his servants the afternoon off, but that frivolous thought soon exited his head. "I'm in a good mood, but let's be realistic," he sang out melodiously. *Interesting little tune*, he thought and started whistling what he had just said. Soon the calash clattered around the corner of the prison walls, and Dr. Warren climbed aboard, grip stowed safely between his feet.

"Where to, sir?" Kwion, his Negro driver, asked looking surly.

"Why, back home, of course!" Dr. Warren sang out cheerfully.

"Hee-yah!" Kwion yelled, clicking the reins.

At the brisk pace Kwion urged the horses on, it wasn't long before the calash clattered onto Washington Street, a beautiful, tree-lined street, and stopped in front of 158, Warren's house. It was a modest colonial by royal standards; it wasn't nearly as big as some of his peers' houses, but Warren figured if the money continued to roll in as it had been lately, in a year or two he could upgrade and leave this dump— maybe move to the South End where all the truly wealthy lived. The house was set a ways back from the street and surrounded by a lush yard and beautifully manicured garden. The southern flair of the house, like the expansive front porch and intricately carved roman columns, made the good doctor's house stand out from all the other basic cape cods and decidedly Victorian residences.

After dumping his frock in the vestibule, Warren secreted himself in his ornately paneled study, poured himself a snifter of Sir Pengrove's Plum Brandy, and counted the wad of federal notes again with miserly avarice. Warren's study was his pride and joy, his safe haven, his lair. It reeked of elegance and boasted fine leather furniture, King Louis XIV antiques, leather-bound volumes of books, and carpets from the Orient. Warren especially liked the smell of his study when he would first come in from another room; the smell of fine cigar tobacco to him was the smell of his wealth and accomplishment. He made a fastidious entry in a maroon-colored, bound ledger, and was in the process of opening a hidden safe when a knock sounded at the door. "What is it?" Warren called out annoyed that somebody would have the audacity to interrupt.

"Aye haf'ta go to wor'gaih," replied a muffled voice.

Dear Lord, Warren thought. "Hold on a minute! I'll be right with you," he called. The good doctor stowed the money in the safe and locked the ledger in a drawer.

He opened the door and there stood one of the night guards from Sing Sing, looking indignant. "Where wer'h ya' all day? I thought ya' wer'h comin' back?"

Annoyed, Warren replied, "I had to stay and actually work, unlike you and your guard cronies that sit around and get snookered all night. Sorry if I don't want to live like some poor slob."

"Ah, fo'ck off then, I don'a need this. I'm goin' to wor'gaih."

"No, No don't go," cried Warren, alarmed he had pissed off Brian, and he wouldn't return. Grabbing the young man by the hand, he pulled him close circled his arms around the fine silk robe he had bought as a gift for Brian. Whispering in his ear softly, Warren crooned, "You needn't work anymore. I'll call on Warden Lynds in the morning and explain to him your new position as my grounds keeper. Of course," he added hastily, "you won't have to do any actual gardening," and added a lecherous laugh. "I'll provide for you, Brian. I will, I promise. I love you, remember?"

Brian pulled his head from Warren's shoulder where the man had forced it and looked into the tear-filled eyes. "Ya'," replied Brian in disgust that this wrinkled old sod was bawling. *What a queer,* thought Brian as old man Warren led him to his ornate and expansive bedroom and ordered Brian to remove the robe. Brian complied. Warren rubbed his hands in anticipation, smiling. The delicate, teary face had all been but replaced with a new iron façade of lust and aggression. Removing a small bronze case from his nightstand, Warren pinched out a large amount of powder onto area of his other hand where the thumb and index finger meet and snorted it up greedily. The rush of ecstasy gave the elderly man an immediate erection; drawing his lover close, he locked his lips onto Brian's in a passionate kiss. Brian shuddered in disgust, but in the interest of self-preservation, he ardently kissed the older man and then did his bidding. Dr. Warren, the master choreographer, positioned, moved, posed, and postured Brian until well after the sun surrendered to the moon.

Chapter 15

My new job entails that I sit in a dusty, poorly lit warehouse on the edge of Westchester County and cobble boots for the Dandy Footwear Company. The warehouse is a large marble structure, built using materials quarried from the Sing Sing quarry and using prison labor. It is reminiscent of the cellblock, being a large rectangular building with small windows high in the eaves, and armed guards, employed by the company, milling about. The small windows offer little light, and even less ventilation, and as a result, on cloudy days, smoky oil lamps have to be burned, adding to the pollution of the already poor air, laced with the curing chemicals of leather and airborne leather particles from the vigorous scraping that goes on on the other side of the factory.

This job is much worse than my old one for Stone Guild. At least I got to work outside. Now, I feel like I go from one cage to the next, while growing weaker with each passing day. I am afraid I will wither away. *Lord save me!* I sit at a cramped table and cobble the soles of the boots to the over cut, the extra leather from the part that encases the foot. Twenty other inmates do this; all chained together in one long row, manacled to our workbench at the foot; or in my case, the hoof. We sit hunched over, diligently working, not wanting to draw negative attention to ourselves by looking around or stopping. So there I sit over the rough-hewn wooden table, tacking small brass tacks into shoddy materials using only 15 tacks per boot, five less than the standard 20, which is one of the main reasons the Dandy Footwear Company is able to out-compete its competitors for the Army contract: it cuts corners with materials and uses prison labor. I have a quota of ten pairs of shoes an hour, or 100 pairs a day. So at the beginning of each day, I am issued three thousand tacks in a small leather sack, tacks counted by one of the brighter trustees the previous evening. At the end of the day, the foreman, Riley Cuckold, collects the empty sacks and hammers, and there damn well better be no tacks in the sack. He personally spot checks the number of tacks in each shoe to prevent inmates from putting a few less in some shoes and saving them to fashion weapons from. The men are so damn scared of the spot checks that each one religiously puts in the correct number of tacks. The newly assigned inmates that don't know how to count learn really fast.

Based on the number of shoes my section assembles, my best guess is that the factory produces about six hundred and twenty-four thousand pairs of shoes and boots a year, or two thousand pairs a day, more than enough to supply the Army over the course of a year and to leave ample pairs for commercial sales in the United States and abroad. After only a week, I was able to fulfill my quota with no problem, but my big hands had some trouble adjusting to the small tacks and the tiny hammer used. After ten hours of sitting tacking shoes, my back hurts something fierce, and eyes water from squinting at the soles to make sure placement of the tacks is correct. My feet don't hurt with the same intensity they used to, but merely ache constantly. I have asked, and been granted permission, by Warden Lynds, on advisement of Dr. Warren, to be able to carry a cane around. So I limp to and from my work detail, being excused from marching lockstep. I just have to lope behind everyone as best I can. This sentence…this life…this is my cross to bear, even though it was done in the name of king and country, what I did was not righteous in the name of the Lord, and he is punishing me for it. So, with all the pureness of heart my black soul can muster, I bear my cross every day, even with crippled feet.

Chapter 16

My new work detail with the Dandy Footwear Company gives me ample time to reflect on how I came to end up in this wretched circumstance. *Tap, tap, tap* sounds my miniature hammer as I tap in another tack; another tack towards the 15 tacks in this shoe, and towards the fifteen in its mate. Another tack toward the three hundred that must be pounded in per hour, or the five tacks per minute, or one tack every twelve seconds. Remove tack from the leather sack with left hand. Place in wooden sole. Tap in with right hand. *Tap, tap, tap...*

The cogs in the machine that landed me here started turning in 1847. The Prussian people, sick of the king's rule, started banding together and there was talk of unrest. Naturally, the people's unrest reached the king's ears, and he ordered *us* to step up our efforts to quell the strife. The actions of my comrades and myself further precipitated the unrest in Prussia, and in 1848, the people revolted. Mobs tore through the countryside, and my old refuge and former headquarters, Schloss Rheinfels, was overrun by angry Prussian citizens. Most of my former associates were killed by the mobs, or later sought out by the new government officials and executed. Fortunately, I saw, as you Americans put it, the writing on the wall, and fled Schloss Rheinfels in the dead of night on my fearless stallion, Stahlhand, with only the clothes on my back and a small wooden clock that my father made. I traveled west through Prussia and Belgium and southwest through the French and Spanish countryside until I reached the Mediterranean Sea where I followed the coastline west until I reached the Atlantic; there I hopped a ship in Port Huelva. My training as an operative for the royal family enabled me to slip effortlessly across the borders, similar to milk flowing through cheesecloth. And, thus, I just disappeared from Europe like I never existed.

I found out later that there was a full-blown revolution in Prussia leading to the dissolution of autocracy and the formation of a National Assembly. The National Assembly campaigned for a constitution, and Kaiser Friedrich Wilhelm IV granted a constitution of the Reich. The king saw change inevitable in the Germanic States, and was forced to give in to the will of the people despite the efforts of people like me for the past half century. The king was rendered powerless, in a larger sense, and there was no more need for people like me in the fatherland; besides, if caught, the National Assembly would've rewarded my eight years of faithful service to king and country with death.

I arrived on the Spanish coast in June of 1848. After inhabiting the high Prussian mountainous area covered with thick forests all my life, I didn't blend in with the bronzed Spanish people living around the coastline. The miles and miles of golden sand beaches and craggy coastline thrilled me; I had never seen the ocean before. The vastness of the great cerulean sea thrilled me to no end. I liked to gaze from the shoreline to where green met blue and fantasize about the country that was waiting for me; waiting for me to work hard and build my fortune as an honest citizen.

The Spanish coast in the fierce summer sun contained the joyful screeching of black-haired children playing in the churning surf as the nude bodies of erotic olive-skinned Spanish women looked on. I loved the change in climate; the air was humid, wonderfully salty, and hot, so hot my heavy uniform lay heavy on my body with sweat as I traveled down the coast. The many colorful Spanish people sold fruits, nuts, and clothes on roadside kiosks, and small children ran beside my majestic horse trying to sell their wares to this pale looking foreigner. After four days of searching the Spanish coast, I found Port Huelva, a bustling port in southern Spain. The glittering cobalt Atlantic served as a perfect backdrop stretching for miles and miles against the urgency of the merchants and sailors as they loaded hogsheads of goods onto the myriad of sailing ships at the docks.

With a weighed conscience and heavy heart I sold my faithful friend of many years to a merchant. He was of no further practical use. I demanded gold bullion for the trade, and managed three ounces for the eight-year-old stallion. The shifty merchant wore greasy robes and had a large bushy beard. He constantly dry washed his hands and made wild gesticulations as he protested and complained about the trade, but in the end, he grudgingly measured out three ounces. I knew his type: he tells his cronies as soon as a large sale has been made, and they rob and kill the person as soon as they leave the town. I made clear to the man I was not to be considered a mark by flashing the stiletto I had tucked in my belt and catching his eye as I stowed the gold in my purse. The expression on his face told me he wouldn't be pursuing me.

I avoided Stahlhand's curious ebony eyes as I walked away from the merchant's store. I could feel them accusing me, boring into my back. I knew he was bound to spend his remaining days as a packhorse, but if he could serve me this one last time by providing money, so be it. It is the way of the world... service. It irked me, being practical. I couldn't take a horse where I was headed, no matter how faithful he had been to me.

One can't blend in without the correct attire, and the uniform I wore made me stick out like a cardinal in a nest of blue birds. I bartered with a textile merchant for a new wardrobe. After much haggling, bullying and cajoling, I got a reasonable deal. I could tell he was greedy for my exotic-looking threads, for he had never seen workmanship of such fine quality as he did on my clothes. I traded my heavy weather Germanic gear, including my topcoat, wool trousers; leather chaps, riding boots, and white blouse for something more appropriate to this new climate, and he gave me an additional two ounces of gold. He also tried buying my clock. His black eyes wandering over the fine Prussian workmanship with longing. I would sell my soul to Lucifer himself if need be to keep my treasured clock. It's the only thing I had to remember my father (and mother) by. I had kept it by my side since I left home at age sixteen, twelve years prior, and I wasn't about to give it up to some greasy, black-haired Spaniard for a few coins of gold. "Forget it," I told him more than once in Prussian and French as he pestered me unmercifully. He followed me out his shop and down the street, maybe hoping to steal the coveted clock. Tired of arguing with him, I let him know I meant business; without another word I pushed him up against a shop wall in a deserted alley, stiletto inches from his eye, my hand clamped on his throat. Suddenly, he understood my language and slunk off back in the direction of his shop like a whipped dog.

Sporting a pair of canvas britches that only went to my calves, lightweight cotton blue stripped seaman's blouse, beige bandanna, and these strange peasant-like sandals as well as a hemp rucksack slung over my shoulder filled with a woolen short coat, watch cap and a few other assorted textile items I could need later, I set out, ready to leave Europe forever and seek my fortune in a new land. I spent a few days basking in the radiant Spanish sun, turning my pale skin first a bright red then a deep bronze. Unfortunately for me, my brown hair turned a light blonde in the blazing sun, and I stood out against all the other black haired men and women of this strange land. To remedy the situation, I used my bandanna to cover my hair during the hot days and watch cap at night. Complete with my newly tanned skin, I was beginning to fit in quite well. Now all I needed to do was hone my rudimentary Spanish skills.

My former profession taught me the best camouflage is no camouflage, but rather to *be* what you were trying to mimic. Over the past eight years, I had become a master of camouflage, so after a few days of establishing my new identity, I journeyed to the wharf to implement my plan. I didn't know a clipper from a sloop so I arbitrarily picked a funny-looking ship named *Anaranjado*. It was the only ship in the entire port that I could see that had a chimney. It was a larger vessel; I counted fifteen total portholes on one side, probably three hundred feet long or so I guessed with the chimney located in between the first and second of the three masts. The dark waters of the port gently lapped at her varnished hull and the slight breeze snapped at the furled sails and rigging ropes. Although she was of prodigious size, she looked a little worse for wear compared to the other ships in the harbor. Her varnish didn't seem as bright and some of the equipment looked a bit antiquated, but I did not care for that, for I only needed her for one voyage. I figured she must be a transatlantic vessel based on her size and all the freight that was being loaded onto her by the small army of shouting men that reminded me of ants swarming an anthill. I ducked into a small dusty apothecary shop on a side street. The shop was nothing more than a long counter, behind which shelves and shelves of glass-filled jars containing every imaginable substance of every imaginable color stood. A tiny Spanish man in a filthy apron asked as I entered, "What can I do for you today?"

"What do you have for head pain?" I asked.

The man smiled. "I have just the thing for you," he said and began getting down various jars filled with powered substances. He measured the contents from three different jars out on a scale and ground them together with a mortar.

While he went about his business I asked, "That ship, the Anaranjado, where is it headed?"

"New York," he said, pouring the powder into an envelope.

"Thank you," I said, accepting the envelope. I paid him and left.

He called after me, "I hope your head feels better."

I sat and smoked unobtrusively on a barrel, observing the madness of the ship until I located the man in charge—the captain. A few hours, and a couple of cigarettes later, after I had figured the territory I marched right up to the captain while he yelled obscenities at his sailors loading crates into the hold. He was a great giant of a man, almost my height, with a great potbelly to match. The captain wore a tattered blue coat with yellow mariner stripes adorning it and it hung unbuttoned around his great gut. "Excuse me sir," I said addressing him in pseudo-fluent Spanish, "My name is Gregor Opfer. I am a sailor. I understand you are bound for America. I would like to work for passage there."

The hulk of a man turned around to fully face me, "You would like to sail with me, eh?" His eyes narrowed and his leathery face wrinkled up as he casually spit a large glob of tobacco juice in my direction. It landed near my foot splashing some in between my toes. The blood rose in my face, but I appeared not to let it bother me. He rubbed his stubbled face slowly with a giant meaty hand then laughed a big bellowing laugh that shook his entire frame and jiggled his big belly. "What other vessels have you served on boy?"

Without skipping a beat I recited the names of three other ships and captains, "The *Faülkirk* sailing under Captain Stephén Mauersh; the

Meridian with Captain Edward Cook, formerly of the Royal Navy, as well as the now-scrapped packet ship, *Dark Star.* That tour was under Captain Albert Jung."

"Is that right?" the captain asked, showing me his tobacco-stained mouth, full of missing and crooked teeth.

"Yeah, that's what I said," I replied with as much attitude and indignation as I could muster.

"What did you say they were again?" he asked. "I forget easily." He pointed at his head and grinned a not too pleasant grin.

I repeated them perfectly without skipping a beat. "Never heard of those ships, Norwegian ships?" he said thoughtfully rubbing the stubble on his face. Not biting on his lure, knowing fully well he probably knew all the Norwegian ships in the area, I replied, "Ships sailing from the Americas bound for the Dark Continent."

He kept stroking. "Let me see your hands, boy." Slowly extending them, he grabbed them and, upon looking at them, drops one and grabs me by the neck, drawing me close to his ugly face. He fiercely whispered, tobacco juice spraying me, "Listen here *chico*, I don't know where you come from, or what you're doing here, but I want you out of my sight. You can't pull a fast one on Captain Alejandro. Your hands are as smooth and nice as any aristocrats as I ever saw, and you sure as hell ain't any Spanish sailor, though you talk kinda like one."

I listened to him, then calmly gasped with what air I could muster through my clamped neck, "Listen, I just want to work for passage to America…"

I was cut off as he squeezed tighter. "How 'bout I take you to the magistrate right now and we'll see who and what you're hiding from, unless you can come up with something to make me look the other way."

"I suggest you…"

He cut me off again before I could finish. "Suggest I do what?" the captain mocked, his greasy locks of hair falling into his eyes.

I had had enough. Before he knew what hit him I took the index and middle fingers of my left hand and jammed them behind the mandibular joint using an Eastern defense technique I knew. Captain

Alejandro released me and immediately fell to his knees writhing in pain, but couldn't shake my hand from its position behind his jaw. I let up the pressure a little and he was able to get out, "All right...all right! W...w...what do...you want? Arghhh!"

I heard a shout behind me and some of the captain Alejandro's men rushed over to aid their leader. "Call them off or you're a dead man," I whispered in the captain's ear keeping my fingers close to his throat as he squirmed on his knees.

"Men, men, it's all right. Back to your work!" he weakly barked. The men back up a little but still milled about like a wolf pack circling a foe, deciding whether or not to attack. "Now! He'll kill me if you don't."

I nodded in response to the captain's declaration. The men dispersed somewhat more but remained in the very near periphery. I released but remained poised to strike. He got slowly to his knees like a defeated man, and I could tell he was making a decision. I said very quietly in a deadly calm voice, "Do it and you're a dead man. You don't know who I am or what I'm capable of. Now how 'bout it? Passage to America?"

He turned to me, "Let's go to my quarters and get us a drink." I just stared at him and slowly nodded once.

In the captain's quarters we struck a deal. The deal was, I'd act like one of the crew, and, in exchange for whatever work I could offer the ship and three ounces of gold, Captain Alejandro would provide me passage to America. The captain probed me about my urgency for passage to America, and I answered with a slightly fabricated and very vague story and left it at that. I, however, had a few questions for him that he answered very frankly, probably out of fear for his life.

"So now that it's clear I'm not a sailor, what is this ship? It is the only one in port with a chimney?" I asked sipping my glass of port and looking over the rim of the glass at Captain Alejandro. "This here is a converted packet ship. She was built in 1820 and sailed with the Black Ball Line outta Liverpool in England until they retired her in the early forties. The company I work for bought her and converted her to a hybrid." He sipped a bit of port. "The company, Tricheur, is a French-owned speculation company that is trying a new thing the Cunard Line is making commonplace: steam assisted transatlantic voyaging. It has been going on since '19 when *Savannah* first made it."

"You steam across?"

"Not really. Only when there's no wind or we are behind schedule. Most of the time we still use the sails."

"Oh," I said without conviction, taking a healthy swig of port. I still didn't really figure how a steam engine could power a boat across the mighty Atlantic. This was the first I was hearing of it.

"We have two paddlewheels that we can bring up and stow on deck," Alejandro said reading my mind.

"Then how come you're the only ship with this if it's so good?"

"Damn, you sure as hell ask a lot of questions." He drained his glass and refilled both of ours from the earthenware jug. "Simple. Coal is expensive, and we have to scrape the salt from the boilers after three days of use. The salt corrodes the hell outta 'em. It's costly, and to be honest with you, mainly an unproven method of sailing. If I had to venture a guess I'd say that in twenty or so it'll be that every ship'll be outfitted with paddles."

"Very well then. Anyway, sir, I'll do whatever you want me to do. I'll work hard, I will."

"*Salud*, Gregor!" The captain said raising his glass of port, trying to sound sophisticated.

I answered his French toast with the English, "Cheers," and clinked his glass. *I am going to have to watch this old sea dog; he is as wily as the day is long,* I thought, sitting in the man's cramped ship quarters, sipping port and questioning him further. From what I was asking him and what he was answering me, I reckoned he wasn't anyone to be taken advantage of—stupid like a fox. And I could tell the gears in his head were turning same as mine but for a different reason; trying to figure out who I was and how he could rip me off.

Chapter 17

Tap tap tap sounds my tiny hammer as I nail the last tack into my last shoe of the day. Another day has come and gone. Another day of limping to and from the factory, limping behind the lockstepping prisoners, another day of sitting for hours and hours tapping small tacks into boots until my fingers are numb and painful. Today turns out to be a good day, though; we get an egg with dinner. We inmates at Sing Sing get only two eggs a year, so when they magically arrive with dinner it's a treat like no other. Although the egg is overdone and very dry I manage to drag out eating the egg over the course of an hour. One of the inmates on tier three has the audacity to ask for another egg. He is a new inmate and hasn't quite caught onto the rules yet. He will learn. Later in the night, after their usual card game, Savage and his crew drag the man from his cell and beat him senseless. When the man tries to fight back the guards throw him over the railing. The man falls the three stories to the marble floor below and lands with a sickening crunch. *There's another one for the bone yard,* I think despondently, the noise from the scuffle having wakened me. I know every man in Sing Sing is listening intently, eyes darting fervently around their cells hoping they could just wake up from this infernal nightmare. The air hangs heavy with our silence, broken only by the shouts and grunts of the guards as they lug the body back to its cell. I begin praying under my breath for the slain man, "The Lord is my shepherd; I shall not want. He maketh me to lie down in green pastures: he leadeth me beside the still waters. He restoreth my soul: he leadeth me in the paths of righteousness for his name's sake…"

In the morning, Warden Lynds is alerted to, and finds, the new man from the third tier that had hanged himself the night before. Dr. Warren is summoned to inspect the scene. I can see the thin, black clad figure making his way up the iron steps, the ubiquitous cigarette dangling from his bloodless lips. His thin, wavering voice drifts downward, "No doubt about it, suicide. Looks like he hung himself with a belt. Contraband…well good riddance, one more damn criminal the world can be safe from. Cut him down boys! And for God's sake bury him before he starts to rot!"

Chapter 18

After striking a deal with Captain Alejandro, I got to work as an official seaman, but not before stowing my precious clock in the crew quarters. First order of business was helping the other sailors finish loading cargo into the hold. This included supplies for the voyage as well as goods bound for America. Basically, all I did was manual labor, carrying crates and rolling barrels into a giant net on the dock, then hefting the giant net skyward by pulling the rope pulley with a score of sailors. It was beautifully tiring, mindless work. Blisters appeared on my hands and popped, and I reveled in the stinging cleansing sensation every time I lifted a crate or pulled the rope of the crane. We worked all day and well into the night for three days, loading cargo and preparing the vessel to sail across the great Atlantic. During the loading, the captain could usually be seen storming about the bridge shouting orders, spitting tobacco everywhere and grandstanding his nasty disposition. For as mean as he acted, he never fussed directly at me, which was fine with me; I'd rather just remain invisible for the duration of the journey. Invisibility, I found, might be harder than I initially reckoned, for the mentality on this ship (and I imagine on other ships) was, "man versus the sea," and you are either with your crewmembers, or you are against them.

Most of the crewmembers were Spanish-looking fellows; as to their exact origin, I couldn't be totally sure. Based on the array of dialects spoken, I'd wager a good many of them to have Arabic, Turkish, or Greek blood in them. I never did directly ask any of them for I tried to avoid talking to them save when necessary. I did not really care that they were casting me as peculiar. There too many other interesting characters for me to ever really stand out, or so I thought. I just conducted whatever task the first mate, Miguel, assigned me.

Unlike all the other ruffian sailors crewing the *Anaranjado,* who looked like they'd just as soon slit my throat over a bottle of grog, Miguel was a gruff but kind man. I could sense it in his eyes. Behind the sun-weathered, leathery face and patchy black and white stubble on his face, the older man ruled over the ship with fairness and decency with his wise brown eyes. On orders from the captain, Miguel assigned me tasks a non-sailor could do like cleaning the smokestack, whitewashing the hatches and doorways, and swabbing the deck— that's real sailor jargon I picked up. I tackled each task with the gusto of a bee searching for honey and ignored most of the insults handed out by the seasoned sailors as they watched me clumsily go about my tasks. They soon learned not to meddle with me.

In the afternoon, after all the cargo had been loaded, the day before we were to set sail, a man pushed me while I was scrubbing the deck, trying to mind my own business. "Outta the way, you pale-skinned *cabron!"* he loudly exclaimed, bustling by me, bodily thrusting me sideways. I lost my balance and spilled my bucket of suds. The bucket tumbled over the edge before I could grab it and fell into the gently lapping waves of the waiting harbor. The man laughed loudly as he stepped past me and said something to another sailor, who looked down and laughed, too. Hawks don't swoop on mice as fast as I did my antagonizer. As he continued by me, a large coil of rope slung over his shoulder, I whipped out my stiletto and buried it into his calf muscle. He screamed in pain and went down clutching his wounded leg. I was instantly on him.

By the time the other sailors had pulled me off I had broken the sailor's arm and was in the process of delivering crushing blows to his back. Blood poured from the wound on his leg and ran in crazy rivulets over the varnished deck. His screams echoed in the background as a troop of sailors laid into me. Unable to compensate for the sheer number of bodies on top of me pummeling me, I just covered my head and absorbed the blows. First Mate Miguel broke up the fight after much cursing and throwing of bodies. He ordered that the man be taken below to receive medical treatment from the ship's doctor. "Guiremo, take him below. Now!" The men stood around panting and glaring at me the way a pack of wild dogs looks at a rabbit it has cornered. My shirt was torn almost completely off, and the bandanna that had been on my head moments before had disappeared. I ripped off the remainder of my shirt and tossed it onto the deck of the ship. "What are you looking at! Get back to work! Now! Move!" Miguel shouted at the men, his big frame heaving from exertion. The men grudgingly obeyed. Hateful glances were thrown my way. I met each one defiantly. Miguel snapped me from my reverie by roughly grabbing my shoulder and guiding me aside. "Here, eat this. Walk with me," he said grabbing a green and yellow thing from an open crate and tossing it to me. I caught the long, crescent-shaped cylinder and bit into it. The inside gushed, but I couldn't break through the outside flesh. It tasted like nothing. I looked up at Miguel blankly. Chuckling, Miguel took one from the crate. "No, no. This is how you eat these," he said peeling the thick skin back and eating the inside of the strange thing.

I emulated him and took a bite. It was magnificent. I had never tasted anything so sweet and wonderful. "What is this?" I asked in wonder. "It is called a banana, *hombre*."

"Buh-ná-nuh," I repeated.

"Now listen, Gegor, seriously," he said stopping and facing me to look me in the eye, "you cannot pull stunts like that. I know you don't understand the workings of a ship, but we *need* each other out there, and the captain simply won't stand for any kind of strife. You could make things very dangerous for yourself, the captain, and the ship as a whole if you keep it up. Know what I mean?" He lifted his eyebrows and looked at me questioningly. I didn't move a muscle. "Besides, most of these men are violent criminals and very dangerous men. You do not want them to dislike you, because *accidents*," and he stressed that word, "can happen very easily on the open sea." He stared at me and continued after brushing a shock of black hair from his eyes, "I have never seen anyone act with such concise brutality as you did today. You are going to have your differences with these men, especially after today, and they will take advantage of you if you don't fight back, but I can't have you injuring my men over trivial issues like that. Understand?" His voice contained an edge.

"Yes, I understand. I am very sorry for my misconduct. I do not wish to be removed from the ship and should have known better than to over-react on a trivial matter such as that, but I do not take kindly to being *anyone's* tool," I said, my face blank, and eyes steeled.

Miguel's weathered face broke out into a smile, "Don't worry son, I understand. I'll watch out for you. You'll be fine." Through his smile, he didn't seem so sure, but I don't need a nursemaid. My scar flared red, almost as an answer; he slapped me on the back and led me to get another bucket, but not before I snatched another banana.

I later learned the sailor, whom I beat within an inch of his life, was named Raúl. After seeing the damage inflicted on Raúl, the other sailors left me alone for the most part. I could tell there was repressed hostility toward me. For what, I don't know. Maybe because I wasn't a sailor but passing myself off as one, and another ludicrous thought crossed my mind, maybe they were angry with me for thumping Raúl. That thought quickly was trashed for the life these men lead is one of dog-eat-dog, and Raúl's welfare is probably the furthest thing of any of their minds...unless they just want a reason to hate me. I finally settled on the idea that they figured I was a fellow criminal of some sort with a bounty on my head, and they were figuring the right moment when they could capture me and collect the bounty. Either way, I slept with one eye open while enduring their passive-aggressive behavior. The cook would give me a small ration of soup minus the *amines* and vegetables contained within, other sailors would 'accidentally' bump into me throughout the day, and my hammock continually came untied while I was away from it. Through that I bore my cross. Fueled by my determination and the small friendship gestures from First Mate Miguel, I endured. I had experienced far worse tests of character and the prospect of a new life in the land of the free kept my spirits high. A man can endure anything for a short time. Anything.

Later in the day, after breaking Raúl's arm, the passengers boarded the *Anaranjado*. Although it wasn't a passenger ship, Captain Alejandro enhanced his purse by cramming as many passengers as he could into what was originally designed as crew quarters. The old crew quarters were nothing more than an aft hold that the captain had sectioned off with cheap wooden planking into small rooms no bigger than tombs. The passenger cabins were near the captain's quarters, while the crew now occupied a small hold near the bow, where it was bumpier in high seas, or so Miguel told me. I could only imagine what it was going to be like on the high seas. I wasn't looking forward to it. Unlike most packet ships, Miguel informed me, the interior of this ship was like a small maze of rooms and passages instead of one continuous hold. He explained that this was due to the addition of the coal-firing furnace and the additional gears for the paddle wheels.

The furnace room was a smallish iron room with just enough room for two men to have room to shovel coal from their chutes into the furnace. I suspected that the proximity of the furnace room to the crew's quarters would mean that we would never lack for warmth. And although the furnace room wall was adjacent to the crew quarters, one could only access the furnace room through a series of twists and turns starting on the other side of the ship.

I suspected the authorities didn't know about Captain Alejandro's passenger manifest, and that many of these particular passengers were Prussian, escaping the same revolution I had fled. I stood on the deck in the waning light, munching on a piece of black bread, leaning on the deck railing watching the passengers board, maybe thirty-five or forty in all. As they marched up the gangplank I hardly saw the Spanish family of five, father berating the two little boys as they ran ahead on the gangplank with the mother trudging along behind them, forlorn, an infant in her arms; trio of young Nordic-looking lads; or several aristocratic-looking elderly ladies, for I spied the most radiant creature these *ojos* had ever seen. She floated up the gangplank like a heaven-sent angel. My attention was torn with the loud cry of Miguel, "Gregor, get your ass down here and lug these bags to the passengers' quarters!" At least I think that's what he said; sometimes when they spoke too fast I would catch bits and pieces and fill in the rest. Comprehension not withstanding, I hastily scampered down to the dock to do Miguel's bidding, but not before stealing another look at the beautiful figure disappearing across the deck in a swirl of swishing skirts. Unfortunately for me, I did not have the luxury of delivering the fine maiden's luggage to her cabin, and that night I went to bed dejected, but determined to make my presence known to that wonderful nymph before the voyage was over.

The day after we set sail I spotted *her* walking about the crowded ship's deck with a sun umbrella, her immense hazel eyes darting around, drinking in every detail. I was conducting my usual menial chores, scraping the rust off the iron deck fixtures in preparation for painting, when she walked by. *Whist, whist, whist,* sounded my brush as I intensified my work. I soon found my breathing labored beyond my exertions as she approached. I could tell she was by no means wealthy from the clothes she wore, a plain black dress, ivory blouse, and blue frock. But the way those clothes hung off her lithe frame she could've been from the Paris store catalogs. I had never seen such classic, restrained beauty. Her dark brown hair was pulled back and cascaded down over her shoulders where it blew gently in the southern Atlantic breeze. As she glided by me I caught the sweet smell of toilet water, and nearly dropped the wire brush into the churning sea. My heart jumped into my throat and I merely gave the faintest of nods as she passed. *Did she even see me? Fool!* Once she passed I watched her promenade the length of the boat and back around the other side. My daydream was rudely interrupted by Captain Alejandro yelling, "Opfer! You want to be indebted to me for the rest of your life? Back to work, *cabron!*" I hastily resumed brushing.

I came across Miguel later that evening as the sun was setting, an orange orb in the west. He was quietly picking out a tune on his German harmonica, "My friend," I said plopping down next to him, "I saw the most beautiful woman in the world today."

"I say that every time I am in port, Gregor," cackled Miguel, pleased with his witticism.

"She is on this very ship. I saw her today!" I protested, offended by his jest.

"Sure, sure, so what do you want me to do?" he asked in mock seriousness.

I sighed in perplexity, still annoyed at his making light of my amorous conundrum. "I want you to tell me where she stays! I want to see her tonight."

"Whoa, hold on there, my dry-land-loving friend," Miguel said holding up his hands and waving them side to side like one might motion to a street vendor for an item they didn't want, "Don't you know anything about women?"

Frowning, I shook my head, "No, not really…Some." I lamely added. In fact, thinking about it I really had had little contact with women in my profession other than to kill the ones I had been ordered to. There had been no time in my former life for a woman, nor had I ever really felt the desire for one other than the occasional prostitute.

Taking out a small tobacco pouch and some rolling papers, Miguel commenced rolling a cigarette. Without looking at me he slowly said in his usual manner, "Well my friend, first of all I don't even know about this beauty you're talking about, and even if I did, I wouldn't know which berth she was quartered in. Captain Alejandro assigns them on a whim. And lastly, you'll scare the poor thing if you go to her cabin. Women do not like getting accosted in their private quarters by strange sailors! You must attract her and get an invite…Almost, say like, uh," he sprinkled furiously, "moths to a candle. You must be the candle, and she will surely fly to you." He finished putting the tobacco in the paper and looked up at me beaming at his clever analogy. Then Miguel pulled a small vial of a dark, doughy-looking substance out of his pocket, pinched a little sphere out of the vial, broke it up, and dropped it in with the tobacco, licked the paper, and upon inspection, finding it okay, he lit it.

"What is that you added to the tobacco?" I asked curiously.

"Opium from the Orient," he evenly answered while taking a drag. Silence ensued. I had heard of opium; apparently there were clubs in large cities like Berlin where one could go and do nothing but smoke opium. It was kind of like drinking alcohol I had heard, but not really.

"I do not know the ways of women very well. Will you teach me how to go about winning this woman?" I asked sheepishly. The past ten years of my life had consisted of power over people. Gregor Opfer had been omnipotent; now I found myself asking love advice from the first mate of a run-out old packet ship.

The wrinkles next to his eyes crinkled up in thought as his almond colored eyes looked distantly across the quickly darkening sea. Slowly,

Miguel took a large puff of the smoke and held the smoke in his lungs and looked at me questioningly, the cigarette extended between his thumb and index finger. I had never smoked any opium before. *What the hell*, I thought and took the small black cigarette and took a large drag. I held it for as long as possible before exploding in a barrage of hacks and coughs. Miguel pounded me on the back, "My friend! My friend! This is a night of many firsts, eh!" Laughing, he took the cigarette back. We passed the small thing back and forth until it was extinguished.

At first I felt nothing, but soon a warm sensation like being covered with a thick warm blanket on a cold wintry night spread over my body and mind. I felt free and gay. "Miguel, I don't have a head," I exclaimed with delight, then alarm.

"Yes, my friend, this will do it to you." He laughed loudly. "Yes, it will! I picked it up on the Asian Continent last time we were there. It makes you feel wonderful." I just gazed at the infinite number of stars high in the sky with amazement, like I was actually honestly *seeing* them for the first time. Miguel was busy next to me rolling another. They were so far and wonderful, blinking on and off in their wonderfully random mosaic of light. I remembered my father telling me tales about the Gods and the stars. *I wonder if Papa is watching me from the stars.* Miguel broke my thought train as he readied the wonderful little smoky treat and we leaned back against the bulkhead and started passing it again. The smoke settled in my lungs and on my mind, and for a while, we sat in silence, smoking and just feeling the roll and pitch of the vessel. Miguel finally broke the silence.

"So how old are you, foreigner?" he inquired. The question took me by surprise and it took me a moment to figure out he was addressing me.

"Oh, you know I am not a Spaniard?" I asked.

"Of course, any Spaniard worth his salt would know how to woo a beautiful woman, like the one you claim is onboard the *Anaranjado*," he said teasing me.

Reflectively I said, "Well, I guess I just wanted to pass surface inspection for anyone that was looking. I could never totally blend in within a week's time. My training kicked in...I'm twenty-eight," I finished lamely.

"No! No! No wait. You learned Spanish in a week?" Miguel asked mouth agape.

"Sure," I replied. "Actually, less than a week...It was nothing."

"You are a man of many surprises. One being that you are twenty-eight and have not been with a woman!" He laughed and slapped his knee.

My wandering mind focused on what he said. "No, no. I never said that. I have been with women before!" I protested, "I used to visit the village women of ill repute sometimes, and in my former profession, enemies of the state," I stammered thinking of a delicate way to put this, "uh, women prisoners of mine...treasonous women didn't have any rights...and we...we treated them like the dogs they were." I trailed off ashamed of what I was actually vocalizing to another human being for the first time—other members of Die Sonneleute not withstanding.

"Oh, I get you," Miguel said sympathetically, "Masters treat their slave women like that. It is like that where we are going. But no worries, I have known far worse men than you. Believe me, I have come across some scoundrels sailing the seven seas. The water attracts them. I swear it."

"I doubt it Miguel," I said interrupting him, "I have done some terrible things in my time, deeds...memories I must flee from."

"'Tis no matter. I am not here to pass judgment on you, the Lord will do that when the time comes." He changed the subject quickly, "Well, here is how you need to go about attracting this young lady you so covet..."

Miguel proceeded to tell me how to go about winning the affections of this angelic creature whom he had never even seen, and I seriously began to wonder if my eyes had actually seen. Each breath seemed crisper, each star shone brighter, and I could taste the sharp salty taste of the Atlantic as Miguel imbued romantic Spanish wisdom in my callow Germanic mind. When he was through, *quid pro quo*, I began to tell him the story of my life, starting with the disappearance of my father, and the horrible truth *I now knew*, the truth the opium finally unlocked. I told him stories of the corpses that lay now in the cold, German soil, put there by me, all in the name of the fatherland. He listened, nodding occasionally and when it was all over he didn't judge me but merely offered, "Each man must do what he must to get by. Put your trust in God and he will forgive your sins made under the will of man." And from that day forward I put every iota of my being into God's good grace.

The following day, a sober mind greeted me. Unlike alcohol, the opium didn't leave me with a pounding head and churning stomach. Instead, I had the unshakable feeling I was forgetting *something*. I could remember all of Miguel's advice, and me telling him my life's story, but I still couldn't stop thinking I had uncovered something that my sober mind reburied. My duties forced me to write the feeling off as just an effect of smoking the strange new substance.

Chapter 19

The meal of salted fish, hard potatoes, and moldy apples tasted great as I sat and watched the sun drop below the endless horizon. Nothing tastes better than a meal after an honest days' work. I mopped up the fishy brine juice with a small bit of bread I saved from breakfast, and stowed my clean bowl in my jacket. As the shadows crushed the light, and the light danced off its fluid stage, I saw her again. Navigating around the coils of rope, crates, and other detritus a packet ship has on its deck, the object of my affections picked her way nimbly through it all. I took a deep breath. Quickly looking around, I determined the deck was basically deserted save her and me, and the watchman and navigator. Remembering words of wisdom from my crusty old Die Sonneleute controller, "Son, men shape their own destiny; fools wait for destiny to shape them," spurred me to action.

"Excuse me, do you hail from the Rhine region? I think I recognize you," I said scrambling blindly to my feet. *Spectacular, you fool! Fucking gorgeous work!* I think, mentally abusing myself but keeping a huge grin plastered on my face while waiting for a reply.

"Excuse me, but I don't speak German," the brunette beauty answered in French, the aristocratic language.

"Ah, but you must speak German, for you understood what language I just spoke," I replied in French with an even bigger smile on my face now that I was one up on this coy little bird.

"Why, sir, I don't really expect sailors to know the romantic languages," she replied, a small smile playing across the porcelain white face as she answered me in my native tongue.

"Who says I am a sailor, and furthermore who says French is all that romantic?" And from there we hit it off; my mouth talked faster than my brain could process, excited by the prospect of talking to a stunning goddess. For all my bravo and assuredness in other aspects of my life, I felt like a fish with wings as I leaned uneasily against the railing and made small talk.

Finally I gained the confidence to timidly ask, "Could I accompany you around the deck, ma'am? It can be hazardous at times, especially without a male escort."

"Why, yes, kind Herr, that would be most gentlemanly of you. A woman can't be too careful these days, especially on a ship of this nature."

"Ship of this nature, Madame?" I asked with mock seriousness, "What could be bad about a ship with French-speaking sailors?" We both laughed. And so I fell into step with her and we began walking around the ship.

"So, kind escort, what pray tell is your name?" the beautiful lady with her arm in mine asked after a moment of walking.

My face turned bright red as I said with considerable chagrin, "Pardon me Madame for being so rude, my name is Gregor, Gregor Opfer."

"Well, Herr Opfer…"

"Please call me Gregor," I interjected.

"Well, then, *Gregor*," she said emphasizing my name, "that is quite the dashing dueling scar you have."

I absentmindedly touched the long jagged scar running down my face. "Thank you very much," I said, quite embarrassed.

"That certainly explains why you know all those languages. You are university educated," she said. She spoke with a coy little smile that both excited and scared me.

I had a funny feeling in the pit of my gut, like I wanted to vomit, but not really. "True, I did attend university, but that is not where my propensity for language was cultivated," I said enigmatically.

"Oh, sir! Er, Gregor, you certainly are the card!" she cried and laughed a dainty laugh, covering her mouth with her hand. I smiled and stared at my feet, tracing a circle with my right foot before awkwardly changing the subject.

"And what may your name be, if you don't mind me asking?"

Batting her long lashes over liquid hazel eyes she replied, "Helga Kugior of the House of Jëger."

"House of Jëger?" I asked, a funny feeling rising in my stomach. "Yes, that's what I said."

"The same House of Jëger that manufactures Jëger carriage wheels?" I asked, my face going from red to pale.

"Yes!" she exclaimed brightening, "You must know of us then. My father is Otto von Arghsdattë Kugior, heir to the fortune, and president of the company."

Well there goes my earlier assumption of her society status, I grimly thought. "That is amazing; I'm in the company of a true lady," I said with no enthusiasm, but trying to summon some. "Well then, ma'am, may I inquire as to what are you doing on an old ship like this if you are a lady in the House of Jëger?" I asked trying to steer the subject, already knowing her answer. Her eyes clouded over, and I hoped my plan would work; she would be too ladylike to recount her miseries. I wasn't so lucky.

"Right before the revolution my mother and father disappeared. One day they were there; the next they were gone. Poof. Like smoke," she said bitterly bringing the tips of her fingers together on her right hand and opening them really fast. "This happened about a year ago— maybe longer. My grandfather, having heard reports from other states in the Confederation of wealthy people disappearing, and fearing our entire family would be wiped out, took what was left of the family into hiding: mainly myself, and an aunt, and two cousins now living in Maastricht. I have been living in a small cottage in the Moorish countryside for about eleven months. Then, a month or so ago, my grandfather decided I should be sent to live in America with a relation of ours. I believe it's my mother's cousin, or some distant relative like that…my aunt knows. He was found dead two days after I got word of my journey to America. Murdered!" Diverting her eyes, she said quietly, "I had to be smuggled to the coast in the care of the only two servants that did not flee the family. Actually, I don't know if they all fled because they feared for their lives…or…" she trailed off, but only for a moment. "Before he was killed, my grandfather found out it was Prussians killing Prussians! And they dressed him like a swine!" she said almost spitting out the words. "People, citizens would just disappear never to be found again. Friedrich Wilhelm had a secret police he used to instill fear into the Prussian people and kill any dissenters...my family! Dissenters? Never." she said quietly, the pretty features distorted into an angry mask.

"That's terrible!" I said with mock anger, hoping she was done, but apparently she was just getting warmed up. My insides twisted about, surprised at the rage this tiny little thing could summon.

"Since the Diet of '47 and the ensuing revolution, it has come to light that Kaiser Friedrich had a police force in charge of quelling internal rebellion, dissent, and strife—most likely the people that took my parents." She screwed up her face and tightened the hold on my arm noticeably before continuing her tirade, "But with the formation of the national assembly and the talk of the formation of a Reich, the secret police squad is being rounded up and hopefully will hang for their heinous crimes against their own countrymen. From his sources, my grandfather had heard that some of these secret police have gone underground and are operating as rogue agents around Europe, which is why he decided I wasn't safe in Europe anymore." The expression on her face was one of pure hatred. I felt weak. "But, they did not get me. Frankly, sometimes I wish they had. I don't like living in a world where a man can kill another man just like that and get away with it because it's in the name of a tyrant ruler. I wish I knew what became of them...I mean...I didn't even get to bury their bodies," her voice now an almost inaudible whisper.

I knew exactly what had happened to her parents because Agent Gregor Opfer had been assigned the mission of eliminating Herr and Frau Kugior. The image of me throwing their manacled bodies into the fast-flowing Rhine flashed through my mind like a lightning bolt. I jumped. "Everything all right?" Helga inquired.

"Yes. Just the, uh, nearly lost my footing," I lamely mumbled. Herr Kugior promised me riches beyond belief then begged like a dog for his life as I sewed him up in a sack with a serpent, monkey, and cock. His eyes contained the look that only the damned can contain as I completed the last stitches. The heavy weights attached to his ankles caused him to sink quickly below the inky water, and his screams echoed hollowly off the rocky shores as the three animals thrashed and gnashed inside the sack. Upon seeing her husband thrown over, the swine, Frau, who had been nothing but a mask of contempt, cracked and begged to join her husband in death. I would never grant an enemy of the state that pleasure, so I let my partner have his way with her before heaving her nude, bloodied, and muddied, weighted body into the fast flowing river many miles down from her husband's watery grave.

The Kugiors were treasonous scum, and had to be treated as such. They were found to have Serbian sympathies, and to be supporting rebel groups of anti-Prussians with the revenue generated from their lucrative carriage-wheel business. Jëger carriage wheels are on over fifty percent of all carriages that can be found within the borders of Prussia, and on almost one third of wheels in the greater German Confederation. The royal intelligence agency came across documentation that millions of marks of profit from the sale of the wheels had been funneled out of the country over the course of the last three decades; right around the time the German Confederation was forged and the Holy Alliance between Russia, Austria, and Prussia was signed. The Kugiors were trying to undermine the very economy and government that was earning their daily bread; they were biting the hand…

"You're awfully quiet," Helga said quietly as we continued to circle the ship.

"Oh, I'm sorry. I'm just brooding about the horrible state of affairs in the fatherland," I replied before falling silent again.

I could tell Helga the exact room in her once-luxurious mansion where to find a swastika carved behind a mirror. Thankfully for her, she was too naive to realize her precious family mansion had probably long since been looted during the rebellion and subsequent cleansing. Strangely enough, my hatred and intensity for the cause seemed to melt, left on the shores of Europe. I cared no more for the cause I had devoted my life to. We had failed; the cause had been lost. The people had prevailed, and I had to now get on with my life. So there I stood in the middle of the Atlantic Ocean arm and arm with the daughter of identified enemies of Prussia who also happened to be most beautiful woman in the world. *So what if her family were traitors?*

"What are you thinking about?" Helga asked softly.

I snapped back to the present, the deck of the ship. Me. Helga. The *Anaranjado.* "Oh, nothing, I was just thinking. I had to flee Prussia because of the rebellion also," I said, not entirely lying.

"Terrible, just terrible," she said hanging her head and shaking it. "Let's talk about something else."

"Good idea," I gratefully said. I wanted to wipe the images of her mother and father from my mind.

"Good idea," I repeated. Soon I had her in peals of laughter recalling fabricated anecdotes of my childhood, and humorous jokes. I liked the way her mouth formed when she laughed, and her ample bosom shook. She would cover her mouth with her dainty gloves, and those eyes would just shine with radiant amusement. No matter how much I made her laugh, the images of her parents still floated in my consciousness.

All too soon, our stroll came to an end. "Well, here I am. I am going to retire now. If it should so please you, we can walk tomorrow night."

Smiling from ear to ear, I replied in French, "That would please me very much, Madame."

As she ducked into the door leading down to the quarters she turned, "Herr Opfer…Gregor, you are an interesting man for sure." She paused and her eyes twinkled. "Sailor, I don't think so. Gentleman, verdict undecided, but I look forward to an evening stroll with you tomorrow." As I walked back towards the bow of the ship, I felt more euphoric than ever before in my life. My childhood had been a string of humiliations until I learned how to fend for myself, and then I became dead inside for so long as I performed my deadly art. My soul was awakening! I felt good for once…Normal.

The next day my mood matched the weather, foul. Rain poured down in buckets, and the ship bounced up and down like a cork under a waterfall. I wasn't worried about the ship going down; I was perturbed because I wouldn't get to see the object of my affections. I dreamt of Helga last night; I thought about her during the day while sitting in the darkened, swaying hold. Her brown hair, hazel eyes, creamy skin, full features, and ample Germanic bosom all made me want to lock arms with her and walk around the ship until the four horsemen spewed forth from the sky. They say that when it rains, it pours, and I found that to be true, as the heavens continued to empty their contents for the next three days, my mood growing more putrid each rainy day. *How God curses me!* I thought many times during the three long rainy days. My physical being ached to be with Helga, but still I went about my duties in the pouring rain, occasionally having to dash onto the open deck to secure a line or helping to furl or unfurl the sails. "They're out too far!" the captain constantly shouted from his perch at the helm. "Let's go boys! They're going to be ripped to shreds!"

Just as I would get a damp sort of dry, I would be forced back into the deluge. The rain was such that I felt like I was underwater. One couldn't even tell what direction it was coming from. After getting a thorough soaking, I would sit in the hold with the other wet miserable sailors trying to dry off by the few smoky oil lamps. The men played cards, gambled, and drank. I generally lay in my hammock staring at the ceiling or passed some time talking quietly with Miguel. The hours dragged by. By the end of the third day, a few of the men had developed deep hacking coughs, and at night, the hold was filled with a symphony of coughing sailors. The entire trio of days was one wet, miserable experience. The only solace was the hope of catching a glimpse of Helga amongst nature's fury.

On the dawn of the fourth day, the rains subsided and clouds cleared, giving way to a crisp, windy morning in which I went about my daily work with rekindled spirits. The day's chore was a nasty one, tallowing the mooring lines and any other spare pieces of rope that are used for the myriad of things they are used for on a sailing ship. My muscles ached from exhaustion by midmorning as I lifted yards and yards of hide and hemp rope in and out of bubbling cauldrons of rendered fat, and my hands were slick and covered with the grayish-yellow

Local author publishes debut novel

PublishAmerica recently released "The Voiceless Song," the debut novel of Delaware author W. Todd Harra. Set in 1850, this is the story of Prussian immigrant Gregor Opfer who was sentenced to life imprisonment in one of America's most infamous prisons, Sing Sing Penitentiary. Opfer believes his sentence is a penance for the evil life he led as an assassin in Kaiser Friedrich Wilhelm IV's secret terror squad, Die Sonneleute. He patiently endures the inhumane living and working conditions of prison life until a beating by guards leaves him partially crippled.

A graduate of Unionville High School and Elon University where he earned a bachelor of science degree, the author currently resides in Wilmington.

PublishAmerica is a traditional publishing company whose primary goal is to encourage and promote the works of new, previously undiscovered writers. Like more mainstream publishers, PublishAmerica pays its authors advances and royalties, makes its books available in both the United States and Europe through all bookstores, and never charges any fees for its services. PublishAmerica offers a distinctly personal, supportive alternative to vanity presses and less accessible publishers.

For more info, visit www.publishamerica.com

K by 2008

PHOTO BY MARY E. PETZAK

Kindergartners in Delaware schools got right to work on the first day.

the bill wit... giving more time t... ...icts that will not have s... ...or full day kindergarten classes by September 2008.

In drafting the amendment, Sokola told the General Assembly that failed referenda during the past year have required the several districts to delay the start of full day kindergarten. There is also a concern with capacity because of growth in several school districts.

The waiver process requires the local school districts to provide evidence to the Secretary of Education, the Office of Management and Budget, and the Controller General's Office of the inability to implement full day kindergarten. Evidence may include, but not be limited to, two consecutive failed referenda requesting funds for full day kindergarten, lack of classroom space and/or unavoidable construction delays.

Waiver requests are valid

for an additional waiver.

Co-sponsor State Rep. Melanie Marshall, D-Bear-Newark, said the measure sends a message to the business community that "Delaware is serious about investing in its human capital."

Appoquinimink and Smyrna were among school districts that began full-day kindergarten classes in separate early childhood centers as part of a Department of Education pilot program in 2004-05. A study by the University of Delaware found that students in the pilot full-day kindergarten programs had stronger literacy substance. I wiped my sweating brow even though the southern winds were blowing strong and flapping the rigging lines against the ship. Apparently, we had lost some serious time in the storm, so the paddles had been set up and churned away at the Atlantic. It was first time I had seen the two-part beast at work, steam and sails. And, frankly, I was impressed. The black smoke that poured from the smokestacks covered me in a fine sooty layer, and every time I wiped my brow my hand came away with a thin black film. I was inspecting my latest oil slick when *she* rounded the aft starboard side of the deck like an angel flying too low. Her dove-white dress was speckled with flecks of ash from the billowing smokestack and flapping furiously in the wind. She clutched a hat to her head with one hand while holding a furled umbrella in the other. I was located on port side of the ship and shouted in the blustering wind, "Miss.. Kugior! Miss.. Kugior!" She turned, acting surprised like she didn't *know* I would be on deck and smiled and waved. I waved oafishly in return and watched in dismay as she kept on walking round the deck, picking her way as daintily as she could around the cargo secured on deck. When she had rounded the fore end of the ship and was headed my way, a huge smile blossomed on my face. I mentally berated myself for being so stupid as to think she had been curt with me a moment ago. My inexperience with women and courting led me to believe she would come running over to me at first glance. "She's not out here to get fresh air," I murmured to myself as she approached.

"Ah, Herr Opfer," the object of my affections exclaimed as she approached, "fancy seeing you out here on such a blustery day." Smiling merrily, she continued, "It is absolutely horrid that you should have to work in such conditions!"

Embarrassed, I replied, "'Tis not nearly as bad as the previous three days. At least the gracious Lord has blessed us with the sun."

"Very true!" I loved the way her cheeks were rosy and moist from the wind and ocean spray. I didn't know what else to say, so I kind of stood there grinning like an idiot, as tallow dripped from my hands onto the deck. *Say something!* My mind drew a blank.

Sensing my loss for words she injected, "What time does your shift end today?"

"Half past five," I responded.

"Well, then, Herr Opfer, perhaps you can accompany me for another stroll around the deck at that time."

"It would be my pleasure, Madame," I answered evenly, though I was inwardly rejoicing.

"You can come pick me up in my berth then. My Auntie's and my cabin is located on this side," she motioned indicating port, "closest to the ship's wall. There aren't many cabins; you'll be able to locate it. Until then...." She batted her long lashes at me as best she could in the roaring wind and continued on her way like the walk was the real reason she was out here. I tallowed the ropes with newfound vigor.

Later that evening, freshly scrubbed as best I could from a bucket, I knocked on the cheap wooden door of Helga's berth. My clothes stank and had some small tears, but there was nothing I could do about it on the open sea. I could almost detect my own fetid odor but at least my hair looked presentable. I had slicked it back with some of the tallow I had used earlier. The knocks resounded sharply. A matronly old Frau, bearing a striking resemblance to Frau Grüner, opened the door. "Ah, the shipman is here," she spoke in obvious displeasure, glancing back and addressing her niece. Then, she just stood and glared at me form the doorway, her face all puckered up like she had been eating lemons.

I could tell she was judging me, and based on my rumpled appearance, I'm sure the verdict wasn't favorable. I nodded in nervous embarrassment for I wasn't used to uncomfortable social situations such as this. "Yes Madame, how do you do. My name is Gregor, Gregor Opfer." I flourished a little bow.

"Frau Ekop," was the only reply I got as she burst into a fit of coughing. The look of defiance dissolved into one of pain as she nearly doubled over in hacks and coughs. Straightening, she dabbed at her mouth with a soiled handkerchief. I couldn't be sure, but I thought I saw blood on the handkerchief. Apparently, the sailors weren't the only ones affected by the weather.

Not knowing how to respond I just shifted nervously from one foot to the other taking stock of their quarters by looking past the plump little Frau. I could see the cabin to be about the size of a crypt, rust from the porthole bolts streaking the once whitewashed superstructure wall that was now yellow and cracking. The other cheap plank walls had no paint; the moisture of the sea had bowed and warped the raw wood. I was amazed that a woman could muster such haughtiness from her current surroundings, but Auntie Ekop was doing a damn fine job of it. A sudden bustling came from behind Frau Ekop as Helga pushed her auntie out of the way, face glowing with radiant brilliance, "Herr Opfer, how do you do?"

I stood there speechless for a moment, cowed by her beauty. Collecting myself like a marionette puppet suddenly animated, I sprang into wild gesticulations and frivolous talking. I wasn't saying anything of substance, but my mind registered that my body was gesturing wildly with its arms and spewing forth nonsensical talk and giggling. *For Christ's sake, get a hold of yourself, man!* I must've done or said something right, because I managed the tiniest of smiles from Frau Ekop's ice façade before Helga and I set off for the ship's deck.

"Auntie, get some rest while I'm gone. I'll be back in a little while," she called pushing the heavy door closed.

"I worry for my auntie," Helga said as I inhaled the scent of lilac that wafted from her head, "she has been coughing and lethargic for many months now, but since boarding the ship it has only gotten worse. I fear consumption, but at this point, there is nothing that can be done until we reach America." We fell into step on the varnished wooden planks. The shiny deck reflected the moon and stars overhead, and my euphoria grew as Helga talked. "She rarely rises from her bed because she has no energy, and she won't eat hardly a thing. In fact, the only time she has risen and dressed is because she knew you were coming to call."

Helga could've talked about anything, and I would've listened and cherished every word. *She is such a beautiful creature,* I marveled, absorbing every detail of the delicately carved features and relishing the clean linen smell of her clothes

"In fact, in the ways of the old country she would've insisted on chaperoning an excursion like this, but she is far too weak to resist my protests." She looked up at me and flashed a stunning grin.

My heart leaped into my throat, and I nearly choked. "That sure is a shame. About your auntie, I mean," I stammered. Gaining confidence,

I continued, "Once we get to shore I know some remedies my mother used to make back in St. Goar. If I can locate the ingredients in the new country, I can make it, and it will cure your auntie for sure. My brother was once afflicted when we were merely boys with the same sort of thing and my mother cured him in just a few weeks."

"Oh would you do that for me?" she cried in joy. "That would be so sweet of you!" I casually took out my tobacco pouch and began to dexterously roll a cigarette. The slight breeze made it slightly difficult, but soon I was victorious and smoked quietly while my little nymph prattled on cheerfully as we continued to make circles around the darkened deck. I was glad we now talked of happy subjects and not the misery we both had left behind. We were heading toward a more wonderful place, so why not talk of happier things?

Every time we passed the night watchman, I felt like his eyes were boring into my back as we passed. He stood in a shadow, and I couldn't see his face, only knew his presence by the glowing ember of a pipe that glowed softly in the black shadow. Maybe he was admiring Helga's beauty? Maybe I'm paranoid; I shook the feeling off and diverted my attention back to the most beautiful woman in the world. She surprised me by asking, "So why are you really heading to the great land of America?" Her large brown eyes bored into me, and her bosom lightly brushed my sleeve, electrifying every nerve in my body.

I inhaled the last bit of my cigarette and tossed the ember into the ocean. "Well," I said thoughtfully, "The fatherland is changing, and maybe not for the better. My family all disappeared while I was away at university, so I had nothing to really stay for. I decided I'd try my luck in a new country. Maybe make a fortune...start a family...try to forget about my family." I spoke only the partial truth, but I really *did* want to flee the memories of my fractured youth.

"Oh, you mustn't ever forget your family! That is who you are, Gregor! It's your heritage; you are Prussian, and even though you may adopt another country, never forget that!" she cried with conviction.

"Yes, I guess so," I replied quietly, my thoughts diverted from the present.

"Oh, Gregor, you are so silly! So serious!" Helga suddenly exclaimed, and I laughed. She joined in and soon we were laughing and reminiscing about good times we had in the fatherland. I had less to talk about than she, but she regaled me with stories of growing up in one of the wealthiest Prussian families. I heard about great balls, holidays to Italy, England, and France, great athletic events, feasts of unimaginable proportions, festivals, and more famous people that I could shake a stick at. Before we knew it, it was getting late, and a chill had set in. "Well," Helga sighed shivering, "I guess you better walk me back to my cabin."

"Yeah," I said dejectedly.

"I had such a good time. You are perhaps the most interesting person I have ever met," she quietly said, a small smile on her face.

I smiled wider than I had ever before in my life, "Really?"

"Yes, really, and I hope we can walk like this every night after you finish your work. There is so much more I want to know about you."

"Sure thing!" I replied, heart racing. I walked her back to her cabin. When she opened the door, I could hear her poor auntie lying in the stagnant darkness hacking in her restless sleep. The door closed with a bang, but I hardly heard it for my heart was with the stars in the sky. I whistled on the way back to my bunk. Whistled!

The radiant brilliance of Helga opened newfound senses and feelings within me. I had never known such joy and ecstasy. Just the sight of her brought shivers down my spine and caused my heart to race like a thousand Roman horses pulling chariots into battle. I was so blinded by Helga's brilliant radiance I let it blind me from the very real danger I was in, and it nearly cost me my life. It was the first and last time I ever let my guard down.

Chapter 20

The workday ended, and I shook myself from the trance I had worked myself into. It's the kind of stupor one finds oneself in when doing a repetitive task over and over. One need not think about it but merely let their hands labor without thought. I needed not even to count the tacks; I could pick up a handful and tell if it was the right amount by weight. Today I had been thinking about the evening on the freighter, the one that nearly cost me my life. If I had died that night, I wouldn't be here today, laboring in this industrial hell. *Interesting,* I thought while shuffling back to my cell.

Once back in my cell, I took off my shirt. My chest is covered with scores of tiny red sores. They itch like the devil himself, but I dared not give in to temptation and itch them, for I knew they would only worsen. I suspect my mattress is infested with bed bugs. Unfortunately, I have no choice but to lie on it; there isn't even enough room to stretch out on the cold marble floor. If I am lucky, the bed bugs will die off next winter. I slowly ate boiled cabbage and turnips in the darkened cell, kerosene lamps throwing just enough pale yellowish light into my cell that I could make out the small type of my beloved book. *"Let us not therefore judge one another anymore."* After most of the lanterns had been extinguished, and it was too dark to read by, I lay in my cell not able to sleep due to the aching in my leg and the maddening desire to scratch the sores. As I lay in the darkness, my thoughts drifted back to that fateful night on the *Anaranjado.*

Chapter 21

When I arrived back to the hold, after my wonderful evening with Helga, my hammock was untied as usual: petty mental games. I gaily tied it back up and contentedly stretched out in it fully clothed. All around me sweating, stinking men snorted and snored in their sleep. The hold with all its crewmen suspended in their hammocks contained the uneasy air that inhabits the earth before a ferocious storm, but I was too wrapped up in my blanket of bliss to detect it, and I slipped into a wonderfully deep sleep, secure in the knowledge that my life was finally changing for the better.

Hands grabbed me, so many I couldn't begin to struggle. Ropes crossed the hammock. I instinctively flexed my muscles and held them as the ropes wound round and round my body. Soon I was tussled up like a caterpillar in a cocoon. Like any professional, I knew shouting would do me no good, but these men still gagged me with a filthy cloth. Amateurs. At least I knew what I was dealing with. They didn't bother with a blindfold: bad sign. My mind cleared like the sky on a cloudless day as it does in times of danger and processed a thousand thoughts a second as they cut down my hammock and four of them picked me up like you might pick up a log. My face was toward the ground but I could see two other men's boots as the men carrying me shifted around. They easily carried me out of the hold and up the narrow passage to the deck. Once on deck, they dropped me, and one of the men that hadn't been carrying me took a covered lantern and flashed into the open sea. I torqued my body around like a landed fish until I was face up. I knew they had signaled another ship, probably a privateer who would return me to Spain for a ransom that they believed to exist on my head. Once they found out I had no such ransom on my head in Spain I would surely be killed. Images of Helga flashed in my mind, and I knew what I must do or I might lose the only thing in this life that was really worth living for. A plan started formulating rapidly in my mind, old lessons from days spent in the physics hall in Heidelberg. I figured it would be impossible to wiggle from my ties right in front of them without them noticing what I was doing, and my alternate plan wasn't much better, but my faith in God would sustain me. The plan was insanity at best, but having no other options, I bided my time and waited for the opening I needed.

A pipe smoker with thick rubbery lips wasn't about to divert his eyes from me, for I was as good as gold bullion, lying there on deck all trussed up and ready for shipment. He amused himself by treating me to a few sharp kicks in the ribs and some profanity, *"Tú chengas, cabron!"* A glob of spittle landed on my head.

Your day will come, hombre, I thought as pain shot through my ribs as his scuffed leather boots came in contact with my side again and again and again. I didn't make a sound into the gag, but merely looked with defiance into his yellowed eyes. He finally stopped kicking me and silently lit up his cheap bone pipe. The small smokestack belched rank smoke, similar to the larger smokestack located behind him. I took stock of the other men, not wanting to forget any of them; their faces I recognized, but had never spoken to, which isn't to say very much, for I rarely spoke to any of the other crew members. Their swarthy Spanish faces I duly memorized and stored away for later use; the sailor with the blue pea coat, the sailor with the glass eye, the bald coal shoveler, Raúl...*Damn him to eternal hell!* I thought with ferocity.

He stood there; arm in a sling made of a filthy torn piece of rag, glaring at me as if to say with his eyes, *You are going to get what is coming to you.* If my thoughts could have been turned to energy I could've easily broken my binds.

My mind surged with anger towards the man I had thumped earlier. *He thinks he is exacting revenge on me! Well, we shall see who laughs last.* As the men nervously spoke in hushed tones and smoked cigarettes, some of them got agitated, speaking in Spanish so fast that I could understand only bits and pieces. From what I could tell, the men were getting worried if the pickup ship would arrive. "...too rough?....danger?...authorities catching them?..." I could only catch small snippets. One of the men tugged on old-yellow-eyes' shirt and he diverted his attention away from me to jump in the conversation, which was getting louder with greater gesticulations. I knew if the pickup ship did not come, they would surely kill me; either way, I had no choice. I silently gathered my strength and rolled off the deck in one deft movement and into King Neptune's waiting arms.

Chapter 22

On the way down, I could hear muted shouts, but they didn't register, my primitive brain focused on survival. The icy water rushed up to meet me and nearly took my breath away as I hit the water like a sack of bricks. I began sinking immediately, the weight of the canvas hammock dragging me down. Instead of panicking and trashing about I methodically began shedding my ties. Having flexed my muscles when I was tied up, I was able to work the ropes binding my torso down to my waist before shedding the whole mess by pulling it down like a large pair of pants. I quickly shed my tunic and pants and fought to the surface. I was worried about the ship passing me before I had shed my shackles, and the stern of the ship was just passing me.

Thankfully, the amateur kidnappers had not bothered to search my person, and I still had both of my knives on me. I slipped the stiletto out of its concealed holster tied around my forearm, and with all the force I could muster drove it into the wooden hull. Thankfully, the stiletto's tempered iron blade was sharp and thin enough to penetrate the thick wood of *Anaranjado's* aged superstructure. The force of the moving ship nearly ripped my arm out of the socket as I plowed through the water, choking on the brine water being forced into my lungs. Turning onto my back I somewhat managed to glide over the surface with as much dignity as a human can. I looked like an oversized water spider being dragged along, complete with a small rooster tail of water spewing out behind my sorry carcass. By bringing my knees up to my chest I was able to free the other secreted knife on my ankle with my free arm. Saying a small prayer to the Almighty for keeping the knife securely fastened to my ankle I took it and drove it into the hull. With two handholds the force of the ship pulling wasn't nearly as bad, and I was able to take a moment to recoup and formulate my next move. Using alternating knives as handholds, I was able to pull myself the twenty plus feet to the deck. The *thump* sound from the razor-sharp knives plunging into thick wooden hull worried me that the men who tried to abduct me would be warned of my presence, but there wasn't much I could do about the noise. The height to the deck of the ship was the farthest mountain I've ever climbed in my entire life. My muscles were shaking and quivery when was only halfway up, but I *couldn't* quit. I just couldn't. Helga was waiting for me. It was hard to get good momentum to drive the knife into the hull because I had nothing to brace myself against; my legs were just hanging uselessly below me, and a couple of times I didn't bury the knife deep enough to hold myself, and I lost a few precious inches. But I kept at it with the determination of a rat dog at work in a hole. *Thump! Thump! Thump!*

I rolled silently onto the quiet deck, fearful I was betrayed by the noise of the knives burying into the hull. I lay inert for a few minutes and saw nothing. Apparently, the men gave me up for a goner and returned to their nighttime duties or bunks. The forms of tied-down cargo surrounded me like great hulking monsters, flapping quietly in the inky blackness as I lay breathing hard from exertion from the past terrifying five, ten, fifteen minutes—God only knows how much time had elapsed since I was taken from my bunk.

Once I was positive that none of my antagonists still lurked about, I rolled into a crouching position and slowly rose up behind one of the anchor devices to peer about. When my breath finally returned, I slipped my ankle knife back into it's holster and crept naked through the dark forest of monster forms. Dripping water formed a little trail and mapped my progress around the deck. I didn't notice the nip of the air on my damp, nude body because my normal mind was not present. The combat senses, honed from years on the streets of smelly little villages as well as in thick Germanic forests, took over, and I was focused on one thing. Really the only one thing I knew how to do well, for it was hardwired into my brain, a part of my being. Killing.

I wonder if Captain Alejandro knows his night watchman tried to make some money on the side, I thought grimly while peering from behind a crate at old yellow eyes. He strolled the decks leisurely enough, but with just enough halting in his step to give away his guilt. He walked almost like a horse does when sensing danger, but rides forward because that is what the master desires. Old-yellow-eyes was dancing the way a spooked horse does, taking great bear-like pulls from the bone pipe. I had much work to do so I couldn't watch his patterns for too long before striking. So, after he paced the deck three or four times I silently sprinted to a large coil of rope, ducked behind it and waited patiently. Sure enough, before long I could smell the scoundrel before I saw him. The fresh, clean smell of the vast Atlantic was replaced with foul cheap smoke: paupers blend. When he passed by, I rose silently behind him and plunged my stiletto into the base of his neck. Effectively paralyzed, he dropped to the deck without a sound, other than a dull thud, and the clattering of bone on wood as his pipe skittered across the deck. In his last few moments of soiled grace, he recognized my face looming over him before the eyes went blank, staring orbs of yellow. I removed his clothing, rank and foul rags, and donned them. I dragged his carcass to the edge of the deck and removed my knife, which I wiped clean on his olive skin before unceremoniously kicking him into the sea. Finally, to totally erase this man's existence, I picked up his chipped bone pipe and heaved it out to join its owner. *One down, five to go,* I thought, grimly hoping I would have enough time before daybreak to complete my bloody cleansing. With a long sigh and nimble mind, I opened up the main hatch and crept down the ladder with nary a sound.

At the bottom of the ladder, I picked up a candle and struck a sulfur match on an iron fastening. The pungent smell of the sulfur filled my nostrils as the tiny amount of light illuminated the cavernous cargo hold. The hold held precious goods from every corner of the earth, linens from Great Britain, spices from the Orient, rugs from the Arabics, gold from the great Dark Continent, and mail. I moved in between the towering stacks of boxes marked with a myriad of languages, stamps, and official seals. At the end of the main hold I pulled open a door and entered the guts of this ancient beast. By the flickering light of the candle stub reflecting off the dingy bare wooden walls, I was able to navigate the tiny passageway. Due to my prodigious height, I had to stoop to enter the passageway, lest I smack my head into the innumerable iron nautical fixtures suspended overhead. I made a left, ducked under some ropes and dodged some barrels and made a right. I came to a door and felt it. It was warm to the touch. The heat inside the boiler room was stifling. Only the stoutest of men could handle the grueling work of shoveling coal into the temperamental boilers. But even these hulks of men were no match for a somewhat smaller, but thoroughly seasoned killer, such as myself. Taking a deep breath, I opened the heavy door as quickly as I could.

Damn, I thought quickly, assessing the unanticipated situation that greeted me. Quickly the stiletto flashed toward the man nearest me. Metal ripped flesh with sucking sound, and I knew I had hit true. I let go of the hilt of my dagger and crouched down in one fluid motion, drawing the knife secured to my ankle. A body hit the floor, the dagger protruding from the eye socket, but I didn't even notice as I sprang up and flicked the knife with a neat little flip of the wrist; a throw perfected from many days of practice at the university. The knife flew through the air with a whirring sound and buried itself into the bald man's chest. With a yelp of pain, he exclaimed, "Holy Maria! A ghost!" before falling to his knees clutching at his chest.

Pulling the stiletto out of the dead man's eye socket I quickly pounced on the bald man like a lion pounces on an injured gazelle. "Repent now, or live forever in damnation," I whispered hoarsely, standing over the quivering mass that once was a man. As his lips moved in silent prayer I pulled his head slightly back and to the left and sliced from just below his earlobe to his midline, effectively severing the superficial veins and arteries. The spray from the neck hit the wall, and I cursed at my stupidity at making such an amateur mistake. But what is done is done. The blood continued to squirt out, but with less pressure as each heartbeat got weaker and weaker until the blood just ran out in a small stream from the wound. The bald man's eyes glazed over and blood came out no more.

After retrieving the knife from the bald man's chest and cleaning both knives off I stuffed the bodies, with considerable difficulty, into the belching furnaces of the boilers. The flames greedily gobbled up their flesh. Oily fat oozed from the carcasses, hissing and popping as the tiny room filled with the repulsive stench of burning flesh and fat. Any inexperienced person would have gagged, but I had smelt too many burning bodies in my former profession to even notice the acrid odor. Using a coal rake, I pushed the bodies to the back of the coal bed and laboriously shoveled a mound of fresh coal into each of the furnaces. The fires roared and the men were engulfed in a fiery pyre. I knew that within the hour there would not be enough of the men left to even discern them as men. I waited a few minutes for the flames to die down in each of the two furnaces so I could add more. The man who wasn't bald was an innocent bystander, but I rationalized with myself: *He covered for the other boiler man while the bald man abducted me. Someone had to feed the furnaces or else their little plan would have been figured out. The man was not that innocent…he was either on the take from the bald man or in on the plan. Either way, I figure he's guilty in the conspiracy.*

The boat was soon going to lose speed when the boiler furnaces were not fed and the crew would be alerted as to something being amiss. Time would be limited in eliminating the remaining culprits. I had no time to clean up the blood on the boiler room wall…not that that would matter in the morning when the men go missing. Foul play would surely be suspected. The clock was ticking for me to finish my vindictive deeds.

The remaining men slept snug with the knowledge they had gambled but came out even. Nothing gained, nothing lost. Their chests rose and fell in the sleep of the guilty as I gyrated amongst sweating, stinking bodies in the crew quarters. The ubiquitous coughing sounded around me as well as the snorts and snores from the slumbering crew. Now was the time to finish my work undetected. Unfortunately the situation presented me with a strange quandary, I wanted them to disappear, but there was no way I could kill, then carry four grown men onto the deck without waking somebody, I would have to kill quickly and cleanly and leave the corpses in their hammocks to sway and rot. But how to kill them? Choking is too unpredictable, even if done properly. The victim becomes conscious and can put up a pretty damn good fight. I didn't want to risk even the slightest noise that might wake the entire bunch up. I sat and pondered my dilemma for a moment before the answer hit me like an eagle swooping down on a field mouse. I hopped up and stole back out onto the deck.

Chapter 23

Once back in the chilly salt air I dashed about the deck like a madman until I finally located it, a large coil of metal cable. The cable was stored in case the *Anaranjado* had to tow another ship through a harbor under it's modern steam power technology and consisted of many fine pieces of metal wire braided together. After working my razor sharp knife along the edge of the cable, almost like I was sharpening the knife, I was able to shear off a six inch razor sharp metal splinter that was about an eighth inch in diameter. Ripping a small piece of putrid cloth from old-yellow-eyes' shirt I fashioned a protective sheath around one end of the splinter and quietly raced back to the crew berth.

The first victim I came to happened to be the sailor with glass eye. I inserted the splinter in his nose and violently shoved it upward as far as I could. Using a vigorous movement, almost like I was stirring with the splinter in his head, I moved it around while holding his head with the hand. Old glass eye never moved during the attack but became deathly still after I pulled the splinter out. A bit of bright red blood trickled from glass-eyes' nose, and I wiped it using my shirt. I checked for breathing and a heartbeat. Nothing. It looked as if he were sleeping.

Pleased that my method worked so effectively, I let the other two enter eternal sleep in rapid succession then descended upon Raúl. He tossed and twitched in his hammock like a man sleeping with much baggage on his mind. I stood over my adversary in the rocking and swaying dark watching him as he slept like the cat watches the mouse nibbling on grains of wheat in a field before making its silent approach. I would've liked for Raúl to know he was going to meet his maker but it was too risky to toy with him. Instead I muttered under my breath,

"Be thankful our Lord and savior bled and died on the cross for you because, unfortunately for you, the Good Book tells, 'An eye for an eye; tooth for a tooth,'" With that, I rammed the long, sharp metal splinter up his nose, twisted and waited until his cessation of breath. When his chest stopped rising and falling, I found I was sad, for he did not suffer for his sins but found some consolation in carving the only symbol I have known to be pure and representative of what is good, pure, and powerful in this world into his forearm. I stuffed a bit of dirty cloth over the wound before rolling his sleeve down to avoid detection of the mutilation and stole silently back onto deck.

The ocean quickly disposed of the splinter, and I plotted my next move. Daylight had to be drawing near. The night had taken on that crisp smell it takes in the hour before dawn. I knelt on the deck and wept to God, praying for his forgiveness and understanding. "I am trying to be virtuous, but those men made it impossible," I wailed softly into the vast inky sky. The stars didn't answer my repeated petitions, but only winked and twinkled in silent response.

The early morning found me smoking shakily in the quiet stillness the air assumes after the deluge. I wore new clothes, a white cotton blouse, canvas short pants, and a cotton lightweight short coat I dredged up from my bag, and had disposed of yellow-eyes' clothes into the waiting sea, the last piece of evidence that could tie me to the killings, other than matching the symbol I carved into Raúl's arm a match to my tattoo. The shouts of the men soon echoed through the old wooden ship as the bodies of the four men were discovered. Miguel (who warranted a special berth, being the first mate) was alerted, and I saw his form move rapidly across the deck and disappear below. I finished my cigarette, flicked the butt into the churning sea, and slipped undetected into the crew quarters. The men were in a frenzy, believing their shipmates to be dead from disease. The ever-unflappable Miguel was waving his arms trying to control the situation. *"Hombres! Hombres!"* he said in a loud tone, not quite shouting. "Do not worry, we will bury these men at sea in a moment's notice, and their cause of death shall not circulate around anymore!" The men had quieted somewhat but still murmured uneasily. Nonetheless Miguel continued, his countenance a mask, "I have seen this before." He said obviously lying, "It is a plague that can only be passed through living men. Since these men," he exclaimed with a dramatic flourish, "are obviously dead, you all will be fine. To be doubly sure though, we will give them the proper seaman's rites this very morning. Do not worry. Now go about your duties, and I will report this to Captain Alejandro. He will surely agree with me, for he has seen everything on the seven seas! Now carry on with your usual duties." The men seemed somewhat appeased by his explanation and quietly broke up, but I knew this quiet was not to last much longer. I was correct.

In the minutes that followed, while up on deck trying to look like I was busy checking the mooring lines of the deck freight, two wild-eyed men burst onto the deck screaming gibberish laced with many obscenities from what my pseudo-Spanish could pick up from their lightning pace. "Quick....quick," the leader of the two, a swarthy Spaniard with only one ear and a purple silk sash tied around his waist panted, yelling to all the men on deck, "you must come quickly! Something...so...happened...boiler room!" The men clamored around, suddenly re-agitated into a writhing, yelling mob. The wild-eyed leader made the gesture to follow with his arm, and the mass disappeared like a stampeding herd of cattle into the ship's belly. I knew those two men had discovered the carnage in the boiler room. There was nothing I could do but wait. Dropping all pretense of working, I sat down and rolled a cigarette. I licked the end and struck a match on the deck floor and puffed away. It took a long time for every person in the group to snake their way to the boiler room for a look. Soon enough, the mob appeared back on deck; I was on my second cigarette.

Captain Alejandro, having heard the new commotion, appeared on deck as the mob of frightened sailors swarmed around him. Having sailed with these men for a number of weeks, I knew they were hardened men. These men had sailed all over the world and had seen everything, and weren't scared of anything...real. These men were criminals, dangerous men who would slit each other's throats at the smallest infraction for the tinniest amount of money. The only reason peace was kept was due to the fact that they all needed each other in order to survive everything Mother Nature threw at them on the high seas. But as I watched this crowd of hardened men I heard shrieks of, "evil spirits!" and, "demons." Fortunately for me, hardened men were also ignorant men, and ignorant men are often superstitious.

I sauntered up to the crowd and fought my way through the thong of people to be able to hear what the captain was saying. "Men! This is not the work of evil spirits," his voice boomed out across the ship, face red from anger, "this is the work of evil men! Now, I am going to find the scoundrels who committed this vile act in the boiler room and the bunkroom and have them executed!" He waved his fist in the air and stated, "These persons or person shall hang from the mast!" He pointed at the main mast. "Do any of you have any knowledge to who might have caused this?" Silence. The silence lengthened and became thick and hot, suffocating me. I gasped for breath. If I had been a lesser man I would've been doomed.

A man from the crowd yelled, "It's the foreigner! It has to be!" In predictable mob mentality, the rest quickly agreed with shouts and shoves, and soon I was jostled next to the captain.

I protested with only the perfect innocence my training could produce, "My fellow sailors," I shouted over them, "what good reason would I have for committing such acts even if I was capable of them? I only want to get to the Americas, and I realize that each and every one of you is vital to me getting there! Why would I harm someone on whom I am dependent? And furthermore, how could I possibly kill *all* those men in the bunkroom without any of you knowing? That would be impossible for any *mortal* man." I let my words ring and stared at them in defiance as they chewed on my insinuation of evil spirits.

A grizzled old sea dog from the crowd piped up, "By damn, you used black magic! I know your kind from the eastern hills, using your spells and whatnot to paralyze men and drink their blood!"

"Black magic?" I replied sounding incredulous, "That is absurd, no such thing exists!"

"The foreigner did it with his magic! Lets make him pay," the old man shouted as the crowd surged forward.

Hands grabbed and tore at my new clothing until Captain Alejandro roared, "Enough! Back to your work now! Juan! Jorge! Clean up the boiler room then get back to work! *Rapido*... We've lost enough time as it is without power, and we need to get back to work! I'll look into this matter and find out who did this grisly deed, and until then you scallywags are going to work like you signed up to or you won't get your cut!" The men didn't move too fast, still milling about in fear and confusion, so the captain helped their progress by drawing a pistol from his belt and roaring, "Now!" The men all jumped to like barrels of powder had been lit under their asses. I jumped to, also, but the captain restrained me with his hand on my shoulder. Within seconds, the ship was back to its normal activity. I stood up with the captain and observed this activity; it had an unnatural air to it, like the men were working, but in a contrived sort of way.

Sighing, I glanced at the captain, "I must be getting back to work, sir."

"Oh no you don't. You're coming with me," he venomously said as he grabbed my collar and dragged me back to his quarters.

Chapter 24

Captain Alejandro sat me down roughly on a scarred wooden stool. I fumbled around in my jacket until I came across a tobacco pouch. Fishing the items out, I began rolling a smoke, my fingers nimbly navigating the project while the captain paced up and down as much as he could in his small cell-like cabin. A couple times I thought he was going to start talking, but he paced in silence, like a caged tiger paces at a zoological exhibition. I lit my cigarette with a random sulfur match I located in the coat and sat holding the cigarette in my left hand and subconsciously running my right hand up and down my facial scar; eyes following Captain Alejandro's every minute movement. Finally, he spoke facing the closed door, "I'm not sure what transpired last night, but there is no doubt in my mind you are somehow involved."

I wasn't sure it was a statement or a circumvented question and chose to remain silent. *Inhale. Hold it, and breathe out.* We sat in more silence as he organized his angered thoughts.

"I wasn't elected to be a captain by being a blundering idiot, and I am not a rash man." He whirled to face me, "But damn it! I will not have this on my ship! Two of my men are missing and four more are dead under unusual circumstances. What do you have to say for yourself?"

I lazily replied, "The open seas are a dangerous place," I took a drag of my smoke, "you should know that as well as any man. Me, I am a novice. I do not know what goes on, only what I heard this morning."

His eyes grew wide and nostrils flared to my response. Remembering what I had done to him on the docks of Port Huelva, he didn't not touch me, but I suddenly found his face less than six inches from mine. His rancid breath washed over my face, "I have known men like you over the years I have sailed the sea. Killers. I can see it in your eyes." His teeth gnashed, "Now I have no idea how you managed to kill six! Six, of my sailors, but there is little doubt in my mind you are to blame for this. Now I must sail this vessel shorthanded, and that endangers everyone!"

"Perhaps the ship is safer without those men, no?" I said gazing deep into his eyes while dropping the cigarette onto the floor and grinding it out with the toe of bone-pipe's boot, for I had saved his boots.

He straightened up and fairly screamed, "I knew it wasn't a good idea to bring you on! *Mierta!*" Then calming somewhat, "Miguel told me you were an all right sort, so I pushed my bad thoughts about you from my head, but now I can see I was made a fool...We are only five days from New York: seven, tops. And you are to remain out of sight for the duration! You are to sleep in the hold with the freight from now on, and for God's sake stay out of the way of the men. They want to kill you, and frankly I wouldn't mind if they did, but somehow I have the feeling if they tried, you'd still be walking the decks while more of my men fed the sharks."

With that statement, my mouth turned up ever so slightly at the corners; I couldn't tell if the captain noticed. If he did, he ignored it, but I kicked myself for showing emotion: *Get a hold of yourself! Do not show weakness.*

"Dismissed!" he barked.

I left the man's infamous Spanish temper roiling, and smiled to myself as I confidently walked from his cabin. *That whole ordeal went as smoothly as it possibly could have,* I thought thinking back on the past...six, seven hours. Cripes, it had only been a few hours since I had been snatched from my bunk. Suddenly seething, I thought of the idiocy those men displayed by their insatiable greed. They conjured up a hell storm for what? They would've each made a few ounces of bullion off my sale to pirates. Fools and traitors, that's what I'm constantly surrounded by, I knew the captain told me not to return to the crew's quarters but I paid no heed to that order as I nonchalantly walked in. Most of the crew is out working for the day, but a few men, from the skeletal night crew, tried dozing in their bunks unsuccessfully in light of all the excitement that transpired this morning. They eyed me warily as I retrieved my precious clock and ducked out. I strolled to the hold and searched about for a hiding space. In a dark corner of the hold, on the port side, I wedged my hemp rucksack with the clock stowed safely in it, in between the hull and a support beam. I covered my sack with a piece of canvas tarp I pilfered from a neighboring crate and retreated out of the dark hold before heading to the mess area for a small pot and a handful of coffee grinds. The mess area was deserted; the cook is also a rigger. I stoked the clay and brick hearth and heated the small bit of water to a boil before adding the grinds. In amongst a stack of dirty dishes in a tub of brine water I located the cleanest pewter mug and filled it with the steaming liquid before heading up onto deck to drink the coffee and loaf in front of the working crew. I wanted to make it known I was someone to be reckoned with.

Chapter 25

Another day, another batch of shoes, another day of having my soul systematically stripped. I lay in my bunk, arms folded behind my head, staring at the ceiling in the still darkness. The nightly beating was about to start. Having been at Sing Sing long enough, I knew that it was about this time of night when the storm would break. The storm didn't break the same time every night, but an experienced inmate could add up all the signs and make a good prediction. *Who will it be tonight? How bad will it be for that poor slob?* I lay with my legs tented, for it alleviated some of the aching to have my knees at a forty-five degree angle. Sighing, I swing my clubfeet onto the cold marble floor and slowly stand, inwardly groaning with pain, and shuffle the two steps to my sanitation bucket. I drop my trousers and am in the process of urinating when I hear the commotion below me: nothing loud, merely some clanging doors and muffled grunts. I lay back down on my filthy mattress, lace my hands together back under my head and listen to the commotion until I drift off to sleep. I dream about the events following that infamous night on the *Anaranjado.*

Chapter 26

I no longer put on the pretense of working, and was sitting by the starboard railing smoking the second day after the incident, staring at a school of dolphins swimming alongside the ship as Helga ran up to me breathlessly. "Gregor, Gregor, you have to come quick!" she exclaimed, wild eyed, her clothes a disheveled mess.

I could tell by her demeanor something was wrong, "What is it?" I replied, alarmed that her usual impeccable appearance was nothing more than what appeared to be nightclothes.

"It's my Auntie; there's something terribly wrong," she wailed clutching me, "I don't know who else to turn to!"

"No, no, you did the right thing," I assured her, supporting her weight while flicking my unfinished cigarette butt over the side. "Is your aunt in your cabin?"

"Yes," she replied. I half carried her back to her cabin. I swung open the heavy wooden door: the smell of rot and decay permeated my nostrils. A small, huddled form lay shivering in the lower bunk emitting a ghastly hacking sound.

I crossed the tiny cabin, leaving Helga clutching the doorframe, and crouched down by Frau Ekop. "Helga," I called, "have you got a candle?" A moment later a candle stub appeared over my shoulder held by a parchment white frail hand. I fished in my jacket pocket for a light. The scene that greeted me in the pale light was not reassuring. Frau Ekop's face was pale yellow, bloated, and moisture oozed from the pores on her face. Blood covered her mouth and stained the sheets where she had been coughing it up. Her eyes fluttered rapidly under her eyelids. "Frau Ekop, Frau Ekop," I said gently shaking her. No response.

Helga, standing over my shoulder said quietly, "She hasn't been responsive since early this morning, maybe six or so."

"That makes it," I did some quick calculations in my head, "about five hours." I sighed inwardly and put my head to the slightly rising and falling chest. The heartbeat was very faint, but it was hard to hear amongst the constant coughing.

"I'll be right back," I said standing and facing Helga. "I'll go see and if I can find some medicines."

"Will she..., will she be all right?" Helga asked as she bit her quivering lip.

"I don't know," I said sighing. "Oh!" Helga cried before burying her head in my thin jacket and sobbing.

I wrapped my arms around her and stroked her thick, brown hair, embarrassed, not knowing what to say. "Maybe something can be done, but I must go see if I can find some medications," I said pulling her away. "You stay and comfort her. I'll be right back. Keep her head moist with a cloth and see if you can't make her drink some water." She said nothing but merely pleaded with me with those big liquid hazel eyes.

I found Miguel on the bridge, looking at nautical maps spread before him. The wind from the open seas flapped the corners of the maps Miguel anchored down with his hands. "Miguel, I need to know where to find some herbs," I said in an excited whisper, looking around to see if anyone was listening, "Helga's aunt is very sick and needs some medications."

Miguel looked up from what he was doing very slowly and stared at me in a calculating manner. I had not spoken with him since before the attempted kidnaping and could only imagine the thoughts swirling around inside his head. Finally, he gestured sideways with his head and tugged at my arm leading me down onto freight deck. "Too many ears around up there," he said nodding in the direction of the sailor at the helm. "I know where I can get you some medications...don't know if they'll help. Medications hard to come by on the seas."

"Do what you can," I interjected, pressing some gold pieces into his hand, "you have been a good friend to me, Miguel, and I thank you for that. I will ask you to do nothing else, for I realize what danger you are in for talking to me. Bring the medicines to the passenger berths whenever you are able to locate them."

He looked at me, nodded and started to walk away. As if thinking twice, he suddenly spun and whispered, "As soon as we make port, swim ashore, or bad things will come to you." I nodded and we parted ways.

Chapter 27

A knock resounded on Helga's berth. I opened the door to be greeted by a small cloth sack. When I opened the sack inside the room, I found a bottle of patent tonic that indicated on the label was for "relief from all gut aches," a clove of garlic, a vial of an indiscernible powder, and an envelope of shredded coca leaves. Inwardly groaning at the uselessness materials before me, I said reassuringly to Helga, "Well, we'll give it a try. These look like they may just do the trick." I felt transparent.

Using two tin cans liberated from the galley, I crouched on the deck next to a small fire built in one can with the other one over it, filled with water. I prepared a solution of the powder, garlic, and coca, boiling the water to prepare a liquid solution. Once the water in the upper can had boiled for a time I strained the sediment out and took the cooling liquid back to the cabin. Frau Ekop had already spit up most of the tonic I tried to administer, and combining these ingredients was a last-ditch effort. I had no idea the effect they would have on her, but given the circumstances, I felt I had few other choices. Darkness was falling as I ducked back into the passenger hallway and entered Helga's berth. "How is she?" I inquired quietly, still holding the tin can filled with my concoction.

"Same," Helga replied, sitting on the floor next to where her auntie lay, stroking the old woman's hair in a methodical fashion.

"Let's try this," I said, gently moving Helga out of the way. Helga's clothes were sweat stained and rank smelling from repeated wear, her hair tied up, rouge strands hanging out, but she never looked more beautiful. I cradled the old woman's head in one arm and poured small amounts of the liquid down her throat. Occasionally, she coughed and spewed some of the liquid mixed with blood onto my shirt. It was slow going. When the last of the liquid was down, she sighed and lay back peacefully. Her coughing subsided and breathing became regular. Helga and I sat in the smelly dark crypt holding hands in the hours that followed. We sat in silence listening to the old woman's shallow breaths and steady coughing. At some point I fell into an exhausted sleep.

Awake. I blinked rapidly figuring out where I was. Helga's head rested in my lap, and established that I was leaning back against the cold wooden wall, head resting on a rivet. I stretched so as not to wake Helga, and found my neck stiff from sleeping in such a position. I gently moved Helga's head; she stirred, murmuring, as I unfolded my large frame to check on Aunt Ekop. She was dead.

At some point in the night, Aunt Ekop slipped into oblivion. Shaking my head sadly, not for the loss of life, but for the creature's heart I was about to break, I turned and knelt to shake Helga. When she opened her eyes, she knew. Those large liquid eyes stared up at me, searching my face, before overflowing with tears. Tears streaked her round cheeks and plopped onto the floor.

After awhile I sat back down on the floor. She crawled a bit closer, buried her head in my chest and wept, pounding my chest in rage, "My family is dead! They're all gone. And I don't even know where this relative lives in America! Only my auntie knew! Oh, Gregor, I'm an orphan. I have no, no, nobody!" I let the tiny fists of fury pummel my muscular chest. Soon she quieted and just wept silently, shaking.

I knew what I had to do. In a moment of dizzy headed euphoria and embarrassment I pulled her tear-stained cheeks from by chest and cradled them in my big hands. She sniffed and looked at me with her cloudy eyes.

"Marry me Helga," I whispered with bated breath. "You have me...we have each other...I...I love...you. You need not to find your fourth cousin or whoever it is in America. We will live together and make a nice home and be each other's family." I felt like I was out of my body watching the scene from overhead as I uttered the words.

She burst back into tears, threw her arms around my neck and wept, "I love you, too! Of course I'll marry you."

I sat in stunned silence, holding her, not quite comprehending what just transpired. We sat and clung to each other as the gravity of it all sunk in: *me, married? Married!* I wanted to sing and rejoice, but merely sat in silence, comforting my love. Strange how one can derive happiness from the same situation that causes another pain.

Chapter 28

Auntie Ekop's body hit the water with a loud splash. It lingered on the surface for a few moments before the white sheet it was sewn up in slipped beneath the waves. A handful of the crew, all the passengers, Captain Alejandro, First Mate Miguel, Helga, and I stood gathered at the railing. I would've felt more comfortable to view the proceedings from a distance, but my current relationship with Helga made that impossible.

"...and I will dwell in the house of the Lord forever," the captain concluded, hat in hand as the last of the sack slipped below the black waters. "And now let us recite the prayer He taught us. 'Our Father...'"

We all spoke the Lord's Prayer in unison with Captain Alejandro, after which he jammed his cap back on his head and stalked away. I had gone to the captain yesterday evening, the evening of the morn of Auntie Ekop's death, and plied him for his liturgical services. He balked at first, but after I explained to him how appearances would look to the other passengers as well as pressing a quarter-ounce of bullion into his palm, he relented.

Everyone drifted away after a time but not before taking one last look at the sea as if to see if Frau Ekop would defy nature and thrash her way to the surface. All the other passengers, none of whom I knew, bade Helga their condolences before retiring to their berths. Helga accepted them all with a dignified grace while I looked on. The passengers ignored me. Helga and I stood at the railing long after everyone had left. The sun stood high in the sky, and Helga appeared to be staring at the birds cruising in the distance. I merely held her, trying to give what comfort I could, but I was not good at these matters of the heart. The appearance of birds meant we were close to land, and I knew what that meant. Helga and I were going to have to make our escape from this ship. Things would get harder before they got easier, I could only hope Helga was strong enough to endure.

Chapter 29

Two and a half days after the funeral, a call went out over the decks, "Land ho!" The ship lit up with an excited buzz by the passengers and seamen alike; the passengers with the excitement at finally arriving in the land of milk and honey, and the seamen for a prospect of taking their pay and carousing about in the streets of New York. The ship coursed with an unusual vibrant energy that night as the men scurried about readying the ship to dock and unload. Helga and I crouched in her cabin in the creaking darkness. Helga, unaware of the potential danger, drifted off to sleep, but my senses were too stimulated to sleep. When my father's clock, which I had brought from its hiding place in the hold in anticipation of escaping, read four in the morning, I decided it was time.

Taking a piece of oilcloth I liberated from the hold, I wrapped my precious clock in it, should I need to get wet. I inspected my two knives, and satisfied their blades were sufficiently sharp for whatever might arise, strapped them onto my forearm and ankle. As a final order of business, I wrapped some apples, a cake of pan bread, and a small wheel of moldy cheese in waxed paper and stuffed them into miscellaneous pockets. "My love," I whispered gently, shaking Helga, "we have to go now."

"What time is it?" she sleepily mumbled, rubbing her eyes.

"Early, but me must leave before sunup," I whispered urgently.

"Why? Why can't we leave with all the others?" she said alarmed. She sat up, fully alert, and her eyes darted about like a cornered animal.

"Shh," I said in a soothing tone. "I'll explain later, but the sailors are going to turn me over to the American government. They think I had something to do with those sailors dying. Notice how I haven't been working?"

"Oh, I thought you had worked off your passage," Helga naively said, trailing off. She pursed her lips and put her finger to it. "Why would they think that?" she said growing alarmed again, voice rising.

"I think it's because I'm different, not a real sailor. To be honest, I don't know," I lied unscrupulously, "but the danger I am in is real, my love. Now be a good girl and get your stuff together. We are leaving the boat before the sun comes up. You can't bring much," I said gesturing to her sea trunk. "It's too heavy. I'll buy you new clothing. New American clothing once I find work. The best clothing America has to offer! I promise," I whispered with more conviction than I felt. She grudgingly got up and grabbed a valise and pawed through her sea trunk, selecting various corsets, dresses, and other sundries, and carefully folding them and stowing them into the valise. It was a painfully slow process, but I knew the only way I could get her to agree to jump off a perfectly good ship with a man she hardly knew was to surprise her with the information and not give her time to think. Sleep deprivation can be a very useful tool, or so I have found, and I smiled to myself for my little victory as I watched the bustle of her dress bounce and bob as Helga sleepily rooted through her trunk.

It was getting 'round five o'clock before Helga nervously toed the ground, hidden from view behind one of the large stacks of crates on the starboard side of the ship. In the sleepy gray morning, the boat was stirring quicker than usual at the prospect of land, so I hurriedly unfastened the ropes as quick as my numb fingers could, fumbling with the large knots. The raft was secured in a derrick near the bow of the ship, and I had sneaked Helga out of the passenger hold and up amongst the stacks of tarp-covered crates under the watchful eye of the night watchman, as well the newly appointed position of watchman's assistant. I told Helga to be on the lookout for anyone as I unsecured the boat, but the sight of land passing by on both sides of the ship proved to be too intoxicating, and she just stared in awe at her new homeland passing by. I too had trouble keeping my eyes on my task, sneaking peeks at the docks laden with crates and dotted with warehouses as well as the buildings with three or four floors off in the distance!

America, we have arrived, I thought as I finally loosened the final knot securing the boat, and with some difficulty, shoved it to the edge of the boat. Panting from the exertion of moving the heavy skiff, I gleefully whispered to Helga, "Hop in my dear, America awaits!" She clambered aboard and sat on one of the benches with her valise nestled between her feet. I, with my clock tucked securely in my jacket, released the half-hitch knot Miguel and strained against the pulleys as the skiff swung crazily over the black water. It banged into the side of the ship with several resounding *thuds* before descending at an alarming pace and splashing into the black river. The skiff peeled off from the large freighter and drifted in a languid circle as I retrieved the oars and threw them in the oarlocks. "Safe journeys," I called to the receding ship with a mock salute. Helga merely sat, cowed in her seat with the juxtaposed black river and gray sky in the background as I rowed ashore. "My dear," I cheerily said to her as I laboriously pulled against the oars, "we have arrived!" She looked up at me with a tired smile and nodded.

Chapter 30

I pulled the skiff ashore as Helga climbed out, bewildered, onto the sandy beach next to an enormous dock. "Hey! Hey! You there! What the hell do you think you're doing?" A voice called to me in English, and I spun around to see a man jogging toward me waving. He wore an ill-fitting brown suit, a bit too tight, complete with a brown bowler perched precariously on his head. The man had a handlebar mustache that jumped up and down as he hollered, and he waved a gold-headed cane at us as he breathlessly made his way across a cobbled apron, transversed the dock, and hurried onto the small beach.

"Be quiet until I tell you otherwise;" I commanded Helga in French; "we are in a strange land, and I don't want them to figure out we're foreign. They'll take advantage of us if they find out." She didn't question me and obeyed like a good girl.

I waited until the man got closer before answering. Before he pulled up near me I could see his face visibly recoil, probably at the sight of my face. Obviously, he was not used to encountering educated Prussian men.

"Friend! We were out rowing last night; just out for a picnic in a nice little meadow my wife here knows," I said gesturing to Helga and the valise. "But *then*," I said with emphasis," the current took us and we were stranded out in the river all night until I was able to summon the strength to row ashore. Where in the hell are we?" I was pleased with the quality of my accent, I could tell by the way the man was looking at me, *sans* expression, and his face lit up with incredulity.

"That's terrible, just terrible!" he said his mustache dancing up and down with excitement. "Why you're all the way over in the Bronx! Bronx River Avenue to be exact. Say, where did you come from exactly?" I pretended not to hear as I rolled the word Bronx over my tongue a couple of times, savoring the cadence of the word.

Feigning anger, I suddenly spit out, "I never want to see this infernal thing again! It is too sluggish to accurately navigate the river current." And for good measure I kicked the boat. "Say, would you like to buy it? I'll give it to you for a reasonable price," I crooned the last sentence with the finesse of a slithering snake.

"Well," the man scratched his head, "My boy. Birthday...'ya know..."

Before long we were walking back to Cyrus McCoventy's office for some coffee. My pocket jingled with two-and-a-half dollars, and I wasn't sure if I had gotten ripped off or not. I was unfamiliar with American currency, but I had gotten fifty "cents" more than the price he offered me, so I figured I hadn't gotten totally swindled. "Here we are," Cyrus said, flinging open a wooden door with a piece of glass in it that had his name painted on it with gold paint. His office was located in the corner of a large warehouse, and I noticed the warehouse contained a strange smell, like a circus almost. I was curious as to the contents, but far too polite, and unversed in American manners, to ask. Cyrus moved stacks of papers off two cane chairs and gestured for us to sit. We must've looked quite the sight, me in my Spanish working clothes, and Helga in her Prussian aristocrat dress, but Cyrus didn't seem to mind the discrepancy in clothing—and was probably too ignorant to know the difference—as he bustled around a potbellied stove in the corner of his office, fussing with a coffee pot. Cyrus' office was quite cramped, I observed, looking around: papers and nautical books stacked everywhere, charts of strange rivers and landmasses covering each of the four walls. Before I had time to study everything in the cluttered office, we were sipping pewter mugs of insipid black coffee while munching on pieces of sugar loaf.

"Why doesn't she speak?" Cyrus asked gesturing his head in Helga's direction. He set the ceramic coffee urn down and sank into a battered leather chair.

"Can't talk; hasn't been able to from birth," I smoothly said. Helga smartly remained quiet, I didn't know how well her English would stand up in a situation like this, and I didn't want to attract unwanted attention, especially since the strange situation Cyrus found us in this morning.

"Mute," Cyrus said solemnly and nodded gravely. He didn't stay silent for long. "So, how you getting back to Long Island? What part of the island do you hail from? Always lived up 'round these parts?" He prattled on and on until I was able to steer his talk in the direction of nautical matters. Turns out he owns an import/export business that deals mainly in the trade of curious animals used in vaudeville acts and circuses. He seemed surprised that I did not know of many of the animals he was talking about, and took the occasion to refill our mugs and show us colored pictures of these animals for the better part of two hours, detailing where each one hailed from, and so on, and so forth.

Finally getting up, I told my new acquaintance, "It was nice doing business with you," I patted my pocket, "but Helga is really tired after last night's ordeal."

"Want a lift to the ferry?" Cyrus asked getting out of his seat.

I motioned him back down, "No thanks, friend, you need to get back to work. You have been more than hospitable. We have used up your hours." He looked at me very peculiarly. I figured the translation had not made much sense and hastily wrapped up with, "Have a good day, Mister McCoventy."

As I spun on my heels and walked out the door, a final question followed me, "Say, I've been meaning to ask, what happened to your face?" The question faded into thin air like our footsteps as we quickly made our escape, our nationality status still secret.

We walked aimlessly up one street and down another until the warehouses turned to houses. Huge, soot-covered buildings dwarfed us as we strolled down the wide blocks in the gray morning. Children played in the street, women tossed laundry water and chamber pots from the windows, and street vendors sold produce and textiles. "Where are we going?" Helga asked, small and scared.

"I'm not sure…wherever we can find lodging," I said, thoughtfully scanning the tall buildings, linens hanging from the iron balconies.

"Get outta there!" I growled, grabbing hold of an arm I felt searching inside my jacket. The arm belonged to a filthy urchin that kicked and spat at me as I suspended him a few inches from the ground. "Go on your way boy, and leave me be," I said menacingly letting the boy down and giving him a shove. He showed his teeth to me and disappeared off into the crowd, looking for another victim, no doubt.

Randomly picking buildings, I started going in and inquiring about lodging. "Any rooms available for let?" I would ask in my near-perfect English. The men and women lazily sitting on the stone steps would invariably shake their heads no. Some would jabber in languages I had never heard, some in languages I understood. After trying countless buildings without luck we plopped down on a random stoop to eat some dinner and let Helga catch her breath. Chewing a piece of moldy cheese, Helga suggested with a very unladylike full mouth in German, "Why not ask the person in charge of the building? These people don't seem too friendly...perhaps they don't even know if there is a room to let or not."

"Interesting," I said thoughtfully, "if what you say is true, then these Americans are strange. I just can't fathom why they would tell untruths like that." I bit into an apple, spit out a seed.

The very next building we approached after dinner, 1287 Lafayette Avenue, I marched right in, dragging Helga behind me. The paint inside peeled away from the scarred molding, and plaster hung from the ceilings and walls in places were the filthy wallpaper was ripped off. It smelled suspiciously of urine, and we had to step over one prone body in the near pitch-black front hallway before I located a hand-lettered sign that read, *Proprietor.* "This must be it," I said, knocking loudly.

"Whadda ya' want?" a voice screamed from behind the door.

"You have a room to let?" I yelled back.

"Goddammit, now I havta git up!" I wasn't sure what that meant, but assumed they were coming to the door, as I heard rustling sounds behind the door. A slovenly, fat woman opened the door, and poked her chubby greasy face out, "Yeah?" she said. She was clearly annoyed at being interrupted.

"We are looking for a room to let. Do you have any?" She slowly looked both of us up and down, clearly confused as to why Helga, in her fancy garb, would be at *her* door. She opened the door a bit wider, and

I could sée that she wore a very fancy, frilly dress that was absolutely filthy and practically bursting at the seams.

"You got it?" she asked staring suspiciously at me.

"Got what?" I replied blankly.

"Money for rent." She looked at me as if I were slow.

"Of course," I replied boldly. "Well, I got one room left, want it or not?"

"How's this?" I asked Helga in German.

"Good as any place," she said bravely, but I could tell by the look on her face she was appalled. I would wager she had never set foot place in a place like this before.

"What in the hell is goin' on here? Wher' you for'ner's from?" the fat lady in the dress demanded.

"Mind your own business," I told her sharply, feeling that if I didn't assert myself now, the fat lady would take advantage of me, smelling weakness. Animals can sense weakness. And the fat lady was an animal.

"Fuckin' pig La'tin," she muttered under her breath. I ignored the comment.

"Twelve cent ah day," the fat lady said and scratched her thigh, letting out a huge belch, "I get two weeks advance."

I gave her the two silver dollars McCoventy gave me just a few hours ago; she gave me four, five "cent" pieces back.

"Come with me," the fat lady said, opening the door all the way to let her bulk pass through. Before she left she turned and called through the door, "I'll be right back, an' we'll finish up." She led Helga and me out the back of the hallway to the back yard where another, smaller building stood. Trash littered the tiny, muddy yard, but the fat lady didn't seem to mind, just wading through it, her dingy slippers getting caked with mud. The fat lady climbed the rickety wooden steps with some difficulty, wheezing from exertion. At the top, the third floor, she swung open the door, "Here 'tis," she said without ceremony. Peering past her considerable bulk I could see a tiny, barren room, measuring, if I had to guess, ten by twelve feet. The only item in the room, other than some trash, was a small iron stove in one corner

"No beds or furniture?" I inquired innocently, shocked there was nothing in there.

She let out a loud gawf, "'Dis ain't no fuckin' hotel. Stillwantit?" She looked at me combatively.

"What?" I asked hotly, getting confused as to what she asked and why she was getting mad.

"Do-you-still-want-it?" she said slowly drawing out each word like I was an imbecile.

"Of course; no need to get riled up," I told her, even though I wanted to backhand her off the rickety balcony to the muddy yard below.

She calmed; her trip out of her room hadn't been for naught after all. "You pay me first of the month. Gotit? If not, you're out. Name's Delores." Without further ceremony, she handed me a long iron key, heaved her considerable bulk around and lumbered down the steps, nearly knocking Helga off in the process as she passed us.

"Well, here we are my love, our own little place in America," I said with as much cheer as I could muster, grabbing Helga's valise and plopping it down. Helga walked around, looking bewildered in her new home. No wonder; she had come from one of the richest Prussian families, used to mansions, servants, and fine dining, and now, here she was in some squalid little apartment in New York City's Bronx with little to eat and nothing to sleep on, and this was all due to my former organization. And she was planning on marrying me. Ironic.

Chapter 31

In the evening, the images come to haunt. It's the same every night: the men, women, and children I'd murdered, then Helga scolding me for deceiving her, and for sowing the seed that killed her. In the darkness of my cell, I picture her lying in a pool of expanding crimson blood, head cradled in my lap, in the filthy squalor that was our apartment. The authorities burst in: blinded by grief, I plead and beg with them in German, and they begin to beat me. "I didn't have enough money for a doctor!" I scream over and over. They think I killed my love, my life!

Their truncheons rain down upon me, and I lie in a broken heap until one of the policemen calls to me on the floor, "Ya' fuckin' piece of Eurotrash. Ya' think ya'r a big man, beatin' an killin' women? That make me a big-airh man by beatin' ya'?" Something in me snaps. Before the men can react, I roll to the back of the stove and grab my knives. It isn't until five seconds later, while I am plunging my knife into the throat of my third victim, that I succumb to the truncheon blows and black out.

Every night, *that night* comes back to haunt me, and sometimes it gets so bad that I wish I could go on tapping tacks into boots and never return to my cell to be alone with my thoughts. The memories may be driving me slowly insane. I can't tell…the pain! What did I do? The anguish! What do I do now?

Chapter 32

Things were going fine. I was living the American dream! Best of all, I had given up my old ways. My knives were tucked behind the stove so I wouldn't be tempted to use them, and I read the Bible every night, poring over the wonderful words by candlelight as Helga cooked our supper. Sometimes, I worried God would punish me for my previous evil, but I supposed that God realized I had done it for king and country, and that made it all right in his eyes. I found work on the docks on the east river, working for the United Coal Company on Castle Hill Avenue. I loaded coal onto barges that would then float the coal down to the southern states that didn't have rail access, and no other means of getting it. It was heavy and dirty work, for I had to shovel coal for twelve hours a day from the hopper into little trolleys that then run down the dock and unload into the barge's hold where more men spread it around. The work was honest, and when I started, I would be exhausted after a long day of shoveling the heavy coal. Before long, though, I rippled with thick muscle that lay wonderfully on my large frame, and my hands were covered in thick calluses. I made nine cents an hour, and was glad to get it, for I had gone nearly two weeks without work, and Helga and I had nearly starved.

Since I had gotten a job, we were able to marry, just two months after landing in America, and two years later, the year was 1850, and Helga was already pregnant with our first. We would sit at night and discuss names, and talk about our dreams for our child. I vowed I would quit the docks, and we would move out West, where I could maybe get a little piece of land, and open a store, maybe try my hand at farming or raising some livestock: anything other than toiling on the docks for a lifetime. Our child would grow up a true American, live the dream; reap the fruit of the land of bounty and plenty! I promised Helga nice things, things she had been used to in the old country. She told me she didn't need them or even want them, but I knew better. Mainly we would just sit and laugh and hold each other. I would put my hand on her belly and feel the life inside her and things were perfect.

Money was tight, so when I came home from work one night and found Helga laid up on our mattress, panting and moaning in agony, I knew we couldn't afford the five dollars a midwife would charge, or the ten a doctor would. Plus, I couldn't leave her, not for a second. I had fairly kept to myself our two years here, a throwback to my old habits, and had no friends or neighbors I knew to call to my aid. I sat and cursed myself as Helga lay in pain. I knew nobody would come help me for no fee, only a friend would, and I had not one, other than Helga.

She grunted, cried out, and sweated all night and into the morning. I didn't even think about missing work as the sun climbed into the sky and then back down again, but still Helga groaned as I poured small drops of water on her parched lips. She grew weaker as time passed. No more did she yell in agony, but merely lay in a tired heap and panted shallowly. And then, just as it was getting dark, my love closed her eyes and groaned no more as a giant puddle of blood began to flow from her abdomen. I tried to shake her awake but I *knew* what had happened. The neighbors summoned the metropolitan police when the heard the screams and furniture being thrown about the apartment. The deputies found my little apartment in shambles and me cradling my wife in a pool of blood.

The judge, a traveling circuit judge for the borough, sentenced me to a life sentence at Sing Sing. "Young man," he said addressing me after my pitifully short trail, "you are lucky you weren't killed in county lockup. Especially after killing three of their own. That gives serious merit to your robustness." I sat defiantly at the wooden table that served as the defense table, glaring at the judge, a shriveled up old man, as he droned on. "The department is crying for blood, but due to the mitigating circumstances your lawyer argued, which I have taken into consideration, I believe you will be a much better asset to this great state of New York alive than dead, working off your debt to society through hard labor. Given a month or so time, I'd be willing to wager, you'll probably wish you were dead." The old man smiled down at me evilly and said, "The people find the defendant, Gregor Opfer, guilty, and sentence him to life of imprisonment in Sing Sing." I wasn't really listening anyway. What did I care if I lived or died? Helga was dead; really, I was dead inside. God was exacting His punishment on me for my collection of sins. He rapped the gavel and my sentence was sealed.

Part II: My Nostalgic Rage

Chapter 33

As a small boy I grew up in St. Goar, a tiny village located in an area of southwestern Prussia called the Rhine Province. St. Goar is located directly on the Rhine River, near the borders of Bavaria and Hesse, other Germanic states. The village derives its name from the Roman Catholic statue of St. Goar Aquitana that stands in the town square. It is one of the smaller villages in Kaiser Friedrich Wilhelm III's realm, population roughly nine hundred in the '20s and '30s. I believe one could throw farther than the length of the village, but I liked growing up there, and knew no better, until the age of ten when my life went to shit. It was in St. Goar, living in that small cottage on the left bank of the *Rhein* that I, Gregor Opfer, grew up a pure *Preussen*.

My father, Fritz Opfer, was a prominent clockmaker; his shop only a few blocks down the narrow cobbled streets from the Opfer household. Fritz was significantly older than my mother, Trudi, and as a young boy I remember him coming home for the mid-day meal, his gaunt frame still wrapped in a heavy leather apron he wore while working, and hands smeared with grease from installing small cogs and gears in his regionally famous clocks. Papa, as my siblings and I called him, was of prodigious height and towered over me. I thought he was the tallest man on earth. His leathery face, wrinkled with age, had crinkles at the corners of his eyes and mouth from the grinning countenance that was always painted on his face. "Papa, Papa, what did you bring me today?" my two brothers and two sisters would shout, running to him every afternoon when he would come home from work.

With a sigh, he would sit me, the youngest, on his knee and produce some sweet or piece of fruit for us to share. "How are your studies coming along?" he would invariably ask us. Then, before Mother could see and scold, our little prizes would disappear, as the five of us would ravenously feast on our treats, while clamoring to tell Papa about school.

The mid-day meal was always filled with teasing and tales of our adventures at school while eating plates of bratwurst, sauerkraut, game fowl, fried pork, fresh garden tomatoes, beets, sourdough-mozzarella sandwiches, and drinking great glasses of dark beer. My mother would spend all morning in the kitchen sweating behind a hot fire preparing the mid-day meal. She was a handsome woman, short, with strong, Nordic features and a rosy face. While she rarely smiled, she was a kind woman who had wed my father at the age of seventeen when Papa was forty-eight. My mother and father were devoted to each other, and my father worked well into the night six days a week to see that my mother and us children were never lacking in anything we needed. In return, my mother doted on him, fixing large feasts every afternoon for him, catering to his every whim when he was home, and raising his five children. After the mid-day meal, Papa would return to his shop and my brothers and sisters and I would tear down the streets of St. Goar, eager to get back to school. Those days, like so many happy days of my life, abruptly ended when I was ten years old. Papa disappeared on a chilly autumn day in 1830, leaving my mother with five children to look after.

The exact date escapes me—seems to me it was a Wednesday—but who can really be sure of these things? He just never came home from his shop for the mid-day meal. Sometimes this happened, especially if he was busy, or lost track of time. At the time, we thought nothing of it; we were merely disappointed to miss the daily handout. But when he failed to appear for supper Mother became worried. "Hienrich and Franz, take your brother and go fetch your Papa. Tell him supper is ready," my mother told my older twin brothers with annoyance.

"Yes, Mother," my brothers dutifully replied. I followed them out the door and we wove through the narrow streets in the dark night to Papa's shop. The shop was three blocks from our house and faced the river on the corner of two intersecting streets. Papa's shop was on the bottom floor of the two-story building, and he rented the upper floor to some frumpy old Frau who had lived upstairs forever. When my brothers and I arrived at the shop, we found it lit up, smoking oil lamps throwing a yellowish light onto the darkened street. I remember pushing the door open to be greeted by an eerie silence. The shop looked like it always did, organized chaos; wood shavings underfoot, gears and cogs everywhere, and a myriad of clocks in different stages of completion shoved into every corner of the place. "Pa-pa, Pa-pa," my brothers and I called out, searching the sawdust-covered shop. After looking in every conceivable place, the three of us stood in the middle of the front room bewildered.

"Perhaps Papa is upstairs visiting with Frau Kriegimmer?" suggested Hienrich.

"Let's go check; Mother is going to be cross if supper gets cold," Franz said and we walked outside to the back staircase that led up to the Frau's apartment.

We knocked and knocked. "Where is Frau Kriegimmer, I wonder?" I said perplexed.

"Yeah," said Hienrich, "she never goes out. I'm going inside," he said testing the lock.

"Perhaps that's not a good idea," I said afraid of walking in uninvited.

"Quit being such a little baby," Hienrich said, brazenly opening the door and walking in.

"Frau! Frau! Pa-pa?" We searched the small apartment and found not a soul.

"How strange," Hienrich chatted on the way back to our cottage, "Maybe they went out to eat somewhere or for a drink at the biergarten and neglected to tell Mother." Our boyish minds conjured up several more innocent theories on the short walk home, none seeming very logical, giving that this was quite out of the ordinary for Papa.

"Well?" Mother asked as we piled in the door. My brothers and I breathlessly told the tale of our adventure, each adding things in such a convoluted manner that Mother finally grabbed her coat and instructed us, "You boys stay here with your sisters. I'll be back in a few moments. I'm going to look for your father myself." With that, she left, and the five us sat in childlike silence around the large wooden kitchen table, occasionally offering another theory as to the fate of Papa.

Hours later, my sisters having retired to their loft room, and my brothers playing cards by the dying fire, my mother was ushered in by the magistrate. This woke me where I was napping, my head resting on the hard wooden kitchen table. "We've checked everywhere. There's no sign of your father," my mother told my brothers and me.

"Well, then, where is Papa?" inquired Franz.

"Maybe he went down to Bingen or Mainz, or maybe across the river to Wiesbaden today to sell some clocks and the ferry broke. He'll turn up tomorrow," my mother told us three boys behind a strained smile. "Now you boys head up to bed; you have school tomorrow and it is late." We clambered upstairs to bed while my mother put the kettle on the fire to make some tea for the magistrate.

Soon after my brothers had drifted off to sleep I crept down the narrow staircase and listened with my ear to the door and could hear some snatches of conversation, "...happening around the country...just disappearing...nothing we can do..." I didn't understand much of what I was hearing and soon retired to bed to sleep a deep innocent sleep.

The next day my father didn't return, nor the day after that. In fact he never returned. I often would wait to hear him enter right before the mid-day meal, or walk by his shop after school in hopes of catching a glimpse of him in the window, bent over one of his newest creations. The courts ruled his disappearance "willful abandonment," on the premise that Papa had run away with Frau Kriegimmer.

"Nonsense," my mother always asserted. "Your papa loved us dearly. And, besides, Frau Kriegimmer was in her mid-eighties; your papa was only sixty-four. He wouldn't run away with an old maid like that."

Chapter 34

Mother, only thirty-three at the time of his disappearance, sold his business in order to pay the bills. My brothers and sisters and I would often hear her quietly wailing when we were supposed to be asleep, "Fritz, Fritz, why did you ever leave me? Damn you, damn you!" Mother never was quite the same after that: always a stoic woman, she now was a broken one, almost like she had lost the will to live. She became very emotionally unavailable and despondent. I often think the only thing that kept her alive were the five children.

Soon the money from the shop sale started running out. We no longer ate meats for the mid-day meal, but rather boiled cabbage, radishes, and whatever else Mother could scratch out of the garden. My clothes turned threadbare along with my siblings', and there was no money to replace them. My brothers, now thirteen, and me now eleven, got jobs after our lessons to help Mother pay the bank as well as put food on the table. I inked the press at the local print shop while my brothers set type on the monstrosity of a press. The owner, Herr Bilgunstrom, was a cantankerous man, short and toady, with wispy hair on his large balding head. Herr wore these ill-fitting, too large black suits and a monocle. When going out, he wore a large black cape with matching black top hat. He had more money than Kaiser Friedrich, for he did all the printing in the surrounding towns and villages and had nobody to spend his money on. Among my school buddies, it was rumored he kept all his money in a large iron safe that sat nestled in a dark corner of his cluttered office. But I could never verify this because it was always tightly sealed. Like many businessmen in the area, he owned a shop in the village and ran his business from the downstairs while living upstairs. He liked it that way; a naturally distrustful man, he liked being able to keep a close eye on his business and his inventory.

One day, soon after starting, Bilgunstrom asked me, "Herr Opfer, won't you stay a little longer to help me fold papers? I'll pay you extra of course."

Another mark, yeah, great, you cheap sonofabitch! I thought cynically, but instead I answered, wiping the ink from my face with an even grimier hand knowing how much my family needed every mark, "Yeah, sure, Herr Bilgunstrom."

My twin brothers set the press for the next day, received their few coins of weekly wages from Herr Bilgunstrom and departed, leaving me alone in the darkened shop to wipe down the plates of the day with foul smelling mineral solvents. Herr Bilgunstrom disappeared into his office, leaving me scrubbing away with the solvent-soaked rags.

After I finished I knocked timidly on his door, "Herr, Herr? I have finished. Where are those papers you want me to fold?" I waited, totally unprepared for what was about to happen next.

Herr Bilgunstrom threw open the door and grinned down at me. Blowing his licorice, liquor-laced breath over me, he grabbed me and threw me down, "Get the fuck down there, and keep quiet if you know what's good for you, boy!" Stunned, I lay on the floor as he reached down and yanked me back up. Roughly pulling my woolen trousers down, he kind of laughed a manic laugh. Then, he grabbed me in a place that made my frightened face register embarrassment. "You like that? Huh, you like that?" he whispered excitedly. He giggled, face flush with excitement. "This is what real men do. You like what men do? Feels good, don't it?" I didn't answer as hot rage and shame burned my cheeks. I clenched my jaw. Herr Bilgunstrom continued fondling, occasionally yelling, "Stop it! Just stop squirming. You like this! Stop it!" The rhythm of his big sweaty sausage fingers became more vigorous. After awhile, I blacked out.

When I regained consciousness, I saw Herr Bilgunstrom looming over me, fastening his pants. When he was done fixing his clothes, he threw a few coins on the floor, "Here, there's a little something extra there for you. Now, don't you go telling anyone our little secret," he said grabbing my collar and pulling my face close to his. "Men don't talk about what they do in private. Got it?" I nodded. "Good. Be here tomorrow, same time." I scooped up the money and fled the store, leaving him in his office sipping from his glass tumbler, face red and giddy. When I arrived home, I gave the money to my mother. "Gregor, this is more than you usually get. Have you been promoted?"

"Yeah, something like that," I muttered, rushing upstairs.

Chapter 35

Even though my brothers and I continued to work for that fucking swine, Herr Bilgunstrom, money continued to be a problem. So, two years after Papa's disappearance Mother married a monstrosity of a man named Pieter van Deose. Pieter hailed from the city of Reutlingen in Bavaria, just south of Stuttgart. He was a traveling patent-medicine salesman by trade who happened to pass through town and meet my mother at the local biergarten during a social. Three weeks later they wed. I could tell she didn't love Pieter, least not the way she loved Papa, and I believe Pieter could tell, too, because soon after they were wed, he took to abusing her. I know she did it for financial reasons. I would lie awake many nights in the boy's side of the upstairs loft I shared my brothers and listen to Pieter come home from the Biergarten drunk, and beat my mother. I still vividly remember her crying, "No! No! Please!" As he would beat her and then her quiet sobbing as he would rape her in the kitchen. I vowed on my papa's life that I would put an end to the abuse of my mother, a woman he loved dearly until the day he disappeared. The only thing I have to remember him by, an Opfer Clock, was lost when I was sent here to Sing Sing. Looters or that fat swine, Delores, probably stole it long ago from my tenement on the lower east side.

The abuse continued at my job. I was assaulted at least once a week. I vainly kept my secret from my brothers, lest they learn of my filthy little secret. Even though I tried to avoid Bilgunstrom, he demanded more and more of me; I was soon running his shitty little business. My brothers were only there for a few hours to set the type on the temperamental old machine, then they were gone to play football for the rest of the afternoon, leaving me in the store to do everything else that needed to be done as well as attend to Herr Bilgunstrom's sordid little demands. Then, when I got home, I had to deal with Pieter, and watch him abuse my mother, threaten my sisters, and make antagonizing remarks to my brothers and me. As a result, I withdrew into myself, began reading a lot. I read everything and anything I could get my hands on: Goethe, Wordsworth, Shakespeare, Dante, Voltaire, Beauvior, Homer.... I would roam the surrounding hills of St. Goar, sit in the ancient Prussian forest, and read peacefully, overlooking the visage of the miles and miles of the king's land with the swirling Rhine snaking through the valley. Up there, I could escape from my reality, my hell.

Chapter 36

Located below my village stood a great feudal castle, Schloss Rheinfels. Local history reads that the castle was once the ruling center for the county of Katzenelnbogen. When the Katzenelnbogen family died off 400 years ago the Hesse-Cassel family took possession until 1815 when the castle became property of His Majesty. Town elders tell of the market that used to be located within the castle walls, and peasants would come from miles around to trade their wares there. "Strange things happen there now. Nobody goes there," they would tell me. Apparently, when the king took possession, he closed it up, and since then, nobody has been seen coming or going except for the occasional glimpse of unidentified men riding black horses in the areas around the castle. "The spirits of fallen knights from the Holy Wars," the grizzled old men would tell us children. "They are looking for their families. So don't venture into the woods alone or they might mistake you for one of their children and abduct you!" I didn't believe any of their superstitious stories, and often roamed the area alone without incident. I would often sit in the meadowlands on the hilly countryside surrounding the castle and read from Goethe or paint, hoping to catch a glimpse of some of the characters said to inhabit the castle. I supposed it is just peasant superstition, for in all my childhood I never saw anyone around the castle's foreboding gray walls.

One such autumn day, after wandering the countryside and reading the works of the Englishman, William Blake, I returned home to find my mother bent over the kitchen table and Pieter raping her in a drunken rage. "Hey, you filthy swine! Get off my mother!" I yelled with all the volume and ferocity my sixteen-year-old frame and psyche could muster.

Turning to me, he grinned, "What are you going to do about it, boy?" My mother slipped through his grasp when he turned his attention to me, and now cowered in the corner, blood dripping from her nose, clutching her dress in front of her.

"I won't let a farmer's boy assault my mother like that," I stoically said and placed my book on the chair nearest me, my heart pounding but trying to show no fear. Pieter was a little shorter than me but much bulkier, a formidable opponent. I had never fought a real fight before, and I knew his huge ham fists would make easy work of me.

"Why, you little shit, I'll teach you to insult me!" he said with a roar and charged. I never stood a chance. My large frame hit the floor when he landed the first blow on my chin. Things went momentarily black before I woke up on my back with him hovering over me raining blows upon my body.

He beat me while I called, "Is that all you have? You have the strength of a disease-ridden-whore Frau!" Pieter beat me until he was exhausted. Bloody and ragged, but my goal accomplished, I dragged myself off to sleep in a barn that night; my mother was at least safe for one night. My nose felt broken, but otherwise I was unhurt except from some nasty swelling welts and bruises that turned a deep violet color the next day.

The next day, when I silently entered the house at dawn, she was waiting for me in the darkened kitchen. "Oh Gregor, look at you," she gasped, "You must leave here. Pieter will kill you if you show your face again!" She quietly sobbed for a few minutes while I held her before composing herself.

I realized what a strong woman she really was. "I am not afraid of him, Mother," I said through a swollen lip, hugging her.

"You must leave now; I have packed your things," she whispered pointing to a leather grip in the corner

"But where will I go?" I asked alarmed, "And who will watch over you?" My two sisters had been married off in the past two years. One was living in München and the other on the Norman coast of France, while my two brothers, the twins, had accepted apprenticeships with a merchant sailing company, the Black Ball Line out of Liverpool,

England. As a result, for the past five months it had just been Pieter, my mother, and me.

"'Tis no worry, Gregor, I will be fine. You are to travel to Heidelberg where you will enroll in the university to receive an education. You have always been the brightest of all my children. While your brothers were always interested in playing football and dealing cards in the alley, you read books and learned many things which I could not even begin to fathom. I have hidden some money from the sale of your dear papa's business and want you to take it to finish your education."

She pressed a large wad of notes into my hand. "But, Mother, what about my schooling here?" I asked stupidly.

"Gregor, that will end this year and you know it. You are ahead of your studies and are ready to enter university." With a sinking realization it suddenly hit me, my mother was right. I felt sick.

"Fine, Mother, for your sake I will go, but I will be back to take care of Pieter. He does not treat you well. I will come back and put him in his place. Until then, do not let him harm you. Understand?"

With tears in her eyes she whispered, "Oh, Gregor, you always were such a sweet boy. Do not worry about me. I will write you at the university."

"Mother I will make you proud," I said with tears streaming down my face. I picked up my grip and stole into the breaking dawn, smashing all the windows at Herr Bilgunstrom's shop on my way out.

Throwing open his sash, the bald little man peered out. Blinking, he called, "Hey! What's going on out there?" I picked up another rock, the size of my fist, and heaved it at him, missing.

"Herr, I'll be back for you; mark my words!" I yelled, and then fled on down the road with his shrill voice receding in the background. When I finally slowed, I was shaking from finally having escaped my antagonizers. Later, opening the grip I found a small Opfer clock on top of my clothes with a note attached to it that read: Dear Gregor, Here is something to remember your dear Papa by. Make us both proud. Love, Mother.

Chapter 37

I shivered and pulled my wool coat close around my shoulders and huddled close to the small fire I had built earlier in the evening on the side of a mountain somewhere west of my village. The days were quite warm in the receding days of summer, but the nights had the unmistakable chill of the impending autumn. A wolf howled in the distance. The day had been long, but I had made good progress, making my way in an easterly direction toward Heidelberg. I munched on some cold fried pork and a few mushy apples I had traded a farmer earlier. The greasy pork tasted good after having nothing to eat all day. The pork made my mouth dry so I left the fire and made my way to a nearby mountain stream and quaffed the trickling water. Then I put my throbbing face into the cold stream. The cold felt good and soon numbed the pain a little. Making my way back to my encampment, I thought about my dear mother whom I had only left yesterday morning. It seemed like an eternity since I had left my quiet village in St. Goar. I pulled the clock from my grip and fingered the smooth wooden curves and wound the brass key in the back of it just so. Not too tight, not too loose. Putting it back I lay down and soon drifted off into a restless sleep.

Morning came with a cold gray presence, and I gathered my meager possessions and climbed down the steep mountainside to a road. Checking my bearings with the dim sun skirting behind the clouds I continued heading south. After walking for most of the morning I came across a farmer creaking along the same direction as I was traveling. Her wagon was laden with bundles of vegetables and boxes of homemade beeswax candles. I stepped into the middle of the road and called to her, "G'morning, Frau. Would you mind if I rode with you for a spell?" The withered old woman driving the moth-eaten mule clicked the reigns for the mule to stop momentarily. She motioned to the seat beside her without a word, and I clambered up into the buckboard wagon. She clicked the reigns and we started off again, the wagon bucking and jolting down the rutted dirt road. The wrinkled old woman sat next to me bundled in many layers, a shawl of brown-dyed lambs wool shrouding her frail shoulders, and a yellow bandanna tied around her head. I thought it strange that she wore so many layers on such a warm day, but I thought it rude to ask and just kept my mouth shut. A few strands of white hair fell from underneath the bandanna. She smelled of every combination of all of God's creatures, and I was thankful for the open air.

After riding in the wagon for a few hours I dug around in my grip for a few apples I saved. Pulling two out I offered one to the old woman. She shook her head and turned her attention back to the road before us. When my father's clock told me it was a little after four o'clock in the afternoon, I tugged at the woman's shawl. "Thanks for the lift, but I'll be getting off here. Here take this," I said pressing a few marks into her hand. She smiled through a mouthful of brown and broken teeth for the first time that day, and I could see why she hadn't spoken one word to me the entire day; she had no tongue. I jumped off the wagon and skirted across a field full of waist high early autumn hay. We had passed a sign for the town of Mannheim earlier in the afternoon, and I figured I was just a short ways north of Heidelberg, and would reach it by noontime on the next day. I jumped over a small stream and made my way into the woods. Now sufficiently away from the road and any highwaymen I began to gather wood for a fire. Once I had a blaze going I roasted the remaining apples and lay back, using my grip as a pillow, and drifted off to sleep as darkness spread across the land.

Chapter 38

Weary and bedraggled I stumbled down the hauptstrasse with the setting sun framing the city in radiant brilliant light. I hadn't made as good time as I had originally thought the day before; I had been farther north than I thought. Pausing, I purchased a steaming ceramic mug of glühwein from a street side vendor and swilled the hot-spiced red wine. The alcohol soothed my nerves, and allayed some of my fears. After asking the street vendor and receiving directions, I located the office to the university with minimal difficulty. *Closed for the day!* Discouraged, I spent a little of my money at a biergarten on a plate of bratwurst and crusty black bread, then slept in an alley, the grip clutched tightly in my arms to prevent any thieves from taking my clock or money.

The next day I returned to the office of the registrar. A matronly Frau behind a desk asked, "Yes, can I help you?" Then, taking stock of my purple and swelled face added, "Herr."

Swallowing, I answered, "Yes, Frau, Madame, I would like to enroll in the university."

Peering down her nose at me, she haughtily replied, "Young man, you do realize classes commenced two weeks ago."

Thinking quickly I replied, "Yes, Madame, but I live in the far northern province of Prussia that was hit by major storms; the roads were washed out and it took me *much* longer to arrive than I originally thought." I hoped my lie would work; it did.

"Well then, I guess you'll just have to catch up to your classmates. Here sign this," she said pushing a register book across the table. I signed my name, and carefully counted out the money for enrollment.

She suspiciously looked at all the money I was carrying, normally only royalty have large sums of money, not artisans' sons, which is exactly what I looked like in my navy wool coat, brown wool sweater and gray trousers along complete with watchman's cap containing my longish hair. "You entering as a first year?"

"Yes."

"Then your courses are assigned to you. You will be able to choose come next semester."

"That's fine," I replied, glad that I didn't have to pick my courses out for the first term.

She consulted a large ledger and scratched on a piece of paper for a few minutes. "Here they are," she said handing me the paper.

"Thanks."

"Good luck," she said and returned to the stack of papers on her desk.

"Uh, excuse me," I said clearing my throat.

Annoyed she looked up. "Yes?"

"Do you know anywhere around here where I can let a room?" Thoughtfully she looked toward the ceiling. "Well, I do have a friend with an extra room who is looking for a boarder. Only twenty marks a month."

She looked at me expectantly; I replied, "Sure, sure, sounds good. Where is her house?" The lady gave me directions to the house, and I left the office clutching the sheet of paper with my courses listed.

Heidelberg sits in a valley with the Rhine River running through the western part of the town. I crossed a bridge with a sign notifying me I was crossing Karl's Gate Bridge, turned right onto Alb-Ueberla Street and knocked on number eight. Another matronly older woman, whom I judged to be around sixty, bustled open the door. Her plump figure was topped off by a rosy face on which a large gray bun of hair perched like a neat little bird's nest. "Yes?" she asked, wiping her floury hands on the white apron that covered a plain navy blue dress. She appeared slightly irritated at being interrupted in her work.

"Uh," I stammered. "Frau Grüner?"

"Yes, and who might you be, young Herr?"

"I come seeking room and board, ma'am;" then hastily added, "a woman from the Heidelberg University office told me of you and your room to let."

Her rotund face dissolved into a smile. "Well then! Come in! Come in! Let's get you something to eat. I am frying up some pork. Would you like some?"

"Yes," I gratefully replied, and my stomach rumbled to reinforce the fact that I hadn't eaten a proper meal in, well, shit, I couldn't remember when. Suddenly re-animated, Frau Grüner grabbed my grip and stowed it in the hall and led the way down the hall chattering away, "Good heavens, dear, what happened to your face?" Without awaiting a reply she continued, "You like pickled beets and biscuits?" Before I could answer yet again she did for me. "Well, sure you do. Silly me! All young men love pickled beets and biscuits. Glühwein, too? It is quite chilly out there…" and she babbled on and on until I was seated at her kitchen table with a heaping plate of greasy fried pork covered with vibrant red pickled beets, shiny with brine, and two huge fluffy biscuits parked on the side of the big pewter plate.

During the meal she told me all about her late husband and just about everything else that had happened during the course of her life. Really, I think she had a room to let because she was lonely and looking for someone to inhabit the house with so she wouldn't have to knock about in the place by herself. "My husband, Klaus, worked for the baron that owns the Heidelberg Castle," she said with a nod of her head in the direction of the massive castle overlooking the town. "But back in '26 fell in the large brewing cask and drowned. God rest his soul." She crossed herself. "Since then I have been living here by myself, occasionally taking in boarders from the university to help make ends meet." She droned on and on about this and that; I was only half listening, too immersed was I in her fabulous cooking. At the proper time in the conversation I told her an abridged version of my history in between mouthfuls of the piping hot food, but mainly let her talk; it seemed to be her forte.

After I inhaled the food and drank two large mugs of her Glühwein we talked business. I was feeling pretty giddy from sitting in a warm room near a roaring fire, my belly filled with food and the wine lubricating my brain, so I would have agreed to just about any terms she put forth. As it stood I would pay her fifteen Marks a month, chop all the firewood, haul water daily from the well in her backyard as well as tend to any repairs the house might need. In exchange I would have a private room and three meals a day if I so wished. "Good, it's settled then," Frau Grüner said grinning. "You are such a large, handsome young man, and so personable, too!" Then, leaning close and whispering in a conspiratorial tone she told me, "I like you so I give you this good deal. I not like you so much," she said with a shrug and frown, "you might pay, eh, twenty, twenty-five marks a month. Come, I'll show you your room." She led me up the narrow dark staircase and opened one of the upstairs doors into a nicely furnished room. The room was whitewashed, and flooded with light coming through a large dormer window that looked out over Alb-Ueberla Street. A straw and feather mattress sat on a rope bed and a large wooden desk and chair filled the room as well as a nice washstand. It was perfect. The entire room was a big as the portion of my loft I had shared all my life with my brothers and it would be all to myself! "You like it?" she asked me as I dropped my grip to the floor with a loud thud.

"Yes, ma'am, this is wonderful, almost like a lodge," I replied carefully. I didn't want her to know *how* pleased I was with the room. "Now do you mind if I sleep for a bit?" The strong glühwein had made me very drowsy. Frau Grüner left and closed the door behind her as I flopped onto the bed and fell instantly asleep.

My, what a strong young man to have around the house, Frau Grüner thought gleefully as she glided downstairs. She had much work to be done around the house and couldn't wait to put her new boarder to work. *Too bad I'm too old for relations,* the matronly old woman fleetingly thought as she got to work cleaning up the kitchen; setting aside a hefty portion of cold pork for young Gregor's supper.

Chapter 39

When I started university, at the age of sixteen I was the picture of health. I was a massive 6' 4", weighing two hundred pounds of sinewy, tanned muscle. I had long, blond locks that fell over a pronounced widow's peak and into my bright blue eyes, and I was constantly brushing it out of my eyes. Since I didn't work as a farmhand all my life, I didn't have the leathery texture to my skin that most young men my age did, but rather smooth skin free of calluses, and muscles from chopping firewood for the family hearth. Women would often try to start conversation with me during my time in Heidelberg, but frankly, I didn't know how to respond so I would brush them off and try to avoid them altogether. Years and years of systematic abuse by Bilgunstrom had twisted my mind into something gross and distorted.

Little did I realize that fifteen years' time everything would be different. The luster from my eyes would be gone, and a head of brownish, balding hair would replace my shock of blond hair. My body would be scarred from numerous beatings and abuses, the most obvious of being a long jagged scar that would mar the strong Prussian jawbone and features, and my rippling muscles would be replaced with a quivering useless mass. I would walk stooped over from small spaces and heavy labor; skin gray and pallid from too much time in stagnant air and darkness. Strangely enough though, a lucid and calculating, strong mind from love, knowledge, friendship, and religion would replace my twisted callow mind. Body and mind switched positions at some point in my journey. But I couldn't see into the future as to what my physical and mental destiny would be, nor can I now, but I still wonder at what point in my life I had it better...

Chapter 40

In the ensuing weeks that followed my arrival in Heidelberg I was very busy with my classes. I had botany, chemistry, physics, citizen society, and a French class. Not only did I have to keep up with the normal course load, but also had to make up the previous two weeks I had missed. Thankfully, I discovered a biergarten on the hauptstasse, Black Rhino, past Karl's Gate Bridge, where I would often drink pints of Karlsburg and Harp ale, eat fried pork, and concentrate on my studies. The Black Rhino had low-slung wooden beam ceilings, a small bar at the entrance, and a few stained glass windows that allowed some light from the hauptstasse in, but mostly it was a dark, smoky little hole-in-the-wall biergarten. There was a quiet, dark corner in the back where I could derive chemical formulas, and work on my sketches of plants in relative peace away from the nosy and talkative Frau Grüner.

The barkeep was an angry bear of man, constantly glowering at everyone like we were all trying to steal something, or cause a ruckus. I tried to avoid him, except to order food and beverage. The place was often crowded with other university students, mostly members of the Duellgesellschaft, or dueling societies. Dueling society members could be easily discerned by the long, jagged scars on their faces; it was a status thing in their organizations to have the scars on their face, or so I'm told. Their houses were located directly above the local watering hole on the hillside, so it was very convenient for them to come down to the local bar for a few pints before retiring for the night. Their massive mansions were always locked up tighter than drums from what I could see. The only activity I could observe when I would walk past them on the matrix of steep stones steps leading up the hill toward the castle was the occasional flickering light behind thick glass. It was a mystery to me as to what went on in those places. They sure as hell weren't very sociable with outsiders from what I could tell, not that I really cared. I didn't really pay any attention to their boisterous trouble making and carousing that often took place in this particular saloon, but apparently they were comprised entirely of members of the Germanic elite, their fathers being mostly rich barons or statesmen. I just ignored them and tried to complete my work in relative peace.

On one particular night I was finishing up some observations and sketches of blooming deciduous plants of the local countryside and eating a plate of venison and potatoes when I noticed some of the scar-faced young men from one of the tables looking over at me. They were all sitting about with steins of ale engaged in conversation, save for two young men. I looked about thinking they might be looking at someone in my vicinity, but upon looking around and seeing nobody in my area of the bar I returned to my sketchbook. I furiously sketched, digging my pencil so hard into the paper it ripped. But no matter how long I drew I couldn't shake the feeling that I was being watched. My face burned with embarrassment at the unwanted attention. I could almost feel those four black eyes boring into me; I didn't want any trouble with those fellows. I was just there to learn unobtrusively.

After a spell, my drawing now a blackened mess, I decided to chance a look. Stealing a quick glance toward the table again I realized it must've been a figment of my imagination. They were all engaged in loud conversation with the rest of their friends at the table. *Damn,* I angrily thought looking at my once nice sketch. I finished up my drawings best I could, closed up my book, and headed out into the brisk night air for the short walk back to my lodgings. The cobbled streets were almost deserted at this hour; only whores and drunks lingered about in the back alleyways. The cool air of autumn blew through the wide streets, and I pulled my sheepskin coat around me tighter to keep warm, and pulled down my wool watchman's cap over my golden locks. Way above my head the dim glow of candlelight shone through the drawn drapes of the houses on the hills.

Chapter 41

The rest of the year I worked like I a man possessed. I couldn't go home when the other members of my class leave the university to travel back to their respective homes for the holidays for I no longer had a home. Sometimes my brothers and sisters wrote me, and I wrote them, but I had no interest in going to visit them on my holidays, for I no longer really know them and their families. They lived happy lives, rolling in the ignorance of mediocrity that so many people roll in like pigs in mire; frankly it sickened me. I wanted to drag myself out of working class mediocrity and make something of myself and that's what really drove me. I wanted to be an explorer and write about my explorations, maybe…I studied every waking hour, and when I wasn't studying I was working around Frau Grüner's house to earn my keep. In the rare moment when I did have free time, I roamed the countryside voraciously reading.

I discovered I had an uncanny propensity for language, and I was learning them by reading my favorite passages from the Bible in different languages. Once I had struggled through those passages and had a feel for the language, I foundered through other books in the same language. As I read more and more in that language, it became less and less hard, until I could read freely in that language. I wasn't able to do that at home in St. Goar for lack of resources, but at Heidelberg the sky was the limit. The university has a wonderful little records room, filled floor to ceiling with every imaginable book on every imaginable subject. I frequently haunted the dusty shelves running my finger over the cracked spines until I'd find just the text I was looking for. I had already learned Spanish by this method, and was working on French in addition to taking a French conversational course.

During the first few weeks of school I had to work hard to catch up to where the other students were but after that I never looked back. As summer turned cool, and autumn turned to winter, I found myself at the top of my class. I had no friends, for I isolated myself from others on my ascent to the top. Other people only slow one down, or so I thought at the time. Needless to say, my journey through academia was mainly solo, save the occasional drinking buddy, until the Neue Dämmerung came into my life.

Chapter 42

The Neue Dämmerung, or New Dawn, approached me one day as I was pulling weeds in Frau Grüner's vegetable garden. The tomato plants already hung heavy with small green orbs, and the bean bushes sported tiny little flowers; there would also be beets, cucumbers, potatoes, and onions to harvest later, all thanks to my tireless efforts in the garden. School was out until the next semester, and I would soon be beginning my second year of university. The sun was high overhead, and I constantly wiped my sweaty forearm across my dripping brow, lest the salty sweat drip into my eyes. I was on my hands and knees in the moist soil, between two leafy bean bushes, when a voice from behind broke the stillness and startled me, "What do you say, Herr Opfer?" The cicadas sang their song loudly in the background, their volume undulating up and down. I slowly straightened my back and dropped a handful of weeds, "Hello there, Herr, how may I help you?" I was cordial, but quite puzzled by this vaguely familiar young man before me, dressed in fine, tailored clothing. He was shorter than me, a little less than six feet tall, topped off by a head of blond hair, the color and texture of corn silk. His strong Nordic features were set congenially, but his piercing blue eyes almost bore through me. "Why don't you walk with me, Gregor?" the stranger said. It was more of a command than a question. Suddenly, I remembered how I knew him. The long jagged scar running down his faces gave it away. He was a member of a Duellgesellschaft, and I sometimes saw him at the Black Rhino. I pretended like I didn't know who he was, and followed him out onto Alb-Ueberla Street. Heidelberg is a small university, and I knew almost everyone in my class, so this gentleman must be getting ready to start his third or fourth year, for I had never had him in any of my lectures. Turning right onto the street, we strolled wordlessly. The scar on his face was thick with scar tissue; bright pink and throbbing with blood. It looked as if it hadn't healed cleanly.

We arrived at a wooded path the locals call Philosopher's Walk and begin hiking up the trail. Only when we had gone a short distance did the stranger begin talking, "Gregor, the Brotherhood has been doing some checking into you. We know you are the top of your class." He cast a sideways glance at me. I grunted to confirm, but said nothing. Scar face continued, "We cannot, though, through our innumerable connections, find what house you come from. But you must come from a reputable house, for commoners can't afford to attend university, nor does the commoner have the mental capacity to grasp the complex theories presented at university. In talking to other Duellgesellschaft, they have also tried to find out about you through various connections, but alas, they have hit the same wall as we have." He paused, but I didn't offer anything, striding hard up the dirt path, puffing slightly. Scar-face continued, "In other words, you're an enigma. You just showed up at the university one day and haven't left. Don't you have family to go home to? Surely you must!" I stopped suddenly in the middle of the trail, annoyed that this person had been meddling into my affairs, but pleased he hasn't been able to find anything out.

"Herr…?" I said, cocking my head slightly.

He replied, "Oister."

"Well, Herr Oister, you seem to be pretty damn interested in my business. And I have to ask; exactly what business is it of yours? You ask me up here," I gestured wildly around with my arms, "to tell me what you don't know about me. You fool. I should teach you not to meddle in other people's affairs," I said and prepared for a retaliatory remark and the ensuing fight. The cracking of my knuckles resounded off the trees in the otherwise still forest as I flexed my muscles, watching for the slightest movement from my Nordic opponent. I had no illusions about beating him, but I could at least get in a few shots before he planted his riding boot up my ass.

Instead of countering my inflammatory remarks, he casually replied, "Herr Opfer, I am here to extend you invitation of membership to Neue Dämmerung." I was stunned. Only the most elite members of society are in dueling societies, and I am a nothing, the son of a clock maker. As if to read my mind, Oister enigmatically said, "You have been carefully chosen, and one day it will be revealed to you why. Neue Dämmerung is the crème de la crème of all the Duellgesellschaft. I am your membership sponsor, Wilhelm Oister; don't disappoint me, Gregor Opfer. The time will come when you will be called upon." He pivoted and strode down the mountain leaving me with my thoughts in the silent forest.

Chapter 43

The time did not come, and soon I stopped thinking about it. Occasionally, I saw Wilhelm in passing and we ignored each other like we were total strangers. Maybe they found out who I really was and decided they didn't want me. Either way, I didn't much care. Autumn turned cold, and winter eventually turned back into summer, university let out, and once again the summer stretched before me like the mighty Euphrates; another academic year come and gone. I occupied my time reading, learning Latin, and repairing Frau Grüner's house. That hot, stagnant summer, Frau Grüner got new frames around all her windows and doors, as well as the new thatching I put on the roof to prevent the little leaks that were becoming more and more frequent. That summer, the summer of '38, at the tender of age of eighteen, I began to realize my potential. I never realized how handy I was until I started fixing up this lonely old lady's house. I made, found, or borrowed all the tools I needed, and by the end of the summer my collection of carpentry tools was quite impressive.

Classes started the next week, and I had completed all the repairs I wanted to complete that summer. My body had hardened from the tough physical labor and my blouses bulged at the seams, and my torso was a mass of defined musculature. As I wiped the sweat from my brow, and stowed my tools into a leather roll on the final day of my thatching, Frau Grüner approached me with a clay stein of beer. "Gregor, you have done such good work," she gushed thrusting the stein of frothy dark beer into my hands.

"Thank you, Frau Grüner," I said, pleased, while quaffing greedily.

"You don't need to do another thing around here!" she cried throwing her arms around me. Startled, then embarrassed, I wriggled out of her grip,

151

"Well, that is very kind, Frau Grüner, but I am happy to earn my keep."

"Oh, Gregor," she gushed, "with the work you have done this summer you have earned your keep three times over. I fix you something extra special tonight!" She twirled around and marched back into the house. I felt warm inside; I hadn't felt this loved in a long time—since Papa died. I felt like I belonged somewhere. And as the week dwindled away, classes started, and summer gave way to autumn I had totally forgotten the words of Oister. But he would soon remind me.

Chapter 44

It was early October, and the crisp wind blowing off the Rhine caused me to clutch my wool coat close around my torso. As I approached the Karl's Gate Bridge, I waved drunkenly to a classmate of mine whom I had passed the evening with, Klaus, and cried into the early morning, "Good health to you my friend! I shall see you tomorrow!" He replied with equal jovial drunken banter, "Black Rhino strikes again, Gregor!" And our hoots echoed hollowly through the narrow alleys and stone streets. It was good to share some camaraderie, something I rarely did. After the pleasant night passed with Klaus, as well as the liquor I had consumed, I felt damn fine. Damn fine indeed, I decided. I peeled off to cross the bridge as a dark alley swallowed up Klaus. The wind whipped down the black river and howled through the valley. I shivered in spite of myself, and longed to dive into bed at number eight Alb-Ueberla Street. Quick footsteps sounded in my ears, and I had only time enough to spin around and see a dark shape hurtling towards me before darkness enveloped me.

Ten minutes, or ten hours later—having no way of telling time—I gingerly opened my eyes and tried to take stock of my surroundings. Pain flashed through my head like lightning bolts, and I quickly put it back down in order to not vomit. Touching my head, I recoiled in pain, a huge knot on my forehead throbbed with the intensity of a cicada's song in summer. Something moved on my leg. I didn't look to see but heard it squeak. *A fucking rat!* I thought and angrily shook the rat off my trouser leg. Gently, without moving my head, I explored around with my hands in the inky darkness. I seemed to be lying on some sort of stone. The air hung heavy with the stagnant scent dampness and decay. The pungent smell of the earth assaulted my nose, *a basement perhaps?* My hands grabbed nothing but empty space, *I must be on some sort of ledge. No, wait...a niche,* I thought as my hands felt earth to the left of me. My whereabouts slowly dawned on my injured skull and the fuzzy brain contained within. *The catacombs!* I realized with blinding fear. *I am stuck in a dark maze with hundreds, perhaps, thousands of rotting corpses!* I wanted to scream out but knew it would do no good. My mind screamed at my feet to move. Thankfully, my body was so frozen with fear, I had a chance to calm down before I started blindly sprinting through the labyrinth.

Ignoring my pounding head, I swung my legs over the ledge and jumped into the black abyss. The ledge happened to be only a few feet off the ground, and I splashed into a puddle without falling. Rats screamed and squirmed at my feet, and shuddering, I spun around blindly in my black cocoon. Fumbling in my pockets for my matches, my hands came up with nothing. "Bastards," I muttered aloud into the darkness. They had emptied my pockets. Small, wet bodies writhed over my boots. I knew I must keep calm so, I took a deep breath I slowly turned in a circle. In the abyss that was the inky darkness I thought I could see some pale yellow light, or then again it could be a figment of my imagination. Either way, I didn't have any better plan so I, with a silent oath, I headed for the light, my hands groping their way in front of me like a blind person. Small squeaks echoed off the stone tunnel I stepped on assorted rat parts, and the catacombs coursed with a raw energy unlike any I had ever experienced. The energy of death enveloped me and my hands clung to mossy, blackened walls causing me to break my fingernails as they scrabbled over stone and bone in my desperate attempt to reach the light before panic set in. And thus my frantic odyssey toward the light progressed with every terse step I made as I wound my way under the city streets of Heidelberg. I inadvertently tripped over a large bone pile and fell into the slimy water. Rats blanketed my body, and I screamed. They viciously bit at my flesh before I could get up, and I knew when I got to light I would find blood. The blood only excited them and the squeaking reached a maddening crescendo. I redoubled my efforts and finally made it to the solitary torch flickering silently on the wall.

I ripped the torch off the wall and waved it around ferociously. The fire spooked the rats, and they parted from around me like I was Noah parting the biblical seas. But the fire also revealed some disheartening information. Now that I had light to see by I saw had three choices, three different tunnels spoking off into the crust of the earth. Having figured their game, I swore under my breath. I could waste hours heading down the wrong spokes or I could extinguish my light and let my eyes adjust to the darkness to see the next correct tunnel.

You bastards are clever, but not as clever as me, I thought smiling as I removed one of my boots. This area of the catacombs proved to have no standing water, *must be moving farther from the Rhine*, I mused as I held the torch to my boot sole. The damp sole, made of wood, quickly dried and the sole caught fire and within minutes had died to a nice pile of ember and ash in the leather shell that was once my nice boot. I blew out the torch carefully and patiently waited for my eyes to adjust to the darkness. The destruction of my boot proved to be fruitful as I saw the light in the correct tunnel and triumphantly relit the torch.

Having no boot now posed a new problem, and I quickly remedied it by ripping strips from my blouse and wrapping the remainder of the blouse around my foot and securing it with the strips. Having crafted a new boot I carefully wrapped the ash pile in the tough brown leather that was once my boot and laboriously made my way down the tunnel. The torch proved to be a blessing and burden, for now I could view the generations and generations of Germanic elders stored under the cobbled streets, their hollow eye sockets staring blankly at the living intruder. I had to blow out my torch eight more times; follow eight more tunnels before I finally met a dead end.

Two torches burned brightly in the chamber the final tunnel opened up into. No skeletons were in this chamber; it was a newer circular earthen chamber with a diameter of maybe twelve feet. A large wooden ladder stood against the far end of the chamber, and having no other option, I gripped the rungs and began climbing. The ladder rested on a ledge about three feet wide, and I pulled myself carefully onto the ledge. Clods of earth crumbled in my fingers and fell to the chamber below. The two torches burned distantly in the chamber below, I heard the pitter-patter of the dirt hitting the chamber floor below and shuddered. I drew a sharp breath and began climbing a second ladder. Dirt and roots fell about me, as my hands numbly gripped the rough-hewn wooden ladder. I must have climbed twenty-five feet before hitting my head on a trap door. It thudded heavily as I pushed it open, and I wearily pulled myself onto the wooden floor and lay panting on it. I rested for a spell before exploring the contents of the room. The tiny room contained one locked door I found after putting my shoulder to it, and nothing else. Despondently, I sat and waited for my tormentors to reveal themselves. They chose to remain hidden. Fortunately, the fear and physical exertion of my ordeal had exhausted me, and I sank into blissful oblivion on the cold, hard wooden floor.

Chapter 45

I'm not too sure how long I slept on the wooden floor, but I awoke quickly and was instantly alert. Not sure of what woke me, I sank back down to the wooden floor. My, how my joints were stiff! My thick tongue explored my parched mouth—too much beer from the Black Rhino earlier. How many hours had elapsed? The lump on my head still ached and throbbed. And I lay in the silent darkness, my head pounding trying to gain some insight on the previous few hours. That's when the drums started, their sound rolled in like distant thunder, low and rumbling. I sat up and quickly backed against the wall opposite the door. The drumming sounded for an eternity, and I constantly wiped my sweaty palms on my trousers, little rivulets of sweat ran from my armpits down my naked torso. I knew they were coming.

Chanting started. At first it sounded like the whistling of the wind through the trees in the forest, but I pricked my ears to it and it was definitely the chanting of men. The chanting continued along with the drumming for another eternity before I heard a scraping sound on the other side of the door, the sound of a bar being moved. The door crashed open, and I cowered as two large figures robed in black loomed in, holding bright flaming torches before them. I could not see their faces or hands for their faces lay hidden in deep shadows cast by deep hoods and on their hands were black gloves. Wordlessly, they each grabbed me under my arms and dragged me into a dark hallway, floored with stones, for my cloth-covered foot bumped and scraped all the way down the hall. The farther down the passageway I was dragged the louder the drumming and chanting got. The hall opened to a large chamber, with vaulted Gothic ceilings where the noise reached a climax. The men dragging me dumped me unceremoniously in a heap before a circular ember pit. I pulled myself to my feet and stood trembling, and absorbing the details. The noise and smoke assaulted my senses, and I felt like I was drunk, swimming underwater. Wall niches were situated around the room, and in each one stood a black hooded man, head bowed, torches affixed to the walls around the room such that the chamber was bathed in very pale flickering light. Strange chains hung suspended from the ceiling, and coats of arms decorated the walls. No windows or anything else gave me a clue as to where I was, but while my body was failing me, trembling with uncertainty, my heart was strong, and I was not afraid anymore.

The two figures who had dragged me, stood behind me. While I couldn't see them I could feel their presence. A figure in the niche directly in front of me stepped forward and held up his hand in a fist. The figures behind me viciously kicked my legs out from under me and drove me to my knees with their hands on my shoulders. The cold stone floor was uncomfortable but I dared not move. The mysterious drumming and chanting immediately stopped. The figure stood opposite me around the stone ember pit, and I looked up at him from my position on my knees. "Gregor Opfer," the voice boomed off the vaulted stone ceiling, "you have been privileged enough to be invited into the secret chamber of Neue Dämmerung. If you accept our offer to join the Brotherhood than you shall be so honored the rest of your days; if not, you will wake up in your bed on the next sunrise and wonder if this," he gestured around the chamber, "was all a dream. Do you accept?" I nodded imperceptibly. "Well?" the figure boomed.

My mind would not communicate with my mouth properly, but I croaked out best I could, "Y, y, yes!"

"Very well then," the figure said and motioned to the two behind me. They dragged me to my feet and stripped me naked, bound my wrists behind my back so that I was standing before the stone ember pit, stark naked in the gloomy dampness. "Brothers!" the authority figure commanded, and all the motionless men in the niches took one giant step forward form their niches, shucking their large black cloaks. I could hear the swish of falling cloth, as the men behind me dropped their robes also. Underneath the black cloaks the men wore suits of chain mail, covered with white tunics, a large red cross painted onto the front of the tunic, with a smaller red cross over their heart. Each man had a large sword in the large brown belt circling their tunic, and over their heads was a white mask with eyeholes cut in it. I could tell each man wore a chain mail helmet, for some of it peeked out from under their masks. The leader too, shucked his black cloak, but instead of a white tunic he wore a blue one, complete with red crosses. He wore no white mask, but had his face painted black with ash, and the chain mail covered his head, his blue eyes burned in silent fury in his head. I stood quaking, feeling small, feeble and vulnerable in the presence of giants. My knees knocked together and teeth chattered. *It'll be all right,* my mind told my body a thousand times over, but my body seemed not to listen.

"At the end of the first crusade a monastic military order was formed to protect Christian pilgrims en route to the Holy Land," the leader boomed. "They called themselves the Knights Templar. As time wore on the Knights gained members and with those members they gained power and influence. They policed the road on the way to Jerusalem and handed out justice in a way that no king could. As their influence spread over the land and their wealth grew to gigantic proportions they began Holy See banking." The embers in the stone pits glowed with radiance and illuminated the leader in an eerie reddish light, I stood, eyes transfixed on him as he continued, "The Knights protected the innocent, protected Christianity in the Holy Land, and fought the rise of evil. Pope Innocent the second exempted the Knights from all authority, save that of God!" The leader pounded his fist into his hands and a loud, *twack,* resounded off the vaulted ceilings as the leather gloves collided. "By the year of our Lord 1307 the Knights were so powerful they could defy any earthly power. And their power of goodness and virtue tempted the devil. The forces of evil combined to crush this goodness. The jealousy of Philip the Fair of France and his Holiness Pope Clement could not be assuaged. They were supposed to be the Almighty on earth, they were supposed to be the wealthiest in Europe, and their envy grew and grew until a certain Friday, October thirteen in the year of our Lord 1307 they had the Knights arrested."

The circle of men around me hissed and a shiver went up my spine. "These soldiers of God were arrested for trampling the cross...homosexuality...and," he let the suspense build before shouting, "worshiping the blasphemy!" The men hissed again. "One by one the knights were executed while the king of France consolidated his power and plundered the knights' wealth. One March 19 in the year of our Lord 1314 the Grand Master, Jacque de Molay was burned alive for his supposed crimes against the cross! Burned with the blessing of his Holiness! Fortunately, the former Grand Master, Tibuald De Gaudin, Grand Master until 1293, formed a secret organization in 1290 within the Knights, preparing for the day when the forces of evil would tear at the fabric of the organization. That organization was... Neue Dämmerung. De Gaudin himself hand selected a handful of his most trusted officers and soldiers to head the organization, and swore them to total secrecy. These men escaped the persecution from the very church it was *protecting*, and devoted their lives to the propagation of good and the dissolution of evil cloaked as good. These men, the founders of Neue Dämmerung, infiltrated, and assassinated both King Philip and Pope Clement by poisoning within six months of Friday the thirteenth." The leader was silent for a moment, letting the final words ring in my ears. "Since that day Neue Dämmerung has recruited men who can continue in the fight against the evil that courses through our societal fabric, and threatens to tear at the very seams of Christianity!

"Now, Gregor Opfer, place your hand over your heart and repeat after me," the leader commanded. The flat of a sword lashed at the back of my knees, and I painfully sank to the hard stone floor for a second time.

"I Gregor Opfer," he recited, and I followed repeated after him, "promise to uphold the secrets...set forth upon me now and in the future...under no lesser penalty...having my tongue cut out...being sewed up in a sack...with a monkey, cock, and serpent....and being thrown into a fast flowing river...and later having my corpse burned...until only ash remains...so that my soul may burn...eternally in hell...furthermore, I promise...to live like the wind....omnipresent and omnipotent...never seen but always felt...striving for the day…when peace and order return to the earth…and my duty to the cross is complete," I finished, my voice wavering but loud, trying to sound as sure as I could.

"Good," the blue-tunic-clad man boomed, "Now, to solidify your membership as a brother in Neue Dämmerung, the most honorable Duellgesellschaft in all of the Germanic states you will receive a Schmisse to let all the world know of your lofty and lifelong purpose." He drew his sword from his belt. It made an audible *shing* sound. My breath left me, and I felt lightheaded. "Do not move," the men behind me commanded, and each man gripped my shoulders. The leader put the sword into the glowing embers for a minute until the metal blade glowed orange. He pulled the blade out and held it before his face, savoring the heat emitted from the blade. He stepped around the ember pit until he was directly in front of me. "Gregor Opfer," he said lowering the blade until it was level with my face, both his gloved hands holding it, "you are now and forever an official brother of Neue Dämmerung." He deftly swiped the blade from below my right ear to my chin. The razor-sharp blade sliced my tender flesh. The hot blade cauterized the wound, but I didn't think about that as the smell of my own burning flesh caused me to vomit. I lay crumpled in a heap, violently vomiting at the leaders' feet as he called to his soldiers, "Brothers, now let us recite the prophecy written by Jesus' own disciple, Saint Peter."

The men, in unison with the leader chanted, "Whereas they speak against you as evildoers, they may by your good works, which they shall behold, glorify God in the day of visitation…for the punishment of evildoers, and for the praise of them that do well. For so is the will of God that with well doing ye may put to silence the ignorance of foolish men…"

I lay shivering on the stone floor and clutched at my wounded face, dry retching. My stomach contents already littered the floor.

Chapter 46

Clang, shhh-wang! The lightweight swords protested as they slashed and clashed against each other. Ferocity ran through my veins as I focused on my opponent, lunged, parleyed and slashed at him. My opponent, in turn, dancing this way and that, countered my attacks, and launched assaults of his own. Our slippered feet pranced lightly across the hardwood floor of the dueling arena as we migrated from one end of the arena to the other. The twenty-six other members of the society stood silently around the rectangular room and watched intently. The room was devoid of any furniture, and contained only coats of arms of famous Templar Knights and distinguished members of Neue Dämmerung. The only light came from small prison-like windows high up on the walls, for the dueling room was in the basement of the society's mansion, and they were just tiny basement windows. The dueling room stood over the ritual room, which I had been shown could be accessed through a secret trapdoor in the floor. From there, one climbed down a ladder to an anteroom where all the chain mail uniforms were kept, along with the big ritual swords. The anteroom had a flight of stairs that led another twenty feet down into the earth and came out behind one of the niches, so it looked when you were in the circular ritual room that there was no exit, unless you went down the hall to the "cell."

There was still enough light filtering through the small prison-like windows that lighting torches was unnecessary, but the torches stood ready in their holders along the wall, waiting for darkness to fall. I was battling the Grand Master of Neue Dämmerung, Albert Goering, and I knew every member was hoping for a crushing defeat of me by him. They got their wish. With a final leap and plunge, and a breathless,

"Ha!" Goering parried the sword right from my hands. It fell to the floor with a loud, resounding clatter. Goering's face bore many long jagged scars from more rigorous duels than the one I had offered, but it was only my second week, and having never dueled before I thought I was getting along quite well. "Well, then, good match," Goering said amicably while walking over to me taking off his white dueling gloves.

I, in turn, took off mine and we shook. "Sir," I smartly said bowing my head slightly to acknowledge my defeat. I left the match along with Goering, and the next two warriors stepped into the arena. We all wore the same white canvas dueling outfits, canvas pants, with a white linen shirt covered by a thick canvas smock. The outfit was complete with little canvas slippers that laced up halfway up the shin and canvas gloves. No masks, the scars were signs of honor.

"Good turn," Wilhem Oister whispered poking me. He bore a large grin on his mug. I turned and made a face, rolling my eyes. "No, I mean it. He's the best fighter here." I gave a quick nod and turned my attention to the match. I vowed to be the best fighter in my society, and had begun to practice secretly in the woods with a wooden pole I had whittled to be roughly the same dimensions and weight. I would secret off into the woods in the afternoons after my classes and practice my choreography again and again until my clumsy moves became more proficient. One day, I vowed, I would be the best dueler, and so I practiced and practiced until the wood left large painful welts on my hands and my muscles ached from exertion.

Chapter 47

Though I practiced my new sport in secret, I wore my new scar, or schmisse, like a badge of honor. And indeed it was so, for only the elite had dueling scars and belonged to dueling societies. Me, Gregor Opfer, was now considered a member of "society." I still chuckle at the thought. Frau Grüner merely nodded and grunted when she saw the freshly oozing wound the first day I stumbled home, exhausted from the trying initiation ritual. I knew she was dying to know how I became a member of something reserved for the children of barons and high-ranking government officials, but she never asked, and I never breathed a word about it.

I drank at the Black Rhino more frequently than I did before; in fact, I was there every single night fraternizing with my newfound friends until the wee hours. Friends! I never thought I would have ever experienced that kind of camaraderie, much less enjoyed it! But I loved it. I ate, slept, and breathed Neue Dämmerung. Usually I would head over to the society's mansion to shoot billiards and play cards, and then we'd head down the hill for a little drink.

One particular evening found me once again at the Rhino conversing with Wilhelm Oister, with who I had become very friendly with since my initiation a month ago. Wilhelm and I were a few steins of beer deep and conversing in low tones in a corner, the members of the other dueling societies conversing boisterously all around us. "That duel the other night was quite impressive," Wilhelm said referring to last night's intra-society weekly duel. He quaffed his beer. "Usually the new initiates get beaten pretty badly their first semester." I sat silent, not biting on his obvious fishing expedition. I had not let on that I was the son of a tradesman, a mere peasant, and I didn't plan to. The fact that

I had never dueled with swords before was obvious my first night, but I was picking the sport up quickly, almost able to hold my own against men that had been dueling all their lives. "Now lets talk about something," Oister said draining his beer and motioning the barkeep for two more. Seeing that, I tipped mine and guzzled the last bit in anticipation of fresh ones. "You realize Neue Dämmerung has considerable financial influence; your uniform," he motioned to my newly tailored dueling society uniform, "is paid for, yes?"

"Well sure," I replied pleased with my new uniform. It consisted of a white blouse, dark blue coat with shiny brass buttons and epaulets, and brown corduroy pants. A wide brown belt and brown riding boots completed the costume. Every society had a different uniform, but what made ours discernable was the semicircle of yellow stitched on the left breast with lines coming off it, representing the new rising sun, or new dawn.

"The organization paid for it, no? Don't they pay for everyone's uniform?" I asked, suddenly confused.

"Yes, and everything else," he replied evasively, sipping the fresh stein of beer a busty barmaid had brought over.

"How do you mean?" I asked, more confused than ever.

"Your tuition, it's paid for."

"What?" I blurted out, almost too loudly over the din of the other patrons.

"Shhh, quiet down Gregor!" He drank some more beer. "There are people, former Neue Dämmerung members, and other compatriots of *the* cause that are interested in our organization, and that's all I can tell you right now. But you will never have to pay for anything while you finish here at Heidelberg University."

"Wait," I said interrupting him, "why are these people interested in me...us?"

"Like I said," said Wilhelm, "I can't tell you now, but when the time comes you will know." He slowly placed his right arm on the table and rolled the sleeve of his blouse up to his armpit. On his bicep a strange symbol was inked into the skin with some lettering around it. I couldn't read what it said in the dim light.

"What the…" I began only to be cut off by Wilhelm.

"When the time comes do not be afraid; you were recruited for a reason," he stated calmly while slowly rolling down his sleeve. His eyes stared deeply into mine and instructed me to shut my mouth. I shut my mouth. The conversation turned to trivial things, more steins were ordered, and soon we were climbing the steep hillside on our way back to the mansion holding onto each other for support, laughing and singing as we tripped and stumbled drunkenly up the hill.

Chapter 48

The next year passed quickly, and before I knew, it was almost 1840. The Christmas decorations could be seen brightly lit inside the Bavarian homes that I walked past, coming back from the market. Small candles adorned great fur trees that I saw through frost windows as I tramped the narrow streets piled high with snow. My fellow citizens, me included, tramped out into the surrounding mountainsides to fell the furs, drag them home, and decorate them in hope that Saint Nicholas would leave goodies under them.

How far I've come, almost like a surreal dream. I was still at the top of my class and hoped to still be there when my class graduated in March. All my fellow society members fled for six weeks to their respective corners of Europe for the holiday, many invited me to go with them, but I couldn't leave my benefactor and friend, Frau Grüner. She let me into her house when I had nothing, and although my buddies pressured me to move to the mansion, I continued living with Frau Grüner. We looked after each other, and I dreaded the day to come when I would leave her. She became like a mother to me; my real mother I still wrote to, with no return address, to keep me secure in knowledge that she knew I was okay.

I had risen to rank of Grand Master, and had the honor of wearing the blue tunic during our ritual activities. I merited the top position, not only for the vast store of knowledge I had accumulated about Neue Dämmerung's history, but also because of my exemplary dueling skills. Sometimes, I wondered if the sword was actually an extension of my body, for I fought like it was. I continued to practice in the woods by myself at least five days a week to keep my skills sharp. It worked; I had not lost a match in ten months, and I planned on keeping it that way. As I turned onto Alb-Ueberla, I thought about the maze of catacombs running under the very ground I was walking on, and how I had become very adept at navigating them because of our ritual activities, even though I stilled hated the rats. Oh, how I delighted in torturing new members, sending them through the catacombs I was repulsed by! "Ah, Frau Grüner, Happy Christmas!" I called merrily opening the door to house number eight and kissing Frau Grüner on the cheek. "I have brought you a present."

Her face flushed with embarrassment, "Well, it'll just have to wait," she bustled back into the kitchen, "You sit down right now young man. We're going to have a proper kitchen feast. I roasted a chicken." She pulled out a chair, and I had hardly shucked my damp jacket onto a peg before she forcefully sat me down in front of the large spread of boiled potatoes, sauerkraut with pork, steamed beans, blackberry jam, sourdough bread, and of course, a roasted chicken.

"My, my," I said laughing and rubbing my hands together, "you sure have outdone yourself this time."

"It's Christmas day, the day of the birth of our Savior. Would you expect me *not* to prepare a feast?" she scolded.

"No, no, not that," I protested laughing, "It's just…wonderful!" We dug in and ate like royalty before the roaring fire. The great fur tree I brought Frau Grüner in the next room scented the house with a beautiful aroma and the tiny candles twinkled on it and snow fell quietly outside.

After dinner I presented Frau Grüner with a small Astrich clock I had purchased in town, along with a box of chocolates, imported from Belgium. "Where did you ever get the money for…" Frau gushed; her eyes wide as she admired the tiny clock face suspended over three small gold spinners set under a glass globe.

"Never mind, nothing is too good for you. You let me into your home, and cared for me the past three-and-a-half years. You deserve a special gift."

"Gregor you are the sweetest boy!" Frau cried and flung her arms around me. "You have a home here anytime you want it Gregor, and I mean it."

Chapter 49

Mother is dead. He finally did it. My poor mother finally succumbed to the brutality of Pieter. "Pieter! Pieter! Je jure par tient le premier rôle et ciel que je vous torturerai…" I screamed my threat to exact revenge in a frenzied rage across the valley in French; the threats and obscenities bouncing off neighboring mountains and reverberating back in my ears from my vantage point amongst the ruins of a 13th century monastery. The monastery is situated at the termination of Philosopher's Walk. *I will make good on those* promises, I thought to myself as I crumpled the parchment letter my eldest sister, Estelle, sent me through the mail and tossed it down the hill into the woods. Estelle didn't say the cause of death in her correspondence; I doubted it was a broken heart. All she said in her letter was something about a fall—*Scheisse!* I knew he had beaten her to death, *knew it.* And no doubt he was going to get away with it from the authorities. *Scheisse!* I clenched my hands in white rage. Well he wasn't going to get away with from me!

The services were to be held that very day, and there was no way, even if I could've attended, that I would've made it to St. Goar. I fingered the fresh scar tissue on the side of my face and sat amongst the remnants of where high priests once sang their praises to God and watched the sun go down. *Just as Pieter is burying my mother today, I will bury him myself.* With a grim chuckle I laid down amongst the cold stones and slept on the top of the mountain, the cold air and wet dew the furthest thing from my mind. My siblings had the same suspicions I had, I could tell from the tone of the letter, but they weren't in a position to do anything about; they were weak. And I must protect the weak.

In the morning as the sun rose into the Heidelberg valley I stumbled off the mountain, cold, hungry, wet, and carrying a heart that now consisted only of stone. I slammed open the heavy door to Alb-Ueberla number eight and startled Frau Grüner. "Herr Opfer," she cried. "What's wrong?"

"Nothing, Frau Grüner," I muttered, trying to escape upstairs.

But her nosiness couldn't let me escape. "But you're soaking wet! Surely you must be cold."

"Yes, Frau Grüner, I am cold..." Then under my breath, I muttered, "Not just externally."

"What's that?" she demanded. "I couldn't hear you."

"Oh nothing, I just said I need to go get changed." I sidestepped the nosy widow and retreated upstairs.

Part III: Membership of the Mordant Café

Chapter 50

Jack Kevin Savage was born in the county Cork, pronounced "Corgaih" by the locals, located on a tiny island in the middle of the Puddle called Ireland. In 1803, when Savage first made his screaming appearance in the world, Cork was a sleepy hamlet on the southeastern coast of Ireland; just a few cottages isolated in the vast green countryside. There was nothing there but Catholics, farmers, and drinkers, what the rest of the world collectively calls Irish folk. The Savage clan was no exception.

Savage's parents were devout Catholics, and as a result, Savage was one of eight children. Savage's parents were poor farmers and the family farmed an English owned plot owned by a Kentish Lord. The good Lord had seen fit that the land was good to the Savage family over the years, and they in turn honored him with piety and prayer. At age three, Jack began helping the family in the field. He knew no other than farming.

And though he received no formal education, Savage always knew there were richer things in life than moving dirt and groveling at the altar. As he grew older, he began to resent his life more and more; he hated being poor, he hated the way the church dictated the way he could live his life, and most of all he hated being a "boy." In the Irish social hierarchy, a man is not a man until he reached middle age; until then he is just a "boy." Being called boy didn't sit well with the fiery young lad, especially by old, withered-up men more than three times his age that addressed him, and treated him like he was livestock.

Jack grew into the archetypal Irishman, flaming red hair, brawny from all his work in the fields, a quick temper, and a predilection for booze, especially whiskey. After the sun set over the distant green fields, Savage would join other young men his age at the only pub in town to toss back a few before the evening meal. If the mood suited him he would just stay there all night long, coming home just in time to begin work in the fields again. His father would often come to the family plot in the morning and find Jack with a swollen lip, black eye, bloody scalp or any combination of the aforementioned. He would just shake his head, but he never questioned Jack about his battle scars because, frankly, he was scared of the boy's volatile nature. The boy was still in his late teens but could easily kick the tar out of the hardened Irishman, and he knew it. So, Mr. Savage prayed for Jack every night, extra on Sundays, that Jack would settle down, find a nice Catholic wife, and provide himself and his wife with little grandchildren like some of Jack's other siblings had. Mr. Savage often wondered if Jack had the temperament of a bear due to the aftermath of long nights of drinking or because the boy was just plain daft. Mr. Savage figured the fault lay in him and his wife for not raising the boy properly, for his brothers and sisters were even-tempered, virtuous citizens. But as long as the boy showed up each morning to work the land, Mr. Savage held his tongue. Unfortunately for Mr. Savage, Jack had other plans, and they didn't include obedience, piety, and hard work.

The town pub was a small haunt, located three dusty streets and a couple of fields over from the Savage household. It was a low-slung taproom with a straw roof and thick stone walls. Jack hated the proprietor, Mr. Nichols. That piece of shit, Nichols, always called Jack, "boy," and Jack hated him for that. Technically, Nicholas was not a man himself, but thought differently because he owned the only suds house in town.

Jack, until this point, had tolerated the blatant disrespect because he didn't want to be banned from the pub, but it rubbed him the wrong way. *Someday,* he always thought, *I'll give that fat fuck what's coming to him.* Jack would sit at the wooden plank bar over a draught of Bass and glower at the slob stamping around behind the bar, shouting orders and insulting everyone that walked through the door. He was the most offensive, vile creature ever created, Jack decided.

Mr. Nichols, Jack would grudgingly admit, did have one thing going for him, a big-breasted, brown-haired beauty of a wife that cooked for the pub. She was gorgeous; Jack often wondered what the slight little pixie wife saw in the big, fat drunk, sweating hulk of a pig husband. Patti Nichols was a little older than Jack, and could've done a lot better in life. The word around town was that Patti's old man had practically sold her to that boar when she was fourteen. Ten years later and somehow she still had not fled in fear of her life. Jack figured she was either too scared or too ignorant to leave him. Catholic guilt. She was, after all, the cook. If a patron wanted ham, potatoes, and boiled cabbage they were in for a treat, but if a patron wanted anything else then they were shit out of luck. Mrs. Nicholas had one menu all the days of the year. It was speculated amongst the townspeople that she was too dumb to learn to cook anything else. Granted, she was a little slow, but probably not *that* slow.

The Nichols boy was practically a slave to the old man, and as the night would wear on and the old man would get drunker and drunker he would start screaming, "Ay' Gunny, git thu' fo'ck up on that roof, an' put some ma'hr straw in it. It's leakin' like-ins' the devil!" The young boy would scramble like a little monkey up onto the roof with armfuls of hay in the incessant rain to try to curtail the myriad of leaks in the seedy establishment. Most of the time the patrons were too damn drunk to realize the place was leaking anyway. One rainy night, Jack was sitting at the plank, sauced. He had been drinking at the pub since four o'clock in the afternoon, it being foul weather and all, and he was downright piss drunk. Gunny had already made countless trips out into the rain to plug leaks and his work wouldn't end until the pub closed sometime around sunrise. The foul weather brought all the Cork farmers out of the eves—can't farm in the pouring rain. The pub was absolutely packed. The boisterous Irish crowd was very drunk, and the atmosphere was stuffy and festive. And Jack was glad for the excuse to step outside and relieve himself.

After taking a leak, Jack steadied himself against the building's stonewall and took another swig from the locally distilled whiskey. *Damn I'm pissed,* he thought. The rain, gentle now, had cleansed the earth and it smelled fresh and clean. Jack decided to stand for a few moments more in the cool night air. As he lurked about in the shadows drinking from his bottle the backdoor flew open and out came Patti with a steaming pot of water. *That is one lass I'd like to give it to,* thought Jack drunkenly watching the bobbing breasts as they practically popped out of the gingham dress as she picked her way deftly through the wet grass.

"Give ya' ah' hand the'r Patti?" Jack asked in his thick Irish brogue.

Patti emitted a little yelp and dropped the pot. "Jesus Jack, ya' scar'd me!" Patti said, putting her hand over her heart and other hand against her forehead. Jack stepped out of the shadows. He could see Patti was sweating heavily from laboring over a hot fire all day. Beads of perspiration hung heavy on her forehead and the top of her chest. The gentle falling rain mixed with the sweat and it dripped off her face onto her dress. He noticed the moisture was causing the dress to cling suggestively to her body. "No thanks, I need t' git back to wor'gaih," Patti replied, wiping her face with a bare hand before bending over to pick up the pot.

"That fo'cker wor-gaihs ya' too hard," Jack spit out sullenly. "Ya' need to lea'fe the swine."

"Jack, we've been through this bef'ar," Patti replied. She sighed, tired from the day so far and the rest of the night that stretched before her. Though she was too religious to admit it out loud she felt a strong sexual tension between them, and had for sometime. She found the scrappy lad handsome. And his eyes intrigued her, even when drunk there was a spark exhibited in them that nobody else in the quiet village had; the same spark a caged, wild dog has. Jack had been making passes at Patti for about a year now. They started off casual enough, a stray remark when her old man wasn't listening, and then the quiet whisperings. Jack had never been lewd or inappropriate in his overtures, but Patti knew how much he cared for her. He had told her he loved her. She knew all too well how much Jack hated her husband; hated how her old man treated her. But she was scared to leave her husband, he was all she had ever known since she had been a mere lass. *How would I live without Ferdi?* She often thought naively, discounting the fact their one and only child had been conceived out of a rape, and for that reason she never had any maternal instinct towards the boy. In fact he wasn't even an issue.

"Here, drink this, cu'hr what ai-hls' ya'," Jack said and extended the clear bottle filled with the amber liquid.

"Fine then, Jack, I'll drink a snoot within's ya's." Patti took the bottle and took the swig of an Irishwoman, about three jiggers' worth. The fiery liquid filled her belly and spread to her extremities. She knew she should get back into the pub and continue working before Ferdi came out looking for her, but something kept her out there talking to Jack. Ferdi would probably beat and rape her later for being slow in the kitchen but it would be worth it to talk with an actual human being for a little while. So Patti took another swig and passed it back to Jack and soon the two were laughing and the bottle was nearly empty. The rain had stopped for the moment and the cool Irish night dried the sweat on Patti's brow as they talked a little longer. Jack had to use all his self-control to keep his gaze level while talking with the petite pixie, for those large breasts just danced and jiggled as Patti laughed. They paused and stared at each other. An uncomfortable silence hung in the air. Jack leaned in and kissed her, she didn't pull away and soon responded arduously. The bottle, with only one finger of liquid left in it, dropped, forgotten, to the ground. Jack pressed closer to Patti and her ample bosom, the passion electric between them. "Oh, Jack, don't. Stop," Patti breathlessly whispered between their fervent kissing. She tried to pull away but his grip around her waist was too firm. He began kissing her neck, Patti moaning uncontrollably drowning out the distant noise of laughter from the pub. Patti's breathing was ragged and intermittent, her hands exploring Jack's young, muscular body.

"Come with me," Jack panted and grabbed her hand. He led her to the woodshed, his mind fairly screaming in anticipation. Jack had fucked many of the village girls over the past few years; the Catholic demure act was just a façade, as Jack had found out many times in his nineteen years of age. Give one of the town girls a drink or two, and her dress would be up over her face in no time. This was different. Patti was a woman, though only five years Jack's senior, she was a woman by experience. The woodshed was cold and damp from the weather, but Jack threw Patti on top of the musty wood and attacked her.

Patti's skirt was around her neck, and they both were on the throes

177

of ecstasy when a drunken bray sounded from the backdoor of the pub, "Patti! Patti. Whe'r ahr' ya' wench? Whe'r thu' fo'ck ahr' ya'?"

"Don't stop, don't stop!" Patti frantically pleaded with Jack as she increased the rhythm. It was almost as if Nichols could sniff her out in the woodshed. There was hardly time to finish up before the drunken beast could wander across the yard and Jack wasn't about to stop. "Hurry Jack," Patti panted into his ear.

"I'm tryin'," he grunted. His thrusting became more vigorous.

Less than a minute transpired before Ferdi Nichols yanked the shed open and found a young patron of his establishment on top his wife. He let out a roar of betrayal, "Bollocks! Savage ya' fo'ck, ya'r gonna die!" The fat beast grabbed a stick of kindling and took a swing at Savage, who by now had jumped to the back of the shed holding one hand in front of himself defensively and using the other to stow himself. Meanwhile, Patti still lay on the woodpile, legs in the air.

"Oy! Fo'ck ya' Ferdi, ya' couldn't fo'ck ya'r wife prop'arhly if usin' muy dick, an' Lucif'ar himself pushin'!" The inflammatory comment just pissed off Nichols more and he renewed his blows toward the young Irishman. Savage ducked as the piece of wood danced dangerously close to his cranium. Jack finally managed to get his pants buttoned and crouched down to free a knife from his boot while Nichols lined up another blow. Nichols swung and missed.

He let out a loud, "Omph!" as he followed through. Before Nichols could get the stick back up Jack jumped and closed the gap between the fat Nichols and himself. He buried the knife up to the hilt directly in the middle of the fat man's rib cage. The slightly dull, and somewhat rusty knife cut deep into his chest and severed the aorta. Nichols staggered back clutching the handle sticking from his chest as a crimson stain widened around the wound. He made some choking sounds before collapsing to his knees and falling face first into the woodpile. Nichols was dead in less than a minute.

"Patti, I've got ta' go now. I'm leavin' this God fu'hr-säken' place. Fo'ck Cor-gaih, fo'ck Ir'lan. It's time fu'hr me to go."

"Oh, Jack please take me with you!" Patti pleaded, horrified by her late hemorrhaging husband lying inert on the floor, blood pouring from all his orifices. "I can't stay he'ar eith'ur." She struggled to get off the top of the woodpile, stepped over Nichols fat corpse and straightened her dress.

"Gunny? What 'ill beco'm of the boy?" Jack asked even though he really didn't care.

"Ferdi's parents 'ill care fu'hr him! He'll get tha' pub. He'll be fine in Ir'lan," Patti pleaded, suddenly anxious to be rid of all of the horrible memories of her servitude to Nichols.

"Fine then, we leave now," said Jack. A large smile formed on Jack's face as he studied the frazzled, but still beautiful, bird he was about to run away with. Something stirred in his pants but he ignored it; there would be plenty of time for that later once they were safe from prosecution. "C'mere," he said, and jerked his head in a small motion that insinuated secrecy. Patti put her ear near his mouth and listened to his plan.

Patti snuck back in the pub to grab what she could, and within ten minutes of the murder they were walking across fields and through forests, lest the local constable pick them up. No doubt Ferdi Nichols would be discovered shortly after their departure once the flow of booze ceased to the thirsty patrons. Jack and Patti fled the few short miles to the coast that night and within a few short days had jumped a ship bound for New York City, America. The year was 1822.

For a short time Jack ran with the Lamprey Gang of Five Points, but soon turned to a career in personal security, a job secured by the gang leader, Pointy O'Kelly. Savage, on orders from O'Kelly, went to work for a wealthy Irishman named Keith Riley. Riley, an aristocrat of sorts, clandestinely bankrolled many of O'Kelly's endeavors to keep the Irish a formidable power in the city. Savage's size and vicious nature made him the ideal enforcer and bodyguard for Riley. And from early 1823 until the summer of 1825 that's exactly what he was.

That summer, the summer of '25, one of Riley's associates, a one Captain Elam Lynds witnessed Savage administer a brutal beating in Riley's basement to a man that owed Riley money. Riley and Lynds personally watched the beating after a wonderful business meal. It was the "after dinner entertainment" Riley told Lynds about in between bites of juicy porterhouse steak and sips of whiskey and water. Later in the evening, they stood on the compact dirt floor in the basement of Riley's brownstone and smoked cigars, imported from the Caribbean, and chatted as Savage pummeled.

"You know, Keith, I could really use a man like that. My prison, Auburn, although a prison, is a dangerous place, and I need someone to personally protect myself as well as administer terror to the inmates to keep them in line," Lynds casually remarked as a geyser of blood spurted from the man's mangled face. Riley took a long pull from his cigar and held the smoke in his lungs thoughtfully. "The state has commissioned me to build a prison in Westchester County on the Hudson this upcoming year, and if you could supply me with men like this man then perhaps we could reach some sort of mutual beneficial agreement," Lynds said and took another sip of brandy from his cut crystal snifter.

Riley took extreme measures to mask his Irish accent and as a result talked very deliberately but sometimes his telltale brogue would intercalate. "Tell ya' what Captain, as a gesture of my good faith I'll *give* you this man right here. He'll be loyal to you like a wolfhound mother guards her pups, and I'll send ma'hr like him." Riley sipped his brandy, silent, too shrewd to *ask* for anything, but waiting for Lynds's generous counter offer.

Lynds fairly beamed with anticipation and good fortune. Clapping Riley on the back he boomed, "Keith, old chap, anytime you need someone to disappear just send him up to me at the new facility. The government has given me full authority over that place, and I promise you anyone you send up there will never see the light of day again…unless you want them to of course." Faces both glowing from their mutual good fortune and the brandy they laughed.

Savage interjected to their conversation, "Mist' Riley, s'ahr, this he'ar man claims he ain't got the mo'ney." He wiped his bloody hands off on his pants and rubbed his knuckles.

Riley swirled his brandy around in the snifter pensively and cocked his head. "Kill him," he said. Then, turning to Lynds, "Let us go upstairs and fetch another brandy; shall we?" They ascended the stairs as Savage finished off the inert man tied to the chair.

Later that week, Savage and his bride of three years, Patti, packed up their belongings from the squalid tenement they were living in and moved up to Westchester County. Savage started as a regular guard and soon became head of the nighttime guard detail at the newly built Sing Sing penitentiary. Over the ensuing years Savage became Lynds's most trusted employee, carrying out his benefactor's orders with savageness befitting his name.

Chapter 51

Unlike Jack Savage, Jepatha Edward Bambury, was not an immigrant. He was the first generation son of Jasper and Elizabeth Bambury, who had emigrated from the Scottish Highlands, specifically Ullapool. The Bambury family settled on the Blue Ridge Mountains in a small town named Asheville. They settled with many of the other Scotch-Irish inhabiting the Appalachian Mountains where they banded into small clans reminiscent of the old country.

Jepatha was born in a small log cabin in the North Carolina wilderness in May of 1810. By the age of ten he was an experienced hunter, trapper, and farmer. His parents always told him, "Jepa, ya'll in'hair't this pee'ce 'o land some day so you must la'rn how to run it. The land shan't fahr'give sloth." Elizabeth was perhaps the crueler of the two. She beat the little boy over every little thing. The beatings were vicious, she used her small bony fists to punch and kick Jepa for the slightest infraction, and if she was feeling extra mean she'd use a leather strap. From as early as he could remember Jepa guessed his mother had no soul. Those eyes of hers were like two gray pebbles and she never smiled, at least Jepatha had never seen her smile. She just wasn't there.

Jasper, on the other hand, smacked the boy around a bit when he did wrong, but he would just give him a little slap. He would however, watch the beatings his wife administered to Jepatha and not lift a finger to stop then. What he lacked in physical abuse he made up for in verbal abuse; constantly telling an impressionable young boy, "Ya' were 'n acc'dent ya' were. How kin we feed three mou'ths? Huh? Huh, answer me ya' li'l shi't!" Having the work ethic of a Quaker, though he was raised a strict Catholic, hammered into him since childhood molded

Jepatha into a diligent worker, but a repressed boy. He soon grew to be an angry, explosive, and vindictive young man.

The first sign of Jepa's volatile nature were passive aggressive little tricks he started on around the age of nine or ten. He would hide Jasper's boots some nights, put frogs in his parent's bed, steal other classmates' candy at school and a myriad of other small things. Before long he graduated to out and out aggressive behavior, thumping other boys at school, throwing ink in girl's hair, and spooking horses tied up outside saloons in town. His behavior was chalked up to "boys will be boys" and life went on on the mountain. Jepatha graduated from the sixth grade and began working full time on his parent's land. Once he was alone most of the time working the fields nobody observed his erratic and aggressive behavior and the townspeople figured he had grown out of it. They figured wrong.

The behavior reached its crescendo one muggy day on the family trap line. The Bambury trap line snaked five long miles through the woods in the immediate area surrounding the Bambury cabin and provided the family with copious small game. Jepatha always begged to walk the trap line. His father thought it was because he was trying to be a good worker, but the real reason was that Jepatha loved to torture the small animals caught in the traps before killing them. He couldn't wait to walk the trap line each day and see what small prize he had snared, and if his father happened to do it Jepatha would sulk for the rest of the day. He would spend hours and hours out on the trap line skinning muskrats alive, rupturing fox's eardrums, and drowning possums. It gave him great pleasure to wield this kind of power on these creatures, and since his parents ruled him with an iron fist it seemed only natural to Jepatha that he should do this to the small creatures. Sometimes, when he was plowing the fields, or mending a fence he would think back with relish to past particularly phenomenal torture sessions and wish longingly for the next morning when he could get out and try new methods and perfect old.

Then the trap line started reaping less and less game. Jasper couldn't figure out why, game was still plentiful in their area. But unbeknownst to Jasper, the reduction was due to all the mutilations his son was doing to the animals, but he figured Jepa was setting the traps wrong. So, he decided to shadow Jepa and see what he was doing wrong. Jasper waited a bit when the boy set off one morning, just long enough to give Jepa time to begin torturing his first victim of the day. When Jasper happened upon his boy, he was busily cutting the feet off a squirrel in a small sunny clearing in the forest near their cabin. The thing writhed in agony and fury trying to escape its tormentor, emitting a high-pitched scream. The old Scotchman, however stern, was no sadist and was appalled by his boy's behavior. "Jepa! What in the hell ya' doin'?" he cried

The boy that turned and looked up at him with a toothy grin certainly was no son of Jasper's. The boy that faced him was somebody different, somebody evil. Staring at him with his grin and his dead eyes, the boy replied, "Atoning him from sin, Father." Then calmly resuming his work, he talked toward the ground while sawing away with his buck knife, "You see, all of God's creatures have sinned. You taught me that, Father, and I have been chosen to cleanse this squirrel before it meets the great creator."

Jasper got over his initial shock and grabbed his boy, jerking him roughly off the ground. Then he laid into him, punching him, slapping him, and shouting obscenities while the footless squirrel squealed in agony, covered in its own blood. Jepatha stood and took the beating, not moving a muscle. Jasper, angered by this display of arrogance, intensified the beating, raining blows down upon the young man. As the beating intensified, Jepatha began laughing. The harder his father beat him, the more he laughed. As his nose broke, he was nearly doubled over with laughter. When his shoulder popped from its socket from a blow from his enraged father, Jepatha fell to the ground, tears of hilarity coming from his eyes. His father stomped and stomped as hard as he could until the laughing stopped. Then he smashed the squirrel's head with a large rock and walked away from the clearing in the forest as blood leaked from his son's head.

Jepatha didn't know how long he lay in the clearing, but it was dark when he came to. He bit his puffy lip and wrenched his right arm back into its socket. Tears formed in his eyes. He knew what he must do.

Jepatha picked up his buck knife from the edge of the clearing where he had dropped it during the beating and sauntered off in the direction of the cabin. The lifeless eyes of the mutilated squirrel watched Jepatha walk off, the blood now coagulated on it's four bloody stumps, and flies covering the carcass and buzzing their winged symphony. The cabin was dark when Jepatha came to it. His pants were dewy from the wet grass, and a chilly northern wind blew through the fields and thickets of trees. Jepatha didn't seem to notice and lumbered like a walking dead man toward the smokehouse. As he ground the large knife on the whetstone inside the musty confines of the smokehouse he hummed a little tune he learned in church five days ago. Large salted sides of meat surrounded him. The blade made a rhythmical *shhhick* sound as the blade ran across the stone again, again, and again.

The time of reckoning is at hand, Jepatha thought mildly inspecting the blade. Satisfied, he wiped the black residue on his shirttail. The blade reflected off the moonlight as Jepatha crossed the yard to the cabin. He had never felt more alive than he did at that moment; it was the first time his life stretched before him with clarity he had never known existed. He slipped silently into the cabin and crossed the plank floor of the common room. He knew where to step so the boards wouldn't creak. The fire had burned down and only a small red pile of embers remained. The house was quiet as a crypt but not for long.

The neighbors found Jasper and Elizabeth Bambury on Sunday after the family failed to show for church, not that there was much left of them. A wagonload of church goers creaked up to the house in a buckboard wagon, dressed to the hilt in their Sunday best. They figured a member of the family was sick and were doing their Christian duty by stopping by and offering assistance. Many hoped Mrs. Bambury would offer them a cool glass of lemonade for it was an awfully hot day, complete with Carolina blue skies. The sight that greeted them was one that only the devil himself could've wrought.

The buzzards and flies had had their time. They had been skinned and hung by their feet from a ceiling support on their porch. The smell from the rotting corpses was too much for even some of the most hardened mountain people, and a few of the men vomited at the gruesome sight while the women shrunk in pure terror, fleeing the scene on foot rather than wait for the buckboard to get turned around. A few brave men elected to go inside to see if the boy's body was there. The scene that greeted them was not a pleasant one. The house looked like a slaughterhouse; blood everywhere, and the skins of the slain lying in the bed where the carving happened. There was no sign of the boy, and the men speculated the Indians had carried him away to live the rest of his days in servitude. Indians did that sort of red devilry they all agreed angrily.

The Bamburys were given a proper Christian burial, and their cabin was duly burned to the ground. The local men stood and watched as the cabin was reduced to nothing but smoldering ash. Of course, the local army outpost was notified of the Indian attack, and for the next five months a contingent of soldiers scoured the area for the offending Indians. Nothing was ever turned up, and over the generations the locals soon forgot about "the great slaughter of '26."

Jepatha woke up in an unfamiliar place. He realized he was covered with blood, so he discarded his clothes and stole new ones from a farmer's clothesline after scrubbing his body clean in a stream with handfuls of sand. He was confused as to where he was, and upon walking for some distance he came to a town called Chattanooga. Jepatha couldn't remember how he had gotten there, or for that matter, the events of the past few days. He figured his parents, having had enough of his behavior, had kicked him out of the holler, or maybe they couldn't feed him anymore. Either way, he reasoned he had to do *something*. He had often heard his parents talk of this great city up north called New York. Apparently his parents had visited it when they first came to America, they landed there from the old country. They had, in some rare moments of frivolity, told him fanciful tales of the bustling place of magic where, "A man could buy anything he wanted under the sun." Having no other lucrative options Jepatha headed north. Walking mostly, but hitching rides with the rare traveler, Jepatha walked for sixty-three days, finally arriving at the city skyline on the morning of the sixty-fourth day. The great buildings belched smoke into the air, and from across the river it appeared to be like an ant colony, teeming with people, ships, and wagons.

There were more people than Jepatha had seen in his entire life, more people than there were birds in the sky! He wandered around the grimy city, poor, hungry, and frightened for days before a kind man by the name of Pointy O'Kelly took him under his wing and taught him, as he called them, "the ropes," of city life. O'Kelly liked the country lad for all his naiveté and wonder, but something about him scared even a hardened criminal like O'Kelly. The boy would get this faraway look in his eyes sometimes, the same look he got when enforcing for O'Kelly's operation. When that look came over him, he wasn't human; he was a machine, a killer. So many nights O'Kelly thanked the higher powers that his country boy was playing for his team, and not one of his rival gangs'.

Bambury's legend as an efficient killer and general enforcer for O'Kelly's operation grew. Some whispered that Bambury must have polar water flowing through his body, for he never showed emotion when he was conducting "official business." He had the cunning of a fox and was as lethal as a water moccasin and single-handedly expanded O'Kelly's territory, leaving a nasty wake of destruction. He was brutal, vicious, and untouchable. Which is why Bambury was soon yanked from the petty gang life and sent up the river, by direct order of Keith Riley; O'Kelly was sorry to see him go. The year was 1835 when Bambury walked to the train station and boarded the train for the ride alongside the Hudson River, forever leaving the city. He had killed thirty-one men.

Every Friday for the rest of his life Jepatha Edward Bambury would write a letter to his parents begging them for their forgiveness, and maybe finding it in their hearts to let him return to his beloved holler on the Carolina-Tennessee border. They never forgave him, or at least acknowledged it to Jepatha, for he never got a letter back from them.

Chapter 52

Allan William Warren, Jr. was born in the borough of Manhattan, on the lower east side, on a sultry winter day in the tumultuous days following the revolution. The high snow banks and freezing weather prevented the local physician from arriving at the home of the Warren family in time, and as a result Mrs. Warren died during childbirth. Mr. Warren loved his wife dearly, and despite his and his maid's best efforts, she still bled out after delivering the infant. Mr. Warren dismissed the maids with the infant and sequestered himself in the room for the rest of the night; covered in blood and ranting like a madman. The next day he called a cabinetmaker.

It's not like the doctor's presence would've made a difference for he was an ancient British doctor who probably would have only administered leeches and bled her as she struggled to expel the screaming infant from her womb, so Mr. Warren, a patriot, didn't blame her death on the bumbling incompetent man, but merely the fact that God called her back to his kingdom. "It was her time to return home," Allan whispered to himself in late spring, when the ground had sufficiently thawed, as his nineteen-year-old bride was lowered into the ground. Screaming infant in his arms, Allan Warren threw a wildflower into the grave and never spoke of her again.

Young Allan grew up raised by servants, for his father, being a great war hero and all, was a busy statesman and rarely at home. The Warren family had accrued more wealth than they could ever spend during the past four generations from the slave trade. They owned over twenty ships that took slaves from the dark continent of Africa to the Caribbean Islands and Americas. Allan Warren's great-grandfather started the business and Allan had inherited the profitable business.

When war broke out he nobly loaned his ships to the cause of the Continental Army, himself commanding the flagship of his fleet. Warren, a shrewd seaman, turned out to be a wily foe for the British commanders and all their naval training. They never were able to catch him, and though they sank more of his ships than he sank of theirs, they were still highly irritated that a common merchant was able to out fox them. This cunning persona Allan exuded served him well throughout his life as a businessman and statesman, but not as a father. Young Allan grew up alone in a large rambling house filled with many fine possessions and antiques. He was clothed in the best clothes and ate the best foods, but the boy was lonely and isolated for he was not allowed to play with "the commoners," as his father told him. And his father made sure he did not go outside and play with the children on the street as he gave strict orders to the staff. So, young Allan was left with only Negro servants for company.

At the age of five Allan started boarding school, The Cirrus Omega School located in Boston. Allan excelled in the sciences and graduated from secondary school at the age of sixteen at the top of his class. It was not a hard feat to do since most of his classmates were quite the ragamuffins. But be that as it may, Allan was an outcast, socially, emotionally, mentally, as well as physically. Where as the other boys were cocksure, strapping, and moderately intelligent young lads, Allan was the exact opposite. He was a brilliant, but frail young man who was an emotional wreck. He grew more and more distant from the other students, and soon became a total social outcast. When they opted to go out to the local taverns to drink and pull women, Allan would stay in and scribble away with his quill by candlelight theories in physics, mathematics, and biology. Later, he would lie awake in the long dormitory that housed all the boys of the secondary school and listen to the moaning coming from the other beds, as his classmates would fuck local whores. He would clutch the thin wool blanket over his ears trying to drown out drunken sounds while the chilly Boston air howled through the eaves.

At the age of sixteen Allan Warren graduated from his hated boarding school and enrolled at the College of William and Mary.

Mentally, he was years ahead of his class and his intelligence caught the attention of the famous Dr. Gilpinder Stuart, renowned anatomist and physiologist. After a lecture in a field of breakthrough biology only seven score years in it's infancy, microscopic biology, Dr. Stuart approached the pupil who usually slouched in the back of the lecture hall, tri-cornered hat pulled over his face, and asked him, "Master Warren, I should say, the essay you wrote about microscopic biology as the vehicle for future developments in the field I found to be fascinating."

The young man stared somewhat hostility at Stuart, or so he thought, and answered, "Glad you did, sir. Many of my classmates find this theory of noble juices, as proposed by Hooke, to be mere folly. Surely, they say, nothing that small can, make up such great beasts that inhabit the earth, the fools!" With that, he gathered his papers and pencils as if to go.

Dr. Stuart was quite put out at the cheekiness of the youth and turned as if to go also, then, on second thought, turned and spoke in a low voice, "Master Warren, what I found most interesting was your theory of a collective communication, leading to a larger effect...something you called 'quorum sensing,'" Stuart pulled out a clay pipe and began chewing on the end, "Do you have any proof of that?"

Warren looked at him funnily, "No proof sir, I don't have a laboratory, it...it was just an unsupported hypothesis of mine."

Stuart's slate gray eyes twinkled with merriment at that statement and he bit so hard on the end of his clay pipe the tip broke off. Ignoring the pipe, he leaned in close to the sullen young man and whispered, "What if you could prove it?"

The thin young man stared right back at the wrinkled old face capped by a powdered wig that was ridiculously too small for his head and asked incredulously, "But how?"

"Come with me, my boy, and I'll tell you about it." With a wave of his arm and a snapping of his cape the withered old doctor led the young man across the college toward his office and laboratory. He moved with amazing speed for an old man Warren thought trying desperately to follow the quick, black-clad figure scurrying ahead of him.

Dr. Stuart produced a large iron ring of keys from under his cloak and unlocked a large iron padlock to a door on an academic building Warren had never seen before in his relatively short time in Williamsburg. The building was located behind a thick of woods on the western part of the campus. The door was set in the stone foundation and appeared to be part of the cellar. The building itself, a derelict clapboard structure with closed shutters and weathered woodwork, looked deserted and nothing like the other beautiful buildings adorning the small collegiate campus. When Stuart swung the door open to reveal the interior, Warren gasped in fright and delight. Before him lay a cellar the likes of which Warren couldn't have imagined. The walls of the room, which was about double the size of an average parlor, were stone; wooden cabinets lining the entire room. The rough wooden planking that sat under the cabinets and served as counter space held large glass jars filled with organs and other specimens. Three large bronze incense burners smoked at various points around the room, and the sweet smell of the smoke mixed with the pervasive smell of underlying must and death—a smell that fairly assaulted the senses. Warren noticed when he stepped into the cellar that, unlike most other cellars, this one had a wooden floor instead of a dirt one. A small cluttered desk sat in the far corner, to which Stuart made a beeline, only after securing the door behind them. Perhaps the most disconcerting aspect of the room were the four large tables set in the middle with partially dissected people on them, three Negroes and one white person. "What is this place?" Warren asked in awe.

"Why my laboratory, my boy. Please come," Dr. Stuart said motioning to a seat filled with parchment in front of his desk, "and have a seat." Moving all the papers and thick volumes, he cleared room on the seat and placed the stack on his desk, spilling a vial of ink in the process. "Confound it all!" Dr. Stuart muttered under his breath. The floor creaked under his boots as Allan Warren wound his way through the bodies, staring in wonder. "Sit! Sit!" Dr. Stuart commanded excitedly. So Allan Warren sat.

"Now what you proposed in your paper is exactly what I am doing here in my laboratory," Dr. Stuart said putting on a pair of spectacles while rooting through his papers. "In all my years I have never seen any student come up with such an original theory, one that I personally have been trying to prove for years myself. How old are you son?"

Warren said, "Sixteen, sir," then looked around with some trepidation. "What is it, sir, exactly, that you are trying to prove? My essay was just something I made up off the top of my head."

"Remarkable, absolutely remarkable," Dr. Stuart muttered under his breath. He did a lot of muttering, and usually accompanied it with scratching at his ill-fitting wig. Then, as if snapping back to reality, he stopped scratching the wig and looked Warren directly in the eyes, his gaze like a serpent. "Mr. Warren, I am trying to prove that the human body is made of smaller units of matter that communicate with each other in a microscopic manner that we unconsciously don't even realize. Your theory of 'quorum sensing,' or that a collection of smaller units of matter communicating make possible a larger unit, is exactly in line with what I am doing. So I propose," a huge grin spread across the wrinkled old face, smoothing the wrinkles almost, "that you work with me." Dr. Stuart quickly added, "I'll make it worth your while, my boy. I have heard you have certain ambitions for…er, say… medicine. And I can *guarantee* you a place in any school in the *world* if you embark on this endeavor with me." He licked his lips and smiled furtively.

Warren sucked his breath in, and thought for a brief second, "Fine sir, when do I start?

Dr. Stuart chuckled, "Why, right now, my boy." Getting up from behind his desk Dr. Stuart walked about his sub terrain laboratory, lecturing as he went. "Now, *you* will be in charge of getting corpses for my work. Important job, important indeed! The general public does not understand the *merit* of what we are doing and therefore considers this kind of work ghoulish. So you must use whatever means necessary to obtain the bodies in the utmost secrecy!" He pulled his ridiculous wig off, threw it on this desk, and waved his finger in the air to illustrate his point. "Even the college doesn't know the extent of my work, for if they did I would surely be banned from the campus," twirling around to face Warren and putting his hand on the foot of one of the Negro corpses Dr. Stuart said with fire in his eyes, "but with time the world will realize the importance of our work! The advances in science and medicine we can make if we can understand the sublime nature of the human body! Imagine possibilities!" Dr. Stuart continued his tirade, and soon Warren realized he was working with a madman, a genius, a philosopher…a lunatic, but it was too late to back out now. "Say, my boy," Dr. Warren asked, snapping Warren back to reality," did your theorem include differential systems?" But Warren soon realized it was rhetorical rhetoric, and tuned Dr. Stuart out as he continued his rant.

In the ensuing months Warren spent many nights in the local graveyards digging up corpses that had been freshly interred that day. This was the one method of body procurement he hated the most, it made him feel like such a criminal, but Dr. Stuart emphasized the importance of a large volume of bodies, so Warren continued. He always made sure to replace empty coffin and carefully pile the earth back in place so nobody would ever be the wiser. Dr. Stuart told Warren in their initial interview, "The Negro is inherently different from the white man, but there is such an abundance of them in the area that I would be a fool not to take advantage of their deaths. I just modify my results so they extrapolate to a white man's body, so get me niggers, too!"

Therefore Warren made a contact with a local plantation owner on the James River, and whenever one of his Negroes died from disease, overwork, or a beating from the overseer, Warren would dutifully make the twelve-mile ride to the plantation and load the corpse up in a wagon. The plantation owner was thrilled; now he could profit from every aspect of his slaves' lives, even their deaths…no matter how disgusting it was that his young gentleman wanted the bodies. The plantation owner never did ask where the young man lived or what he wanted the bodies for. Frankly, he didn't give a damn; out of sight out of mind. Lastly, Warren made some underground connections with local criminals in the area, and would pay them for bodies they would bring to a secret rendezvous location just off Central Meeting Road some two miles from the college campus.

All in all, Warren did a fine job keeping Dr. Stuart supplied with bodies. Soon Dr. Stuart began teaching Warren how to dissect the corpses and collect data. And after the doctor was finished with the corpses it was Warren's job to dispose of them in a nearby swamp. "We must be quick about our work or they'll get too rotten," Dr. Stuart always told his young apprentice. And so Stuart, and his undergraduate associate, Warren, pioneered work in differential tissues and their growth, their work wrought from the scores of cadavers they dissected and experimented upon during Warren's tenure at William and Mary, and nobody ever the wiser to the eccentric genius and sullen apprentice.

Warren's already fragile, eggshell mind, coupled with the stresses from his new work drove him to drink, and many nights he could be found in Chowning's Tavern, a few pints of ale too deep. Slowly but surely Warren became a functioning alcoholic. The whole time Warren participated in his groundbreaking scientific research he was sinking deeper and deeper into the bottle, becoming depressed sometimes for days on end. But he found the bouts of mediocrity could be remedied by new patent medicine derived from an Indonesian plant named the coca plant. A drinking mate of his had turned him onto the wonderful new medicine that was all the rage in the Netherlands and came in a granulated form, having been chemically distilled from the actual plant fibers. The medicine worked miracles! Now he couldn't wake up without this magic powder. It cured sleepiness and hangovers…even his depression.

By age seventeen, Warren was teaching Dr. Stuart's classes so the reclusive little old man could spend more time in his laboratory with his rotting corpses. Warren would often show up to these afternoon lectures drunk, having just staggered over from the tavern, screaming at other students for their idiocy while talking about theories wrought from the great minds of Galileo Galilei, Ole Remmer, Edward Jenner, and Thomas Young. After a fistfight broke out during one of Dr. Stuart's lectures that Warren was supposedly teaching, the administration caught wind of Dr. Stuart's little game and that ended Warren's lecturing career. Warren's drunken and arrogant behavior infuriated all his classmates, and further alienated him from them. So, when he graduated in 1808, at the age of eighteen, two years ahead of schedule, with a great wealth of intellectual knowledge and academic kudos, he had not a human friend on earth, save for the eccentric Dr. Stuart who was more of a partner, and a couple of drinking friends at the various taverns. Dr. Stuart kept his word, and it took only a small note of recommendation from the world-renowned Dr. Gilpinder Stuart, and young Allan was accepted to Oxford University in England to study medicine.

Warren hadn't spoken to his father since leaving for William and Mary two years prior. Holidays, Warren would just stay at the college and study or hobnob with the local aristocrats at the taverns. The money never stopped flowing from New York, and that is what young Allan Warren told himself was important. Frankly, Allan, Sr., didn't much care about his boy, and it was just easier to send money than his love and affection. Upon receiving the news his boy was leaving for England, Allan, Sr. sent a letter of congratulations as well as money for a first-class ticket for England. So, as he had been doing all his life, Allan Warren, Jr. sailed for England with a full pocket and empty heart.

Warren completed the four-year term at Oxford with little difficulty. Unlike all his previous experience in an academia setting, the other pupils at Oxford were almost as bright as he, and he had little trouble making friends with actual *peers*, instead of the, "Fucking dullards I'm used to dealing with," as he would tell his Oxford cronies. Perhaps his most valued friend and confidant was Walter Prig the fourth, a German citizen from Hesse, whom had originally been born in the shipping town of Liverpool, England. Prig's parents, wealthy land barons, had sent Prig back to his native country to receive the best education. Prig and Warren lived together in a small loft apartment in the town of Oxford only a few blocks from the school of medicine. Prig liked to drink more than Warren, and the two soon could often be seen carousing at the pubs. Warren turned Prig onto his scientific miracle medicine from the Netherlands and soon Prig couldn't imagine life without the fine white powder; he even took to sprinkling on his eggs and grilled tomatoes at breakfast to cure his raging headaches. Warren, formerly a reclusive and sullen man, blossomed into a semi-normal functioning human being with the newfound human contact he experienced at Oxford. No longer angry and sullen, Warren could carry on a conversation, make the rare friend, and even laugh on occasion, so when it came time for his class to graduate and Walter to return to Hesse, Warren was crushed. With a heavy heart and ever-familiar sullen disposition the newly christened Dr. Warren packed his bags and headed back to the Americas.

Like many physicians, Dr. Warren was a brilliant man, but lacked in the personality department. "It's like, he's just…not there," one patient described him to a friend, "he just can't empathize with my problems. I doubt he even cares." And this particular patient was correct. Dr. Warren didn't care; all he was interested in was science and drinking. Back in America and surrounded by fucking dullards, Dr. Warren began drinking more than ever. As his drinking problem got worse the use of his patent medicine, *Dr. Swügechewnz's Patent Cocaine Powder,* became more frequent. Dr. Warren began using it so frequently he arranged to receive a case a month from the Netherlands. The drinking affected his desire to work, and Dr. Warren drifted from town to town up and down the east coast, unable to set up a stable practice. After ten years of struggling to make a living in various towns and cities across the eastern seaboard, Dr. Warren returned to his father's house in New York broke. Allan, Sr., disgusted at the shadow of a man that turned up on his doorstep without a penny to his name, used his contacts to set his son up with a steady job for the state of New York as a surgeon for the prison system.

In 1822 Dr. Allan William Warren, Jr. was assigned to Auburn prison under the direction of Captain Elam Lynds. The stocky warden with piercing eyes met his arrival on his first day at the stark prison, located in Cayuga County. Dr. Warren offered his hand, but Lynds merely spun and began walking and talking over his shoulder, "Sir, my name is Captain Elam Lynds. Obviously, I am the warden for Auburn Prison. We had some problems with the last surgeon and he was dismissed two months ago. Let's get one thing clear," he said spinning around. Dr. Warren had to stop quickly in order to not run into the man, "You are not here to mollycoddle these men. They are hardened criminals. You will tend their needs, nothing else," with a hint of a twinkle in those slate eyes, he added, "and believe me, if your treatments are not totally without pain I will not be offended." He started walking and talking again. "See that building over there?" he asked pointing to a house on a hill. "That will be your quarters along with the head of the guard detail. And this," he said stopping in front of a squat clapboard building with no windows, "will be your treatment facility. Anything you need submit to me in writing. You get paid $14.67 on the first of every month. Questions?" Not receiving any, Lynds said curtly, "Good day to you, sir!" Without further ceremony he strode across the yard and disappeared into the administration building.

Warren sighed, went inside, unpacked his surgical instruments, and mixed himself a little gin and water. The inner turmoil that had haunted him for so many years had finally subsided, but only partly because of the fact he had finally found a steady job.

Dr. Warren had unlocked the secret to his own sick soul some three months ago when living at his father's house in the city, but this secret must be kept closely guarded, for he knew, that, if found out, he was liable to be thrown out of the community, or worse yet, killed. Warren had recently discovered he was a homosexual, and the increasingly frequent visits to certain houses of specialized ill repute balanced the void left by his departure from Oxford. Really, he had found that the only panacea for his tortured mind was the intimate company of another man. Just the thought of it brought a smile to his face. Men were so easy to get in the city, but he may have a problem here at Auburn, for he simply couldn't buy them, he would actually have to woo one—maybe a prisoner? Until the time that he could get a man, he figured he could stay mentally balanced with his magic white powder.

Tourists who paid a dime to tour the prison, would often see a hungover Warren emerging from his office where he had passed out the night before. The good doctor's office had become somewhat of a social hall at night and he would usually pass the night with a gaggle of guards, all of them snookered. The visitors usually witnessed him stumbling off in the direction of the main cellblock; grip in hand, blood running from his nose, shouting nonsensical greetings. Over the course of the next few years, Dr. Warren proved himself to be such an apt surgeon as well as subversive administrator of torture to the prison that when Warden Lynds was commissioned to build a new prison in Westchester County he named Dr. Warren as chief surgeon. When the prison opened in 1828 Dr. Warren was thirty-eight years old. "Sing, sing a praise out to Jesus. Sing, sing your prayers to the Lord. Lest you evil doers of the world get on your knees and quiver, 'cause you'll be sing signing all the way up the fucking river," Dr. Warren quietly sang to himself on a hot, dusty summer day as he walked through the gate of Sing Sing for the first time.

Part IV: Die Sonneleute

Chapter 53

They wait until nightfall to come for me. The rain pours down in buckets, drumming a staccato beat on the roof. The lightning occasionally lights up the definition line between the black sky and black landscape immediately followed by deafening bursts of thunder that roll across the low northern Catskill Mountains sounding much like a battery of cannons. The thunder covers the approaching sounds of *them*. And just like the horsemen of the Apocalypse will come forth to cleanse the earth, they too came to bathe the prison of my presence…I guess they figure I'd resist now that they were wise to my history.

The cell door crashes open with a reverberating clang. I wake up instantly. Confused, I look around; it is pitch black in my cell save the soft yellow glow thrown into the cell by three guards in the hall holding smoking oil lanterns. The gentle rain I fell asleep to some hours ago has intensified now. The light emanating the three guards' lanterns masks the identity of two figures in the foreground but I quickly figure out who they are by their respective voices.

"I got an interesting letter today from across the puddle from a friend, Walter Prig the fourth. Dr. Prig attended school with me as you know, and lived in Germany for some time before returning to Oxford to teach." Warren pauses and a small ball of light rose from his cupped hands as he lights his cigarette. Continuing, the small ember of his cigarette dances around his face, "He had some very informative things to say about those markings on your arm." With those words my blood chills, and I instinctively reach up to cover the tattoos on my right bicep.

"I was first intrigued by the symbol on your arm," Warren purrs in a menacing tone while the other figure remains black and silent, framed by the guards' lamps, "and made a sketch of it to send to Dr. Prig. You know the lines that make two ninety-degree turns opposite of each other and cross each other? Sure you do. Anyhow, Dr. Prig informed me your symbol is something called a 'swastika.' Apparently," he pauses for dramatic effect and the ember glows brightly, "this swastika is a symbol of the sun. A symbol standing for power and strength used by the Egyptians as far back at 2500 before the year of our Lord, and one now used by many royal European families for decoration. Apparently the Tsarina, Alexandra Fyodorovna, is especially fond of decorating the royal mansions in that motif. You know," he says casually, "she is originally a Prussian princess and if I'm not mistaken, daughter of Friedrich Wilhelm III." A cold sweat now bathes me; small droplets of sweat drop from my forehead. I swallow and say nothing, but continue to hold my bicep as Warren continues his tirade, "And it appears that the lettering circling your swastika, *Die Sonneleute*, marks you as a member of an organization called 'The People of the Sun'."

Dear God save me. I feared this day might come when my identity would be found out and I would be persecuted. Save me for my sins committed against you, I fervently thought.

The other darkened figure interjects in his familiar gravelly voice, "So this means, Opfer, that you are suddenly a very dangerous man, and the state of New York has sent you here so that I can keep the good citizens of this great state safe from riffraff like you. Which means that you are a threat to the integrity of this institution and my reputation, so you must be moved outside the normal inmate population."

Jack Savage and my enemy, Jepatha Bambury move in front of the warden and prison doctor, the light framing their sadistically grinning faces. "Lets g' sc'ahr face," Jack pleasantly growls in a malice-laced voice. They roughly grab me and hoist me up; my almost useless feet can't support myself as they drag me down the tier, an entourage of guards following.

I bow my head as they drag me down the steps to tier one and across the floor and start reciting, "They came upon me as a wide breaking in of waters: in the desolation they rolled themselves upon me. Terrors are turned upon me: they pursue my soul as the wind: and my welfare passeth away as a cloud…"

As I get dragged out into the pouring rain my skin instantly turns to ice as the April rain soaks my body, but strangely it feels good and clarifies my mind. I kick my feet to kind of propel myself through the mud while Savage and Bambury carry on, their hands digging into my flesh. Past the kitchen and to an auxiliary building they carry me. The auxiliary building was built in 1830, just two years after completion of the main cellblock. It is a squat building, set apart from the other two buildings. In all the time I have spent in the recreational yard and in my daily comings and goings to work I have never seen a spark of life from the building. It's almost as if it is abandoned.

The warden takes lead as we near the building and pounds on the iron door. A small slit opens and a man peers out. The light from inside the building escapes; it is the only light in my black surroundings. The slit closes. A rusty locking mechanism squeals in protest and the door screeches open. A guard in the same blue uniform as the others in the regular cellblock stands blinking into the night. "We're ready for him, Warden," he says and beckons us in.

A guard at a battered wooden table jumps up. "Sir, good to see you," he shouts.

"Take it easy, Neville, good to see you too," Warden Lynds replies. The same guard that opened the main door closes it, leaving the one guard to return to the main block. Savage and Bambury stay. The guard who wasn't Neville crosses the little guardroom and sorts through his ring of keys. Selecting one, he opens the barred door on the other side of the room. Bambury and Savage drag me unceremoniously into the room, which has nothing in it. Savage props me against Bambury. Closing the barred door behind him, leaving Neville in the guardroom, the nameless guard scurries to the middle of the room and lifts a heavy padlock off a trapdoor. Sorting through his keys again, he selects the correct one and works the key, releasing the mechanism. With a loud bang he swings open the trapdoor. Juxtaposed against the white marble of the tiny room's floor the gaping black hole before me appears to be a portal to hell.

Bambury continues to prop me up complaining, "Can't you even stand up, you damn Prussian shit?" I don't answer and let him continue to bear my soaked carcass. Savage disappears into the hole and soon some dim light appears from within the belly of the beast. His voice wafts up, "Al'ight, send him down." I am dropped abruptly down into the hole into the waiting arms of Savage, my body banging painfully against the steep metal ladder on the way down. Savage drags me past several cell doors down the dirt-covered corridor.

Emaciated hands grasp the bars, and the soft calling of a voice rouses my senses, *Does the silence rule apply in here?*

"Here ya' are ya' fo'ck," Savage says. With a kick he boots me into an empty cell. I crumple to the ground with the sudden amount of weight put onto my crippled feet. The cell door slams with finality.

Warden Lynds saunters up to the door, "So, Mr. Opfer I am so pleased to have one of his majesty's own People of the Sun incarcerated here at Sing Sing. Welcome to the hole. This is where we put...problematic prisoners that don't respond to, uh, conventional discipline methods as well as those that are extremely dangerous, like you, *Mr.* Opfer. Once you have become too feeble to be dangerous to my guards or the citizenry of New York you may be leaving the hole. But...don't count on it, and, until then...enjoy. With a nasty laugh he turns and ushers the others up the steep ladder. The trapdoor bangs shut. I slide to the floor slowly, back against the wall, cold, wet, shivering in my tomb, my blue eyes blinking in incredulity.

What is wrong with these people? I have caused no problem since coming to this prison, yet I am constantly sought out for brutal humiliation. Feeling around in the pitch darkness I find I have more room that my previous cell. This one is probably about eight feet by five feet, guessing from my rough estimates. The only thing it is lacking is light, fresh air, and a cot. *Great, fucking great, every immigrant's dream.* With that thought the wailing begins.

Chapter 54

Back up in the guard's room of the unidentified small cellblock, Warden Lynds and Dr. Warren warm their hands by the fire while the four guards look on. Dr. Warren turns to face the others. "Seat, have a seat men," he says motioning to the battered wooden chairs matching the condition of the rickety table. The four men sit. Warden Lynds turns from the fire and begins, "All right, I am going to fill you in on inmate Gregor Opfer. I realize he has never threatened any guards, and other than his noise infractions some nights, has an exemplarily prison record." While the warden speaks the good doctor busily rolls a small cigarette. Rain drips from his Van Dyke beard and soaks the paper. Annoyed, he pitches the mess into the fire and begins the process again after wiping at his beard with his equally damp shoulder. Meanwhile the warden continues, "I doubt you realize it, but Opfer has been sufficiently trained so that he essentially could escape at any point, and kill as many guards on the way out as he wanted."

Savage interjects, "S'ahr?"

"Go ahead."

"Well s'ahr, how 'bout even with 'em bum feet?"

"Good question, Savage. We're really not sure of this man's capabilities, but there is a good chance he could still manage, feet or not. Apparently he's extremely resourceful. Dr. Warren here has already explained this organization to me and he can do a better job than I ever could, so, Dr. Warren?"

Turning to Dr. Warren he finds him, back to fire, swigging from his silver flask. Stowing his flask, Dr. Warren retrieves his smoke balanced precariously on the edge of the pot bellied stove and scratches his head. "Well, men, according to my doctor friend in England who has some knowledge of this organization warned me to exercise extreme caution when dealing with this man. The People of the Sun is an organization that was assembled in the late 18th century sometime by the Prussian King, Frederick William III after an assassination attempt by a Hungarian national. The king, paranoid after the attempt on his life, organized a secret police force to protect him and root out any anti nationals located in Prussia and the surrounding Germanic states. The men are apparently recruited from the top universities in the country and subjected to rigorous training that turns them into lethal killing machines. They are the best and the brightest and can usually be readily identified by a scar on their face, remnants of a membership to a dueling society from their university. Although all dueling society members aren't members of this Sonneleute organization, all Sonneleute are members of a dueling society. Follow me?"

Everyone in the room nods. Warren licks his lips and continues. "They are skilled in hand-to-hand combat and can apparently use knives like no other." Warren pauses and takes a drag from his cigarette while gathering his thoughts. "These men are trained to blend in; they are essentially chameleons, a lizard that changes color to blend in according to it's surroundings. If Opfer were ever to get out, we would never find him. Never," he stresses the last word and puffs his cigarette before continuing. "He would simply disappear and there would be absolutely nothing we could do about it, and this I am sure of gentlemen. Inmate Opfer personally told me he can speak eight languages fluently, for Christ's sake!"

Bambury lets out a low whistle, "Whoa, and to think that little fuck gave me no trouble while I broke his feet." Dr. Warren glares at Bambury, finishes his smoke and throws the end into the fire.

Warden Lynds ends the meeting, "So this means, men, exercise extreme caution when dealing with this man, he has fangs. All right, get back to work; I'm going home to bed. It's been a damn long day." The man named Neville opens the rusty door and the four men disappear into the driving rain.

As Neville closes the door he addresses his partner, "Whadya think of all that tomfoolery?"

"Ain't no worry," replies the other man, "he's a fuckin' cripple. Cm'on, on let's finish this game of cards."

Chapter 55

The only sensory input in the depths of the dungeon are few and far in between. The *drip drip* of a slow leak sounds in the distance, like the maddening tick of the doomsday clock. I could run my hands over the marble walls slick with moss and slime, feeling their sliminess against my bare skin, or chaff my hands over the rough iron bars but these are things I have already done. Sight is a sense I no longer possess. Blackness surrounds me. I can't even see my own hand in front of my face and must feel my way over to the hole in the floor; the hole that supplies me with plenty of aromas for my olfactory senses. Frantic cries of men slowly losing their minds sound around me, sporadic sometimes, but constant at others…almost following a circadian rhythm of their own. This prisoner's sanity isn't that frail yet, but give it time; the mind is a muscle. Disuse wreaks softness. So here I sit, *sans* sight, *sans* dignity, and *sans* world, just sitting and contemplating *my* crimes…ones I committed and ones I *should've* committed.

The morning was one that just wouldn't break. It wouldn't rain either. It was one of those mornings that just misted so heavily that large drops of dew collect on your clothing, and nobody wants to venture outside, but stay inside beside the roaring fire, warm, safe, and content. I rose before any other of the soldiers, long before dawn, and climbed the ramparts to look out over the town, my home. The swirling wind flapped my overcoat around my ankles and tugged at the matching black fedora. The heavy mist collected and beaded on my jacket, rolling off and plopping on my riding boots. I had set everything up perfectly; the job would go down as planned. I smiled grimly at the prospect. I retraced my steps, picking carefully over the moss-grown stones and alighted the stone steps back into the courtyard. The dreary day passed slowly, but revenge can never come soon enough to the slighted. To pass the time I drilled with some my fellow soldiers in such techniques as hand-to-hand combat, cloaking techniques, linguistics, and equestrian evasive maneuvering. Most of the unit was dispersed throughout the king's country gathering intelligence, and enforcing his will in this time of political unrest so Schloss Rheinfels was strangely empty. No matter, since I wanted to do this mission alone.

After a light supper of beans and potatoes in the castle's great stone dining hall I retreated to my bunk and started reading from the Good Book. "Gregor, are you sure you need no help on your mission tonight?" Igor, a sullen looking, yet compassionate fellow asked interrupting my studies. Igor is a new recruit, having joined only six months ago, and although young, he is more than capable of carrying out Friedrich IV's work. I have already decided he will be my protégé of sorts, but not this night.

Looking up I replied, "No, this enemy of the kaiser is weak, and there is only one of him. He is a fat, toady man, who hoards his money to give to the insurgents. I can handle him myself."

"Gregor, you could handle any man, or several of them at once for that matter, I've seen you walk into a biergarten full of enemies and single-handedly control those who seek to dominate what is not theirs." The boy told me with hero worship.

Chuckling, I replied, "Ah, you are too kind. I have seen your skills and within the year you shall have far surpassed my elimination skills."

Igor laughed and said, "If you change your mind, let me know. I am scheduled to be deployed to the far eastern region for a fortnight."

"Thanks," I said, turning back to the gilded pages as I heard receding footsteps. After the proper amount of time passed I consulted a gold pocket watch, and seeing that it was, in fact, the correct time exited the dormitory and headed for the livery stable.

Shucking off my topcoat, I grabbed a peasant's cape from the hook in the livery stable and donned it, pulling up the hood to hide my appearance and profile, not like anyone would be out on a miserable evening such as this. I patted Stahlhand's nose, and he snorted and stamped his hoof in anticipation. I have found that whispering into his ear while patting his flank calms the beast and readies him, so I did just that. When he is ready, I loaded a large bundle of fags onto him and lead him out the back entrance of the castle and into the little valley running perpendicular to it. After fifteen minutes of vigorous walking I came to the edge of the forest that intersects with the small road leading to St. Goar. The mossy rocks and wet tree limbs have soaked my clothes and muddied my boots but my mind is focused on my goal, and I don't even realize the physical discomfort. "Come on, boy," I said, firmly pulling on Stahlhand's reigns. We step out of the forest and start moseying down the road toward town. If the sun had been out on this day, this would be the time of day it would be ducking behind the horizon. Another fifteen minutes of walking brought my faithful friend and me to the outskirts of the town.

I tied Stahlhand to a bush, just out of sight of the main road in the surrounding forest and sneak off, avoiding the main street. I slipped through alleyways like wind through the trees and made it to my destination, Bilgunstrom's Printing Shop, without detection. I stood in the shadows across from the building for some time making sure nobody was watching before I crossed the street and ducked into the alley next to the building. Grabbing a large wooden rubbish crate I used it to boost myself up and latch onto a windowsill. I dug my leather riding boots into the small space between the iron drainpipe and wall and got a foothold. With the foothold I was able to pull myself up and into a second story window. With soft footfalls I made my way through Bilgunstrom's apartment and to the narrow staircase that led down to the shop. The stairs are steep and unlit, but I stealthily navigated them. I peered into the pressroom; nobody is visible, same with the front room. With quick movements I checked the front door. "Good. Locked," I thought, and headed for the back office. I knew where the bastard was.

"Who the fuck are you, and how did you get in here?" asked Bilgunstrom with incredulity when a rain-soaked peasant pushed open his door. "What do you want?" he demanded. I said nothing, my face looking down and hidden by the burlap hood. Scared, but still loud,

Bilgunstrom declared, "The safe is locked, and I shan't open it for you! If it's money you've come for then you won't be getting it today, now get out of here before I call for the magistrate."

My head still downcast I said, "Your time has come, Herr Bilgunstrom. I have come to collect." With that, I raised my head and slowly lowered my hood.

Herr Bilgunstrom didn't recognize me at first. "Who are you?"

A malicious grin spread over my face as I said in a low voice, "The boy you once loved...or so you claimed."

"Oh, dear God, your face!" he cried. And recognition slowly blossomed and spread over his fat face. "But, but," he spluttered, "you ran away..." he lost steam and trailed off. He sat staring incredulously at the scar tissue running from eye to neck. Neither one of us spoke while I savored the moment. I could taste his fear and it excited me.

A range of emotions played over his fat face. He was stunned but not for long. With the deviousness of a ferret he congenially offered, "You want money? Is that what you want? I'll give it to you. All of it." He frantically got up.

A leather riding crop appeared from inside my sleeve, and I whipped him across the face and roared, "Sit the fuck down! I do not want your blood money! That precious money that you are trying to buy me off with is tainted with your perverseness. May Satan himself keep your precious gold!" I had worked myself into a frenzy. Keeping my voice low so as not to be heard outside, but by no means under control I asked, "How many lives have you ruined? Be honest. And think carefully, this may be the only chance you have to save your life."

"I, I, I," the now pathetic little man stuttered. I stepped across the room and jerked him out of his chair by his lapels and jammed the handle of the crop harshly into his groin. Bilgunstrom collapsed to the floor writhing in pain. "I is not an answer, you fiend," I whispered and grabbed him by the ears and hauled him back into his nice cushy leather wing chair. The mighty Herr Bilgunstrom who used to rape me started to cry, cowering in the corner of his chair. Tears flowed freely from his eyes and shone in the candlelight while he clutched his injured groin with his fat little sausage-link fingers. Towering over him I asked, "Why does such a man that used to take such joy in using his mouth on me and fucked me, cry when we are reunited? Aren't you pleased I'm back to see you again? You want to see this?" I grabbed my crotch.

He cried louder.

"I didn't think so. For Christ's sake, you used to whisper you loved me as you fucked me!" My face was now mere inches from his; I could smell his unwashed body and cheap lavender toilet water.

"Please, please," Bilgunstrom whimpered, and was immediately silenced by the thwack of the sap as it connected with his skull. He slumped over unconscious.

Quickly, I retraced my steps back upstairs. I picked the finest mirror in Herr Bilgunstrom's chamber. He had many, for he was a vain man and liked to perform sexual acts in front of them with little boys, or at least I'm guessing so from when I... The mirror was a King Louis XIV-style DeCartier piece, very expensive. Turning the mirror around and using my razor sharp boot knife I quickly carved Die Sonneleute's symbol, the same symbol on my right bicep into the back of the mirror. Die Sonneleute did this so that people looking into the mirror in the future would be forever watched by the eye of righteousness and reason. 'Perfect,' I thought to myself and hurried back downstairs. In the darkened corner was Bilgunstrom's safe. I put my ear to it and started twisting the dial. In a few short seconds the tumblers dropped into place, and I cranked the door open. Grabbing all the gold coins, bars, and other documents stashed inside I placed all of the safe's contents into a burlap bag and placed it on the desk next to the unconscious man.

I used the side door to exit into the alley, and snuck back through town to my waiting friend. Stahlhand was waiting patiently in the steady rain that had developed. Recognizing me, he blew steam through his nostrils and neighed, tossing his great head. We made our way back through the town to Bilgunstrom's shop and, once there, I led my large stallion into the alley. I took off the bundle of fags and placed it next to the door. Looking in, I saw with satisfaction that Bilgunstrom hadn't moved. With no little effort I managed to get his fat ass onto

Stahlhand. He didn't like the extra weight and danced around. I quieted him using my method and when he was calm I piled the fags back on until they conceal the body sufficiently. Pulling the hood of my cape up, I quietly led Stahlhand out of the alley and through the town. My eyes darted feverishly around but I doubted anyone spied me, and if they did they look past me, through me. Die Sonneleute members blend in…don't even exist.

Once away from the winking lights of my familiar town I picked up the pace. The rain saturated the cloak and it weighed about ten pounds more than normal, but I didn't even notice. I was too focused on the task at hand. After walking a good distance west, I turned off the road, knowing these woods to be remote. Not that detection would be a problem at this time of the evening, the inky blackness of the night having long since descended upon the fatherland. Deep into the woods, I found a satisfactory spot. Tall trees towered overhead, and the little moonlight that penetrated the heavy fog cast an eerie pale light over the forest floor. I moved the bundle of twigs aside and unceremoniously pushed Bilgunstrom to the forest floor like so much shit. The distance from Stahlhand's back was no small distance and the inert man hit with a heavy thump. I lit a small lantern and began to dig with a wooden spade. The digging was difficult in the hard Prussian soil, and soon perspiration dripped freely from my nose mixing with the black clumps of dirt I heaved in front of me. Soon, I had a small hole about two feet deep and roughly six feet long. 'Perfect,' I thought.

I shook Bilgunstrom. At that point, I was slightly alarmed. He should've woken up by now, not that I'm worried that he's dead, but rather disappointed that I miss out on the opportunity to torture him. I passed some smelling salts under his nose and he woke with a start. "Where am I?" he stammered, inspecting his muddied suit and frantically looking about. "Help! Help!" he screamed into the black night.

I backhanded him hard across the face. "Fool, did you honestly think I would bring you someplace where you could be heard? You're pathetic. Have some semblance of dignity," I spat out as I saw the tears in his eyes once again.

"What do you want?" he cried rising to his knees and tugging at my soaked cloak. Ignoring his question, I looked down at him. 'Excellent,' I thought, for once our roles are reversed. "Take your clothes off you pathetic piece of dog shit!" I commanded.

"W-w-why?" he whimpered. I raised my hand as if to strike him again and he fell back to the moist earth, arms covering his pudgy face.

"Now!" With some jerking motions, he began to unbutton his shirt, hands trembling. I watched with satisfaction at the once proud predator now a shaking little mouse. A minute later he knelt before me fat, white and naked, his flaccid little penis hanging limp and shriveled. "Stand up, be a man!" I commanded, sickened by this disgrace to my Prussian ancestry. As he straightened up I grabbed his genitals and pulled and twisted down, producing a loud animal howling noise from Herr Bilgunstrom. "You like it, you sick fuck? Huh? I sure as hell didn't when you used to force your will upon me. Now I force mine upon you." His eyes were squeezed shut and teeth clenched as I squeezed and pulled so he didn't even see it coming when I took my free hand, freed my knife and cut his manhood off with one slice.

Bilgunstrom looked down at the massive amount of blood that pumped from the spot where his torture instrument had once proudly been displayed. He opened and shut his mouth like a fish but not words came forth. I tossed his genitals into the shallow pit to my right and picked up his semi-clean white shirt and slowly wiped my bloody hands with it and watched him bleed. Finally, a loud high-pitched scream escaped those blue lips as he collapsed. I carefully removed a stiletto from its hiding place in my riding boot and crouched over my victim. A swift motion, and I plunged it into the mastoid process, his breathing quickly ceased and after a few convulsions he lay still. The small wound in his neck was barely visible, bloodless. I normally didn't operate in such a sadistic fashion, but Bilgunstrom was personal.

Unceremoniously kicking his fat pale body into the shallow grave, I dumped the clothes on the body and then got to work filling it in. After the grave had been filled in I piled heavy stones on it to keep animals from digging the corpse up and having my work discovered by an unsuspecting hunter before the flesh had properly rotted off. Finally, I swept over the spilled blood on the forest floor and traced a swastika into the dirt. "For king and country," I muttered, knowing in my heart this killing was not in the name of homeland security, but rather a personal vendetta, and this certainly won't be the last personal killing. I mounted Stahlhand, who had been contently nibbling on foliage through the entire process, and rode him hard back to Schloss Rheinfels where I tumbled into my bed for a fitful night's sleep. That night I slept the sleep of the innocent.

Chapter 56

Sitting in my darkened cell I ponder whether or not fate has destined me to be here now. *God, are you punishing me for the past?* If this is repayment from God I think I'd rather take death, this mental anguish, and being deprived of the senses is slowly driving me insane. God won't let me take death...yet? "I deserve death!" I scream into the darkness gripping the bars. "Yeee-aaahhh," in the form of an insane scream, answers me. *Now I've got them going,* I think, plopping down. Pulling knees up to my chin, I rest it on the fabric of the now filthy and torn black and white stripped suit.

Coming from the darkness two cells I hear, "I can now see all the beautiful sounds played by the queen! The disease-ridden bowery queen of paint and plume, I tell ya', and I'm a prince...a prince that burns. How it burns! Did you know..." I hear the sound of the inmate urinating into the dirt-covered passageway running between the cells, screaming in pain all the while, "Pins an' needles!"

Chapter 57

I awake with a start to the sound of the trapdoor banging open and low lantern light filtering into my abyss. I must've nodded off, because a line of drool runs down my now-bearded face and covers the knees of my pants, soaking both of them. I run my finger over my scar. No hair grows there; it is a barren place. Heavy footsteps sound on the iron steps of the ladder and soon a bright lantern is held in front of my cell. The others have been worked into their usual insane frenzy. "Quiet ya' broug mutha' fo'ckars! Bam'brey, ya' bett'ar be be'in dog wide!" I recognize the rough accent of Savage.

His sidekick, Bambury, pipes in, "Opfer, you wretched little shell of a man. How can you now call yourself a man? Look at yourself. Pitiable. A few months in the hole and you can't even hardly open your eyes. You freak cripple!" He laughs, and I hear liquid swish. I can't see past the bright light, but guess he's drinking a pint.

"We're jest checkin' up on our favorite pris'nar, Opf'ar. Makin' sh'ar ya' don' get no thoughts like givin' the gu'ards ov'r he're any trouble, 'cause ya' know I'm in ch'arge of these gu'ards so, if ya're givin' them trouble then ya're givin' me trouble. He'ar me boy?" I look at him and blink. "Ans'er me!" Savage roars.

"Nessun problema qui voi parte irlandese ignara dei rifiuti dellagrondaia," I insolently spit through the bars telling Savage there is no problem here, and insulting him in Italian.

"The fuck he just say?" demands Bambury, blowing his whiskey breath into my cell.

"He're, hold this," Savage tells Bambury. I figure he's referring to *his* pint. "Ya' speak American ya' god-damn piece of crim'nal trash." Although I can't see them, I can tell he is about to call upstairs for the door to be opened and then I would surely receive a good beating from

216

the two drunks. I neutralize the situation quickly, not wanting a beating in my weakened condition.

"Sorry, sir, sometimes I don't even realize I'm talking in my native tongue," I say, lying to him. The dumb pile of horse manure doesn't even know the difference between a romantic language and a Germanic one.

"He're, gimme that," I hear Savage say. I can hear a sucking sound.

While Savage is drinking, Bambury calls snidely through the bars, "Don't ya' forget who's in charge here, Opfer, ever! I own ya', boy! And I will always own ya'."

He is interrupted by one of my cellmates, "Who do we have here? Has my bowery queen returned to her prince?"

"Shut the fuck up!" Bambury screams at him, diverting his attention away from me.

But the man is on a roll. "See how it burns," he shrilly screams.

He must have whipped his penis out, for the next thing I know I hear Bambury curse and yell to Savage, "Sonofabitch, this bastard is pissin' on me!" I hear a bottle shatter. Savage must have thrown it at the cell.

All the time the nameless fellow inmate is screaming, "Ahhhh," and laughing maniacally.

Savage turns and yells up the trapdoor, "Gimme the keys! Now!" I quickly stand, pain shoots through my legs and the sudden movement makes me dizzy. I ignore the nausea. I steady myself on the bars, and strain my eyes against the faint light cast by the lantern, my legs trembling from the exertion. I see the keys drop down the hatch and Savage unlock the cell door. Both guards rush into the cell truncheons held high.

From the darkened cell, I can only hear the laughter and the prisoner screaming, "Yes! Yes!" Like on the throes of an orgasmic experience. The grunts and muted curses from Bambury and Savage eventually drown out the laughter as it suddenly ceases and the crunch of wood breaking bone fills the hallway. The guards emerge without their caps, uniforms askew, wiping sweat from their brows.

"I can't believe that sonofabitch pissed on me!" Bambury complains as they walk past my cell, climb the ladder and leave the man's cell door wide open. As the lantern light recedes up and the trapdoor closes I am once again surrounded by darkness.

"Hey, hey, buddy," I call to the cell next to me, "you all right?"

"Lots of glass, lots of glass, lots of glass, all 'round me."

A plan slowly formulates in my mind, or at least the beginnings of one as my trained mind comes out of dormancy with the ferocity of a snake striking a mouse. "Lemme have some of that glass." I scrabble my hand over to near his cell. "Here put it in my hand," I command. I can hear him scraping up some glass, then feel him placing it in my hand. I feel the sting of it cutting my hand open. "Thanks," I tell him pulling my hand back and feeling my pieces.

"Yeah, yeah, my reward will eventually exist in heaven," the voice drifts from the cell as I hear him scraping up the glass shards in his cell. I select the largest shard, about the length of my middle finger, and throw the others down my latrine hole. The piece I keep, I store in the corner for later use. Sucking on my bloodied fingers, I once again drift off into the state of perpetual suspended sleep I seem to exist in, and my demons begin to haunt me again.

Chapter 58

I awoke in the early morning hours the day after I had taken care of Bilgunstrom. Consulting my gold pocket watch, it told me the other soldiers wouldn't rise for another hour or so. The dorm room was still darkened, only some gray slivers of light penetrated through the old slit windows in the castle, their bars of light sliced across the two rows of cots. Many bore sleeping men and some were without. I swung my legs over the side of the bed and pulled on my riding boots. I crept into the kitchen area and stoked the fire. When a decent blaze roared to life I put a kettle of water over the flames. While the water came to a boil, I found some coffee grinds and strained out a small cup coffee that tasted like espresso. I quickly drank the strong coffee drink and ate a hunk of crusty black bread before stealing back into the dorm area. "Igor, Igor," I whispered into the sleeping man's ear. Any normal man would've cried out and sat up fast, having been woken in such a manner. But because of his training, Igor calmly opened his eyes, not moving a muscle, and took stock of his situation.

Realizing I was a 'friendly,' and he was safe in Schloss Rheinfels, he slowly sat up. "Yeah?"

"Come on, get out of bed, I am going to need your help today. Grab something to eat and meet me in the stables, I'll be getting our horses ready."

"But I am supposed to be deployed to Baden today," he protested.

"Never mind that," I told him, "I spoke to Weschulz, and you have been reassigned to this mission. You are in Phase III, are you not? I promise, this will be much more exciting than going to Baden on an 'errand,'" I said sarcastically, "You will learn from me today. Now get your gear together!"

"Okay," Igor eagerly exclaimed, jumping out of bed, excited to be going on a real mission.

Ten minutes later, while I was saddling Stahlhand and Auslöser, Igor's horse, the young man appeared across the square munching on a crab apple. "What's the mission today?" he asked when he drew near enough to me in the swirling mist.

Closing the buckle on Auslöser's bridle, I replied, "An enemy of the king has been identified in St. Goar. He is a Russian spy, sending intelligence to the Romanov Empire. Although we have a signed a peace treaty with Russia, Nicholas plans on annexing Prussia in the near future. Specifically, he is here to spy on the king's armed forces and has stumbled across our band of brothers."

Igor looked at me in awe, absorbing the lie. "Wow. I thought nobody knew about us."

"He is very good, and very dangerous," I said emphasizing the word "dangerous."

"Who is the target?" inquired Igor.

Slowly, as if savoring his name like one would savor a steaming mug of glühwein, I said, "Pieter, Pieter von Deose is what he goes by. His real name...is unknown." I shrugged.

"What are our orders?" the fresh-faced recruit whispered. His eyes danced with the prospect of adventure.

"Have you heard what we do to enemies of Die Sonneleute?" I asked scornfully, knowing full well he knew the answer.

"Sure I do! It's the first thing we learned in training!" he whispered louder this time, his long jagged scar glowing bright red from excitement.

"Good then." I mounted Stahlhand and patted his side as he danced around. "Mount up and let's get going." I trotted Stahlhand around some outbuildings and to one of the secret entrances. Before the sun made its full appearance in the east, our black horses raced across the countryside, circumventing St. Goar; long streams of steam flowed from their nostrils like the horses of the apocalypse.

About seven miles due west of St. Goar in a meadow I used to sometimes camp as a boy, we selected a spot. By now the sun was almost a quarter of the way to its pinnacle in the sky. The rain was gone, at least for now, and the mist was burning off. "We must hurry and construct it in order to make the usual removal," I told Igor, jumping from my horse. I gave him a slap on the rump and issued a loud, "Ye-a." He scurried off to the other side of the meadow to feast on whatever clovers and grasses he could find. I shucked my overcoat, the day turning out to be sunny and somewhat warm, and grabbed the two axes I brought. I tossed one to Igor. "Here, start looking for dead timber; it burns the best." We began dragging great logs from the ancient Prussian forest. In no time I had a good sweat worked up from chopping the large logs and branches into ten-foot segments. I found the straightest piece I could, about eight inches in diameter, and shortened it to roughly fourteen feet in length. After sharpening the end, I called to Igor who was hauling a large branch from the other side of the meadow, "Here, sink this, and I'm going to continue chopping, and stacking it."

"That is good," he said bringing the branch over, huffing from exertion. As he dug a small pit and put the pole in upright I continued chopping, then stacked the ten-foot segments in a staggered pattern around the stake. After the initial structure was completed and sturdied, we took all the small branches and twigs left over and threw them in the middle. "Looks good," Igor commented standing next to me wiping his brow.

"Ever done this before?" I asked.

"No, I just finished my training a few weeks ago, you forget."

"You are never done training," I told him sternly. "Wisdom will come when you realize your infinite ignorance."

Flustered, he replied, "Well, you...you know what I mean."

I ignored him and looked to the sky; the sun is well past the halfway mark and climbing down out of its perch for the day. "We will make perfect time. Come." I threw my axe into the grass, and grabbed my topcoat and fedora, donning both. Igor followed suit, and I whistled shrilly. The horses that were peacefully grazing looked up and came trotting over obediently. "Good boy," I whispered to Stahlhand. I stroked his muzzle briefly before grabbing the bridle and swinging my leg up over and into the saddle. We raced off toward St. Goar, skirting the roads and riding like shadows. We rode fast and hard. Hell knows no fury, and Pieter von Deose was about to find out the fury Gregor Opfer could unleash.

We left the horses in the woods. For the second day in a row I sauntered into the town of my birth. The sun was a blood red fiery ball in the western sky causing long shadows to play across the cobbled and dirt streets. When we reached my house I used hand signals to motion to Igor. The house stood only a few fathoms from the outskirts of town so there was some cloaking shrubbery. We approached and upon seeing nobody, I tried the front door. Locked. Motioning Igor around the opposite side of the house, I skirted the right side. The small garden that my mother once managed to turn lush vegetables out of the black Prussian earth stood barren and choked with weeds. The backdoor was obviously locked. I tried it anyway. Igor looked at me with imploring eyes. Saying nothing, but motioning him to stay put, I grabbed hold of the iron drainpipe and pulled myself up onto the low roof. I scrabbled up the tiled roof to the small windows in the loft. Thankfully the mossy roof was dry, and I was able to keep my balance as I pried the swollen wooden window up and wriggled in. This was the way I used to enter to avoid Pieter's beatings in a time that seemed like so long ago—a lifetime.

I crept downstairs silent as a church mouse and heard noises in the bedroom. Careful not to creak any wooden flooring, I opened the backdoor and let Igor in. I pulled my scarf around my face to prevent Pieter from identifying me and compromising the integrity of the mission for Igor. He emulated me. I led Igor back to the bedroom and creaked the door open very slowly. A woman was riding Pieter. his hand moved from her body to the bedside table and lifted a bottle of amber liquid to his lips. Neither of them detected us, so wrapped up in their amorous throes they were. The audacity of this pile of horseshit boiled my blood; having sex with some woman in my murdered mother's bed, in her house! In my father's house! In my house! 'What a parasitic, predatory fucker,' I thought as the anger rose in my chest. The scar on my face was red hot and throbbed with fury. I nudged Igor, pointed to the girl, and drew my finger across my throat. He nodded.

With one large step and a lightning-quick motion, Igor grabbed the girl by the throat and heaved her across the room. She crumpled into the corner like a rag doll. "What the fuck is going on here?" Pieter demanded. He sat up and sounded angrier than alarmed. That would soon change. "Who are you people and what are you doing in my house?" His face was red from drinking, and he clutched the sheet over his white muscular chest like a woman would do.

"You are under arrest Pieter von Deose," I said loudly, "for the charge of treason."

"You have the wrong man," he protested interrupting me.

"Shut the fuck up!" yelled Igor, backhanding him. "You will speak when spoken to!" Pieter rocked sideways on the bed, his large body heaving hard as blood trickled from his nose. He moaned. I could tell his nose was broken.

I continued my charade, "By the decree of His Royal Majesty, Kaiser Friedrich Wilhelm IV, you are to be detained by agents of the State. We are taking you in."

Pieter's pale body, accented by the darkness of the room, half rose and he looked at us stunned. He suddenly didn't look so tough when not facing women or defenseless children. His large body seemed to visibly shrink. The evil scowl was gone, the fire in his eyes extinguished. I reveled in the moment. In a quavering voice he asked, "Well, where are you taking me?" Igor raised his hand. I motioned him to stop. With the speed of a rattlesnake, I punched him in the trachea. With a choke and grappling with his hands at his throat, he toppled off the bed.

"Maybe you will listen to an officer of the State's orders from now on. He said, 'Silence!'" I calmly said, rubbing my knuckles before spitting on the nude man rolling on the rough-hewn floor, choking. A wave of anger washed over me, and I kicked him hard in the ribs; hard enough to make some break with an audible crack. Now the son of a bitch didn't know what to hold, his injured throat or thorax.

The woman in the corner began to scream. Igor knelt in front of her. Using a gloved hand, he grabbed under her chin and squeezed. She tried clawing his face with her hands but he grabbed them both with his *other great, gloved hand and effectively contained them .The woman's feet turned with pain, and she tried to turn her head. Her efforts were in vain for Igor has a vise-hold on her throat. Leaning in really close so his face is mere inches from hers he whispered, "Listen girl, it would behoove you to shut up, if you know what's good for you. Nod if you understand." The girl nodded. Igor let his vice grip go.*

She immediately whispered, "Look all I want is my money and then I'll leave."

I whirled, "For Christ's sakes you're a prostitute? A fucking prostitute!"

She turned her eyes downcast, "Yeah." Then turning her eyes up, "And this Herr owes me five deutsche marks, and he's going to pay me!" Her voice slowly rose in fervor and pitch. Igor read my eyes as I looked at him. He slipped his hand into his pocket and with lightning speed sapped the woman across the back of the head. Her head lolled forward at an alarming angle. A large red spot spread through her thick brown hair like a blossoming flower and soon blood leaked from her head onto her supple pale body.

"Did you kill her?" I asked indifferently.

"I think so," replied Igor.

"Wrap her in this," I said handing him the sheet. "And Igor," he looked at me, "next time I tell you to kill someone, do it right away." I motioned my head in her direction.

He nodded briefly then began wrapping the soiled dove.

That poor prostitute just picked the wrong Herr today, I thought looking down at the figure of von Deose still writhing in pain. "I hope you're happy," I said to him. "You killed that poor whore." He obviously didn't answer.

"Get the horses," I commanded without looking, "and bring them to the backdoor." Igor left quickly and silently, having wrapped the prostitute in the filthy sheet. I took the bottle of booze and smashed it in the corner. I stood for some time over von Deose, not wanting to venture into the rest of the house. I was terrified of what memories I might dredge up and lose myself mid-mission. No, I was much too professional to do such a thing. I turned my attention back to my former

tormentor. "My, my, my how the tables have turned," I chuckled and bent down face to face with Pieter, easing my stiletto out of it's boot holster. I slowly pulled the scarf down and said, "Surprise." Even with the long jagged scar, Pieter instantly recognized me and gasped, still trying to breathe. His activity got more frantic, pathetic if you asked me. "So you kill my beloved mother then invite whores into her house? Well, Pieter, I'd say your day has come." He frantically shook his head, eyes wide with fear. Before he knew what was happening I had the long knife inside his mouth. The thin, razor sharp blade cut his tongue out in two seconds. I couldn't have him telling things to Igor right before Everyman arrived. I stuffed his shirt into his mouth to stifle the screams and keep him from bleeding out. "Keep it there so you don't bleed to death," I told him calmly. Then I sapped him lightly. He slumped over, knocked out for now.

With much effort I dragged the prostitute and Pieter to the backdoor. The prostitute was a good thirty pounds heavier than Pieter's two hundred. "Too much time spent accepting drinks from Herrs at the biergarten," I mused as I threw her corpse across the threshold. Igor arrived in the semi-darkness and we threw our victims over the horses' backs. "I'll be right back; there is too much blood in the house we must destroy it, mark the garden," I commanded Igor. I rushed back into the bedroom and threw a match toward the broken bottle. Flames instantly ignited, greedily licking the dry wood. With a heavy heart but clear conscience, I exited my house for the last time, stepped over the hasty swastika of rocks in the garden and rode hard back into the ancient Prussian forest.

The extra weight of the passengers nearly doubled our riding time, and we had stop once to let the horses drink. While they were resting, I checked to make sure Pieter was still alive; that bastard didn't deserve to die yet. My pocket watch notified me that we reached the meadow at a few minutes before midnight. Igor unceremoniously dumped the woman of ill repute off his horse into the grass. I heaved Pieter off; careful not to drop him so his neck broke. I stripped his clothes off and then slung the inert man over my shoulder and walked to the edge of the pile and handed him to Igor, who stood in the middle of the woodpile. He dragged Pieter over the wood and held him up against the pole, as I too waded in and began running the length of rope around his body.

He really looked pathetic trussed up on the pole, buck naked, his small endowment shriveled and lifeless. The large muscles that once pummeled me to a pulp were now small and insignificant. Coagulated blood collected in his beard, all the blood loss of having his tongue cut out, and the bloody shirt kind of hung out of his mouth like a new red tongue. His belly was red and chaffed from the movement of the horse. He was pathetic, I decided. Pieter's head sagged to the side. I slapped him. Nothing. "You bring any smelling salts?" I asked Igor patting my pockets realizing mine were at the castle in my footlocker.

Nah, didn't know we needed them."

"They come in handy sometimes," I said producing my stiletto once again, "but if you don't have them this trick usually works." I took my knife and dug the tip into the bottom of his foot, on the instep into the lateral plantar. Sure enough, Pieter snapped his head up and tried to scream. Just a muffled sound emitted through the shirt. His now alert eyes darted this way and that into the surrounding dark forest.

"Igor, you do the honors," I said.

His eyes danced with glee at having the honor to officiate this momentous occasion. He started reciting. Igor the magistrate, judge, jury, and executioner boomed out into the crisp black night, "Pieter von Deose, you have been found guilty of treason; the most odious of all crimes. Therefore the king, His Majesty Friedrich Wilhelm IV has dispatched Die Sonneleute to carry out your punishment for your crimes. The People of the Sun are going to eradicate your soul from this earth by burning it on a surface as hot as the sun's, and in your moment of death you will feel our presence. May God have mercy on your soul, for surely Gabriel has a place waiting for you!" Igor lit a torch and began touching it around the woodpile. Soon the blaze roared high into the witching hour, reflecting off the tears in Pieter's eyes. I watched until the pile of wood collapsed on itself, then went to help Igor's grave digging exertions. When the fire was nothing but a smoldering pile of glowing embers, we rode off into the night, my mission complete, and Igor thinking it was carried out by order of royal decree.

We stopped in St. Goar for breakfast at the biergarten. We feasted on blood sausage, black bread, and creamy milk. When we were done, the barmaid sat down and chatted with us, having no other customers at this early morning hour. "So, you travelers been here long?" Upon receipt of our shaken heads, "Well, last night we had this massive fire on over at the edge of town. Big news, took all night to put out. No sign of the owner. It's suspected he died in the blaze. I guess if you'da been in town you'da seen it."

We shook our heads again then abruptly stood up, and I threw a wad of marks on the table. I glanced back at the plump barkeep casually remarked, "Möglicherweise sah er das Gesicht des Gottes."

"Odd thing to say," the barkeep muttered, collecting the money, but soon forgot it as the morning rush came in to eat. She had money to earn to feed her family, and no time to dwell on strange travelers.

Chapter 59

I wake up in a cold sweat, panting; mind racing like a thousand hoplites charging into battle. Slowly, I am able to catch my breath, and slow my heart rate. The incessant blackness still surrounds me, but the images of Pieter von Deose flash across the darkness in shooting stars of light and energy. I realize what I once did for king and country was in the name of duty. What I did for myself was Satan's hand guiding me. *I am no better than Bambury or Savage,* I realize with a start. But those bastards haven't found the error in their ways; I let the Lord's shining light into my life and changed for the better. The sinners of the world must repent. The images of Pieter von Deose still flash vibrantly in the darkness and suddenly it became all to clear of what I must do; what the Lord is calling me to do. He is calling me to cleanse this den of inequity, and suddenly the irony of it all comes to me. "Full circle!" I scream into the darkness, laughing like a madman and gripping the iron bars, cuts on my hands opening up and blood running down my arms. The laughter and commotion I cause sets the whole row off.

The prisoner next to me mimicking, "Full circle, full circle…" in his brogue, Bowery accent.

The trapdoor above us flies open, and the voice of our tormentors screams down, "Shut the fuck up, the lot of ya'! Just shut the fuck up! We're trying to play cards up here and can't with all this infernal racket!"

Come down here and make us, I silently will the voice. As if to read my mind the trapdoor slams shut and silence follows. *That's all right,* I think, *when stalking a mouse the feline is, oh, so patient, as I must now be. Drip, drip* sounds the far off sound of my insanity. The wailing begins. First low, like the wretched sirens singing to brave Odysseus;

228

then building to a crescendo of men verbalizing their own personal mental hell. Time holds no bearing in prison. The only indication I have in the hole that time is passing is the serving of our daily meal. Do I sleep? Frankly I don't know. I live here in a cocoon of suspended animation, circadian rhythm be damned. But I am waiting, and when the next meal comes I will be ready; I have figured out their Achilles tendon, so to speak.

Patrick O'Leary, one of Lynds's guards for the hole, I know is relatively new. He is the Achilles tendon that is going to set Gregor Opfer free. Unbeknownst to him, I watch him when he brings the tin plates full of the garbage they pawn off as food, down once a day. I lay crumpled in the corner of my cell, not moving, feigning a catatonic physical state so I can watch unobtrusively. Since he is the new man he has been assigned to slop duty and the lack of inmate-to-guard violence—surely there has been plenty of guard-to-inmate violence—in the hole has made him complacent. I figure most of the men down here have been down here so long they are no longer a danger to anyone…their minds have turned to mush. I am the only real danger, and my mental state is hanging on like that last autumn leaf clings to the bare black bones of a winter tree…But the guards, even Savage and Bambury, know not what I am *fully* capable of, cripple legs be damned.

It's the same every meal; first I hear the sound of the trapdoor opening and soft footsteps descending the metal ladder. In the distance the light from the lantern bobs off the stone walls as it slowly makes its way down the hallway. The light gets closer and closer until young Patrick stops in front of the bars, puts the wooden bucket down with his right hand, but keeps the lantern hooked in the crook of his left arm. Then he rummages in a canvas sack slung over his shoulder until he reaches a tin plate. Then he picks up the ladle with his left hand, holding the plate with his right, ladles a plateful and slides the plate under the bars. This I know because I've seen it everyday for…I don't know how many days. Too many, to be sure, but this time I am ready for young Patrick and his cumbersome ways.

This meal is no different from all the rest; the trapdoor slams open then slams shut, footfalls sound on the ladder, the light of the lantern draws closer, and a broken Gregor lies crumpled in the corner. Save tonight, I have the shard of glass. The cold, sharp glass is reassuring in my hand. I realize I have been gripping it too tightly by a tingling feeling emanating up my arm. Surely my hand is bleeding from the sharp glass, but I pay it no heed; my senses are focused on my approaching prey.

Patrick glances into my cell before putting his equipment down, "Ro'uf day, eh? Aw, Co'm'n ya' fo'ckin' far'ner. Wake up, f'uhr Christ's sakes!" Then laughing to himself, he puts the bucket down with his right hand. Busy with his task, he doesn't notice me sliding across the small expanse of my cell until I am almost to the bars. When Patrick's right hand snaked under the bars to slide the plate in I grab it and twist with lightning fast speed. The arm breaks at the elbow with an audible *pop*. I have enough strength in my upper body to quickly thrust upward with my right hand and stab at Patrick with the broken glass while still holding his broken arm with my other arm. Patrick only had time to let out a strangled gargle before I plunge the large shard of glass into his trachea. A look of astonishment crosses his face as pink bubbles spew forth from his silent mouth and blood pours from the ragged hole in his neck. Not wanting the poor bastard to suffer, I draw the sharp shard of glass across his throat, severing the sternocleidomastoid muscle and effectively cutting the internal and external jugular veins as well as the ceratoid artery. As I draw my bloody fist from his throat, blood spews forth into my face in a great spray as the still pumping heart expels blood in great geysers from the wound. Feeling around the late Patrick's belt, I locate a large iron ring of keys and set about trying each one until I find the one that works on my cell.

"Dumbass, never locate the ticket to freedom of an imprisoned man within reach," I mutter under my breath as I click the lock and take my first step toward freedom on my crippled legs.

The flurry of activity around my cell has obviously attracted the attention of all my fellow cell mates, and of course they have worked themselves into an insane fury of screaming and pleading. It is mayhem, but mayhem works in favor of those who plan for it. The screaming and insane shouting from all the other poor souls in the hole covers the sound of my cell door swinging open on its rusty hinges. I leisurely take my time wiping the blood from my body and donning the dead man's clothes. His blouse and jacket are soaked with blood but anyone looking from a distance hopefully won't notice. Flipping the truncheon, and hefting it to gauge its weight I decide it will have to do. It's a cheap government issue that isn't very balanced, but I had fought the forces of tyranny in the fatherland with worse improvisational weapons than this, so one measly guard upstairs will be no formidable obstacle with this piece of shit weapon. I don't want the crazies impeding my escape...just yet. "Hold on," I tell them softly, "you'll get your chance." I put the key ring in my pocket.

I lift the trapdoor just a crack and peer out. The other guard upstairs has yet to detect danger, I observe. I swing the door open and it slams back against the floor, opposite the hinge, with a resonant *bang*. I crouch just a few steps down the ladder and wait. Surely enough, the noise of the trapdoor startled the other guard and when Patrick doesn't emerge, he crept over to investigate. I can hear him calling as he drew nearer, "Patrick? Patrick?" A slight tremor laced his speech. His calls become more frantic as he moves closer to the opening in the floor, "Patrick! It's not funny. Lynds will have your job if he finds out about this...Come on up...Stop with the tomfoolery and come up and finish the game...Patrick?"

Just as he is about to turn and run for help I leap out of the hole with as much force as my cripple legs can muster, and lay a crushing blow across his nose. We both hit the floor at the same time; me collapsing after my legs crumple from landing on the floor, and the young guard from the disorienting blow. He lies on the floor writhing in agony, scrabbling to find his truncheon with one hand and holding the mass of flesh that used to be his nose with his other hand. I manage to haul myself to my knees to administer a few more vicious blows to his face and cranium. Soon my truncheon shines with blood, and the guard moved no more. Looking around, I notice I have painted the walls with tiny droplets of the guard's blood, but that does not matter to me anymore; atonement *had* to happen. No matter what the price. As I collect myself mentally to figure my next move, the pool of blood surrounding the guard's head slowly expands.

After the shooting pain in my legs and feet subsides, and I am able to control my breathing I hobble over to one of the tiny windows inside the shack. Using the sleeve of my new, blue wool uniform, I wipe at the dirty window until I can see out of the filthy pane. It is the twilight hour and only the faintest hint of light laces the sky. *Darkness is always a good ally,* I think grimly to myself, still unsure how I am going to make my great escape from the prison proper. The cell I had been contained in technically did not exist, according to Warden Lynds, so I will have no problem sneaking about the interior of the prison compound because nobody will be coming to count later, but I needed to grow some wings to get over the high prison exterior walls.

Chapter 60

I am going to have to plan as I went along I decide, something I *hate* to do, but in this case is necessary. But first things first; I grab hardtack and jerked beef from a tin plate on the wooden table and wolf the hard dough and beef down as fast as I can chew the tough delicacies. The guards' card game still lay out, and I dropped crumbs from the biscuit onto the table. The real food tastes good after the near liquid diet I had been on for what seems like an eternity. With horror, I realize the hard food is loosening my teeth. Scurvy has ravaged my body from my meager diet. With a bloody *pop*, a tooth comes out. No time to worry about that now, as I stuff the remains of the bloody biscuit and meat into my blouse pocket.

At the rear of the shack I use my truncheon to smash out a board. *Thank God the maintenance detail isn't as vigorous as the guard detail,* I think with delight as the rotting board clatters onto the ground after a few swift blows. Before I made my exit, I threw the key ring into the black abyss and heard iron hit iron, and then the scrabbling of hands. I duck out and find myself between the shack and the imposing outer wall. The air is sweet and warm, and memories of springtime in Prussia as a child, and the spring days I spent with Helga walking the pastures of the island borough come flooding back. *Those low down scoundrels have kept me locked in that infernal place for a year! They were waiting for me to die in the hole!* And the sickening realization of another lost year of life washes over me, but I must forget that now and focus on the mission. My training takes over and my body goes on operative overdrive.

The outer wall is a fourteen-foot-high, solid-marble monstrosity with guard towers spaced at the corners of the prison, as well as one in the middle of the great wall that runs perpendicular to the river. If I try to scale it, I will surely have several musket balls buried in my back before I come within four feet of the top, and that's with *good* legs. Ignoring the outer wall, I skirt in the shadows cast by impeding darkness. My limp combined with malnourished muscles makes for slow going, and I often have to stop and catch my breath, resting my hands against the cold ramparts and sucking in great gulps of air. After only a few minutes the small amount of beef and biscuit comes up in a bout of violent vomiting; my stomach, not used to the solid food, is revolting. The violent stream of steaming liquid brings me to my knees in the shadow of the wall, where I remained for sometime on all fours until my stomach stopped trying to exit by way of my throat. Feeling considerably better after a spell, I continue.

The guards in the towers are secure in the knowledge that the prisoners *cannot* escape from the main cellblock, and therefore never glance into the shadows to see my crippled form ducking behind random carts, carriages, crates, and hay bales. I hear them festively calling to each other across the empty yard, joking with each other about this and that. After snaking across what seems to be miles of wall, I finally hear the Hudson River flowing with its usual vigor on the other side of the wall. Pressing my ear against the cold marble, I confirm that I am on a river wall. By now, darkness has descended, and I am able to move more freely about without fear of detection. On my hands and knees once again, I scrabble around in the dirt until I find what I am looking for, a storm drain. The sound of gurgling water emanates from the monstrosity of crude cast iron. Tugging at the drain cover with all my might, it doesn't budge even an inch. Luckily, the stable is located on the river wall, only a few feet from the drain, and I crawl over to it.

The inside smells the clean smell manure and hay dust. The horses shake their heads and some whinny softly as they detect my approach, but sensing no danger they do not make much noise. I open the first wooden stable door to my right, and déjà vu. Stahlhand, my faithful equestrian from a thousand years ago, stares back at me. "Damn, you look familiar," I whisper quietly to the Stahlhand-look-alike while gently stroking his muzzle. He snorts through his nose loudly, but is obviously not threatened by my presence for he lets me lead him out into the prison yard, trotting happily behind me. On my way out the stable entrance, I grab a length of hemp rope and once at the storm drain loop the rope twice through one of the jagged holes in the cover. Tying off one end of the rope to the big black horse's bridle, I hold onto the other end. I give the horse a quick hard slap on the rump; he neighs in anger and rears up, letting a whinny of displeasure out. The cover moves a foot or two off the hole. I quickly untie one end from the spooked horse's bridle and shoo him out toward the middle of the yard. As I slither into the dark hole like a snake, I hear the shouts of the watchtower guards as they see a horse galloping around the prison yard. I figure the other members of the hole will soon emerge from the shack; then the guards will really have their hands full. With any luck Gregor Opfer's disappearance will go unnoticed until daylight, and by then it'll be too late.

The fast moving water surprises me as I fall into the icy water and am swept along. It's no use fighting, the slimy, moss covered terra cotta tube offer no handholds, and soon I am dumped unceremoniously in the black waters of the Hudson. Spluttering and coughing, I drag myself onto the muddy bank and lay gasping for air and marveling at my escape. *Stop it! Your gloating will land you in irons once again, you fool! You were once a professional. Act like one,* I mentally chastise myself. I strained out the water as best as I could in the heavy wool uniform and commence to crawl upstream, the least painful way of traveling in the sucking mud. I crawl along the bank until I'm sure I can't be detected and hop across the train tracks in my laughable gait. I widely skirt the prison walls, hearing lights and commotion, and head in a westerly direction. *My fellow inmates must've made their presence known,* I think grimly hearing shouts and the occasional shot from behind the marble façade known as Sing Sing. Walking parallel to the road leading to the prison, I come to the main road, Spring Road, and scurry across the road, hop a fence, and make my way across a farmer's field. A strand of pines makes a great hiding place, and I nestle down in a bed of needles and sleep fitfully in my wet clothes.

Dawn comes fast and finds me waiting patiently in the gray glow of the early morning. Soon enough, the night guards file by on the way to their homes in the nearby village of Ossining. Eventually, I spy the familiar slouching figure of Jepatha Bambury staggering down the road, a little drunk, swinging his dinner pail from side to side. His skin is pale white, almost transparent, from a life spent out of the sun. He whistles a little tune walking alone down the lonesome road. I follow him from a distance walking parallel to him in the woods. Jepatha stops and buys an apple from a roadside vendor, a filthy beggar wearing a ridiculous powdered wig that must be at least forty years old from the looks of it. As Jepatha takes a bite of apple, I observe him knocking the beggar's wig off his head with a swing of his lunch pail then laughed to himself before continuing down Spring Road. A short distance later he makes a turn onto Acker Avenue and disappears into a small, whitewashed clapboard house.

Acker Avenue, located on the outskirts of Ossining, is surrounded by nothing but farmland and wooded areas for as far as the eye can see. The street consists only of two rows of tidy clapboard houses lining the lane, facing each other. My guess is that the houses are workingman's housing, probably mainly for the guards. Children laugh and play in the yards and women hang laundry and hoe their gardens in the balmy springtime New York weather as I observe the street from my vantage point in the woods. Nobody plays in Bambury's yard, nor hangs laundry. *Perfect!* I think to myself, not wanting to factor women and children into this man's punishment. Like the spider spins his web and waits for the fly, so did I spin my web and wait for my fly.

At dinnertime, when the sun is high in the sky, the yards empty as the families gather around the table for the big afternoon meal. I use the opportunity to circle around Acker and approach Bambury's dwelling from the field that backs up to his rear yard. The stealth I used to posses is gone due to my crippled legs, but I still manage to arrive at the backdoor undetected.

Bambury's house is totally unlike the other houses I've seen on Acker Avenue; the yard is choked with weeds and debris. It looks like he pitches all his empty liquor bottles into the backyard from his backdoor, as they all lay a good heave from the door. The house's paint is peeling in most places, and several of the wooden shingles are askew.

It's the only house on the entire street *in disarray,* I think testing the doorknob, *emotional turmoil manifested in personal property?* The knob turns easily, and the unbolted door swings open. A smile crosses my face, *No, he's just a fucking drunk. He's not smart enough to be a head case.* The house has but a few pieces of furniture, and the hearth is cold to the touch. Moving quickly from the room serving as the kitchen and living quarters, I ease my way over the rough boards to the door I assume to lead to Bambury's personal quarters. The latch releases with ease, and I feast my eyes upon a passed out Jepatha Bambury, sleeping off yet another night of boozing. As his chest rises and falls with peaceful snores, a wide grin encroaches my countenance and my eyes steel.

"Wake up, you miserable fuck," I say leaning over and backhanding him violently across the face.

Bambury must've sensed danger because he tries to sit up abruptly; not the reaction one would expect from a passed out drunk. "What are *you* doing here?" Bambury exclaims, eyes widening with fear.

Chuckling I reply, "Come to repay a few debts." I purposely let my Prussian accent bleed into my speech making my w's sound like v's, "You know, the whole eye-for-an-eye thing." I point to my legs. I watch him to see if he would make any movements as if to escape, but he just sits there on his bed, dumbfounded. His rich brown hair fell in his eyes, a stark contrast to his parchment skin, and is no longer neatly combed like it usually was.

"But, but how?"

I laugh; the idiot is so scared he can't even talk. Bambury is only a man of composure when he isn't being fired up, so to speak. "Never you mind. Your precious prison isn't as secure as you thought, especially to a trained agent. Dr. Warren warned you of my, ah, talents."

All the sudden his demeanor changes and he spits, "You stupid, scar-faced foreigner. Do you really think you can waltz in here like this? I'll have your head on a stick before the day is out!"

Patting the excited man on his bare shoulder I soothingly say, "Ah, but *Mister,*" I emphasize the word scornfully, "Bambury, who can help you?" I gesture around and act confused. "There is nobody here, and believe me; you won't make a sound, and that's a promise." I menacingly laugh, drunk with my newfound power and the irony of the role reversal. "Speaking of the good doctor, would you by chance know where he lives?"

Bambury insolently says, "No."

"Wrong answer."

Chapter 61

As I walk through the fields, parallel to Spring Street, headed north toward Dr. Warren's house, I think about the past few hours. Bambury had been quite a tough little bird. I had trussed him up and promptly cut out his tongue to prevent him from making too much noise. All he could do after that was make a sharp whistling sound; nothing near loud enough to alert the neighbors. I had tied him to a wooden chair in front of his fireplace while I built a fire. The blood-soaked rag in his mouth dripped crimson drops onto the floor it was so saturated with blood, but I didn't mind I wasn't going to be the one cleaning up the mess. While the fire crackled, and I waited for some good embers I rooted around in the kitchen, ravenous for a little something to eat. I found some moldy bread, and toasted it on the open fire to kill the mold, and had a nice little snack of toast and cheese while Bambury sat in the middle of his kitchen and bled. After my snack I helped myself to Bambury's civilian clothing; his brown knickers, white blouse, and Bowery cap fit nicely, and I admired myself in the leaded mirror for a bit. I was glad to get out of the blood-crusted guard uniform.

By this time, the embers were nice and glowing, and I returned to my prisoner. "Well, now, Mr. Bambury, since you did this to me," I said with growing anger pointing to my legs, "I'm going to disfigure you in some way." With that, I pulled off his woolen trousers and stuck a poker in the fire. He struggled, but all for naught.

Soon the poker glowed red. Holding the instrument in front of my tormenter's face, I asked, "How would you like to be less of a man? I can guarantee you that when your friend Savage joins you in hell, he will be less of a man, too!" He struggled and made noise, his normally dead eyes alive with fear. Laughing, I touched the poker to his scrotum.

The smell of burning flesh filled my nostrils as Bambury twisted and turned in his chair in agony, tipping the chair and passing out. I removed the cloth from his mouth and a mixture of blood and vomit poured out. I righted the chair and waited for him to come to. I repeated the process a few more times burning his biceps, belly, and neck. After the last burning he didn't wake up for a long time. I decided he had repaid his debt to me as well as he could in the time we had allotted; I would be merciful today like King Solomon. "Here," I said putting a quill in his hand. They were tied together in front of him, almost like he was praying. "Write down Warren's address on this and it will be over. Refuse, and we'll go on for the rest of the day. I know how to keep going without killing you," I told him gravely.

His eyes shone with pain and fear so, with a shaking hand he wrote out on a piece of parchment I put under the quill, 158 Washinten Ave.

The dumbshit. I shook him, "Do you mean 'Washington'?"

He nodded.

"You better not be lying, because I'm going to find out, and if I have to come back and get the correct address I'm not going to be pleased. Get it?" He nodded in resignation and hung his head. I could tell he was telling the truth, so I was merciful and quick, and broke his neck. The sadistic son of a bitch didn't deserve the quick and easy way, but I figured he had suffered enough. My stomach just isn't what it used to be.

Chapter 62

I whistle a little, pleased I still have some of my skills intact. I come to a farmer's fence and hop it with some difficulty. Quietly threading my way between two houses spread a rooster's crow apart; I cross a road and head into a place called Nelson Park. Couples stroll hand in hand; it being mid-day and all, and children sail small sticks and toy boats in a small pond. Larger boys yell and curse at each other in a boisterous stick ball game. One fellow rides by on a curious metal contraption with two wheels; he seemed to be operating it with his feet. I try not to be too conspicuous by staring, lest he remember my limp, but I make a mental note to inquire into what that invention actually is. Emerging on the other side of the small park, I find myself on Washington Street. Number 158 is a large white monstrosity of a house. It has a wide porch flowing around the house, with big Roman pillars holding up the second story's roof. And the windows; they are everywhere. The grounds of the good doctor's house are well manicured, better kept than the king's own grounds. It being early spring and all, the grass is just greening up, and dogwoods sprouted small pink and white blossoms. Birds sit in the trees and twitter accusingly at me, as if they know I don't belong, while squirrels hurriedly chase each other across the lush lawn. *Dr. Warren must be a wealthy man,* I muse to myself before disappearing into the immaculate garden in the back to wait for the arrival of Dr. Warren later this evening. As I sit crouched amongst the shrubbery and trees in the backyard I study the gigantic house. *It has to have at least ten rooms,* I think to myself before being lulled to sleep by the sweet-smelling flora and singing insects.

Sure enough, when I awake it is dark. The damp earth fills my nostrils with a pungent smell as I shake my head to clear the cobwebs and get my bearings. I lift my head out of the dirt and peer through the brush to the house. The leaded windows cast the distant glow of candlelight upon the house's grounds. I watch for a bit and occasionally see a dark shadow bustle by certain windows. *Maid? Warren himself?* I muse wiping some debris and filth from my face. I have no way to tell time, no change from the past four years, so I just wait. I'm good at waiting; I've had a lot of practice. Soon enough, my patience pays off and the glow from the house extinguishes as its occupants go to bed. It is time.

The moon and stars cast plenty of light onto the backyard; so I lurk in the shadows of the shrubs and trees while stealing toward the house. The back of the house is a bit more modest than the front, and a small porch situated to the right grabs my attention. I easily shimmy up the modest wooden pillars holding up the second floor back porch using what's left of my upper body strength and letting my legs dangle like two useless bratwurst links. Once I have pulled myself over the railing, I sit in silence, my chest heaving and sweat beading on my brow. The lack of physical activity has weakened me considerably; for back in my prime I would've been able to scale the porch without even breathing hard. Once I catch my breath, I duck inside through the already-open French doors. The air that meets me inside is stagnant and stale; the open doors are useless against the odor. The rich hardwood paneling and carpets from the Orient add to the dankness of the interior. As my eyes adjust to the low light I find I am in a bedchamber; the bedchamber of the very man I am looking for! I can see the shock of white hair protruding from under the sheets as they gently rise and fall in time to the peaceful sleeping of the thin man. *The peaceful sleep only the guilty can get from laudanum*, I figure, seeing the half empty brown bottle sitting on his night stand. Another form stirs under the sheets and startles me.

Damn! I just want Warren, but his wife will have to go also, I think. I am truly sorry about this casualty, for she has done me no wrong other than marrying the sadistic butcher, but some missions have collateral damage. I sidestep to the other side and peer down in the dark. Shock and revulsion sweeps over me. Staring up at me is the sleeping face of

Brain, one of the former night guards! I shiver in disgust in the realization of the situation and turn my head as if to block out the conjured up images of the old buzzard seducing a young immigrant who knew no better. As I did, Warren's specs caught some light from the moonlight, temporarily blinding me, but my eyes readjusted once more, and I ease back across the oriental carpeting toward the door. As I cross the dark bedroom, anger rises like a wave cresting before breaking on a beach; I bet the boy no longer had a job and is now a kept man for the perverted Dr. Warren! *You must never let emotion factor into a job; it will only get you killed,* I recalled the spoken words of a former instructor. He told me, *Once the job is done you may rejoice at the conquest of evil, but until the target has been eliminated…Ihr Herz muss an Felsen wenden.* The words bounce around in my head like a thousand angry hornets as I slip silently out of the bedchamber with the stealth of a spirit.

The hallway and staircase are lined with gilded oil paintings and the heads of conquered animals. Ornate King Louis XIV furniture dots the upper hallway, and as I make my way down to the foyer, I can see more. They are monstrosities of pieces; a symbol of Sun King's reign—Sun King! I laugh inwardly at the irony.

All this shit bankrolled by criminals on the take from companies that extort the labor of imprisoned men, I think angrily, pounding my fist on a hunting board in rage thinking back to all the countless hours I broke my back under the Stone Guild Corporation just so crooked government employees like Dr. Warren could accumulate gaudy pieces of antiquity. In the vestibule I find what I have been looking for, Warren's grip. Opening the recently creamed leather case, I find an old scalpel in desperate need of a good sharpening. *Excellent,* I think grabbing the tool and heading back up to the master bedroom.

In short order Brian's throat is slashed. He was no innocent. He was there I was beaten to the point of disfigurement. Brian lay wide-eyed, with a look of shock on his white face surrounded by a pool of blood, framing his head in a grotesque way on the purple satin sheets. The good doctor is in such a drug-induced haze, that he did not even move as Brian made his last gurgling sounds and thrashed about violently.

Smells like sex and shit, I think with disgust and go about the business of ripping up the satin sheets; their fibers protesting with a loud *rip* every time I pull another piece off. I didn't worry about Warren waking as I noisily shred the sheets, for an addict this old, I know, had to take a large volume of his poison to feel 'even' every night. And at his age, he had probably ingested the better part of that brown bottle sitting on the nightstand.

I nearly puke with revulsion as I lean over to pry open Warren's mouth due to the pungent stench of feces. Swallowing a little bit of acidic bile that settles in my throat like a lump, I force the good doctor's jaws open. In order to avoid having my fingers bitten off when he wakes up, I stick a small piece of wood I had liberated from the garden earlier in between his teeth. When I start hacking away with the dull scalpel at his tongue he wakes with a start. I had bound his hands and feet to the bedpost with strips of his own sheets, so the thrashing did little good. Even though he is elderly, I had learned a valuable lesson my days with *Die Sonneleute*: faced with imminent death, even a weak adversary can summon up unbelievable amounts of strength in the name of self preservation. It is almost pitiful as the feeble old man tries vainly flailing about, but soon grew annoying. "Stay still," I growl, irritated that I was slashing about in his mouth causing blood to fill his oral cavity.

It sloshed all over my hands, forearms, and my brand new white shirt that Jepatha Bambury had so graciously given me. Some even spattered onto my face. Wiping at my eyes with my shoulders, I use all my weight to pin him down before incisively removing his speech organ. I smile at my handiwork. "All done," I say in the same cheerful tone Warren had used when removing my braces. "Now sir, you will stop moving about and provide me with some information.

Blood pours forth from his mouth as if he was vomiting it, and flowed freely onto the floor. I tower over the now-pathetic Warren, flopping around in the bed like a landed flounder, as he looks up at me as if to ask, "How?"

Reading his mind, "You should've left town for a little while once you heard the news I was out. Do you think I would forget these?" I say tapping my mangled legs. He chose not to answer. "This," I say motioning over to Brian, "is fucking sick. You perverse old faggot butcher. Well," I continue in the same cheerful tone, "you will repent for your sins tonight, you well know what the Good Book says in Proverbs: 'For their feet run to evil, and make haste to shed blood.' Befitting isn't it? Especially since you maimed these feet." He chose not to answer again. That's when he pissed himself and something inside me snapped. I lost it.

Punching and hitting him, I rain blows down upon his face. Soon his face is a bloody, pulpy mess, only two white eyes distinguishable from the whole bloody semi-solid that used to be the face of a man. I have to restrain myself in order to get the information I have come for. Furious at myself for acting in such an un-Prussian manner of unrestrained, *Americanized* fury I step back and address the blinking eyes, "All right, you miserable piece of sodomite shit. You give me a piece of information and it'll be over quickly. If not…" I trail off to let it sink in. "I think you know what will happen. You read the dossier on my former organization, you know what I am capable of." Putting my face next to his I scream, "Look at this!" I point to the jagged scar on my face and then the ink on my right bicep, "I hope you don't think I'm fucking around. I have killed more men, women, and children than I can remember. One cemetery would not be enough for the amount of graves I have dug in my time!" My voice rising in timbre and volume I continue, "No biblical plague hath wrought as much misery and death as Gregor Opfer! So, you, *sir*," I say the last word with biting sarcasm," should rightly tremble in my presence!"

Shaking from anger, I rip open the night stand drawer. In anger I throw the container of white powder across the room and grab a handful of parchment. I hand him the paper as well as a pencil. "Here, write down where I can locate Jack Savage," I command the writhing mass that was once called a man by some and a monster by others. I produce a knife and cut free an arm. Shakily, he scrawls the house's location on the paper and pushes it back to me, covered in blood drippings from his face. The address looks familiar, I had passed that street when I used to go out on work detail; it was more guard housing.

Stuffing the paper into my stolen jacket pocket, I set about re-tying his free arm to the bed. Soon Dr. Warren is once again secured tightly to his bed. I get down on my knees, fold my hands and begin praying. Softly at first, but then louder and louder until I end the prayer with one of my favorite passages from Leviticus, "...and the priests shall burn it upon the altar, upon the wood that is upon the fire: it is a burnt sacrifice, and offering, made by fire, of a sweet savior unto the Lord." With that, I stand up, and grab a shovel from next to the smoldering fireplace. The bottom of the ash pile held some good glowing embers, and I throw a shovel-full onto the bed as well as one onto the carpet and hardwood floor. Soon the room is smoking, ready to ignite. Faint trails of smoke curl up around the bed and lace their way to the ceiling. The room is quickly filling with smoke and it is time to make my exit. On my way out the French doors, I pause long enough near the panicked eyes of Dr. Warren to say, "Oh yeah, I lied about the quick and painless death. This death is going to be painful and long as you and your house, wrought from the misery of others, burns! May the Lord have mercy on your soul, Allan Warren." I climb down the pillar and lope off into the night before the fire brings spectators.

Chapter 63

Hiding in the same spot I had reconnoitered the building from not more than a few hours prior, I watch my handiwork, something extremely dangerous and unprofessional. But this kill had not been professional, it had been personal, or so I tell myself as to why I was watching the aftermath. Flames flare out the upper windows and black smoke billows into a sky that is indistinguishable from the soot. Servants spill from the doors screaming and shouting. Their shouts cause reason to raise alarm and soon shadowy men, their faces partly illuminated by the blaze, their curses and exclamations punctuating the cracking fire, ring the periphery of the house. The Ossining fire brigade is slow to respond, because how often do fires happen in this sleepy little town? The house is all but caving in on itself when the buckboard wagon, drawn by four snorting and whinnying mares pull up. Men rush to the wagon and begin distributing buckets and form a line to the house. Bucket after bucket of water is passed from hogsheads in the wagon to the burning house and thrown on the insatiable fire. As the inky blackness turns slate, then orange, and the men weary, the house slowly turns from a raging inferno to a smoldering skeleton. My clothes are damp with dew, and I stretch out my arms and legs to relieve the stiffness that not moving brings. Satisfied Warren's death has been the spectacle I wanted, I steal away in the brush to stalk my next victim.

Chapter 64

This one is going to need some preparation, I think disinterestedly as I make my way around Ossining scouting the location for my next victim. I tramp by numerous farms and country homes, warily keeping an eye out for the occupants, but don't run into one living human being the entire day. Nightfall comes once again, as it always seems to, and I make a nest of sorts in a grove of pine trees using the dead needles as bedding. Two raw eggs, pilfered from a henhouse, serve as the only sustenance of the day. I lay back in the prickly bed, too tired to care, and sleep soundly. With the dawn of the new day I resume my search. I tramp around until noontime when I stop by a babbling brook to rest. After quaffing greedily, I lay back and bask in the warm sun for a spell; then wearily get back up. By now I have made a huge crescent shape around the town; if I don't find anything soon I will have to improvise with something less desirable. That doesn't suit me, but improvisation, correctly done, is the mark of a professional.

Around evening time I find the perfect location at the north end of town, near the main highway, the one that travelers coming through the area ride on. It is a little clearing with a large willow tree growing near the road, at the midpoint between two sides of the field. A low stone fence runs the length of the field between the road and the tree, and the branches of the magnificent stretch out over the fence. The tree is not more than a stone's throw from the road and the perfect location for the demise of Jack Savage.

Chapter 65

Now that I have a location I need tools. I find them at a fairly large farm, Jackson Farm according to the hand-lettered sign at the end of the dirt drive, about a half-mile from the field and as the sun went down. I bide my time and waited for the farmhouse to grow dark. I know I have to work quickly, and everything has to go according to plan or the plan will fail. If it works, it will be the most successful mission of my career.

When the last faint glow of light extinguished from the farmhouse I count back from a thousand, ensuring everyone is asleep, before stealing onto the property. After looking into the smokehouse and spring house, I finally find the tool shed. I chance squeaking the door open to let a little moonlight in, in order for me to see. In the pale light, I grab a rucksack off a wooden peg and fill it with the various instruments tonight will require, hammer, nails, spikes, rope, saw, awl, whetstone, and a thick woolen horse blanket. The cracked and worn leather rucksack creaked in protest as I struggle to tie close its bulging form but I persevere and swing the swollen bag onto my back and head for the barn.

This is going to be the trickiest part, I think grimly, *for if the farmer is alerted I am going to have to kill him and his family to preserve the mission.* Gritting my teeth, I pray the horses will not make noise and wake the innocent farmer. The worn boards of the barn feel smooth on my hands as I grip the oversized door and slowly pull it open on its rusted iron hinges. Thankfully, this industrious farmer oils the hinges often and it makes not even the tinniest squeak as it swings silently open. The smell of equines and molded hay assaults my olfactory senses as I step silently in.

The horses, three of them, snort and paw at their respective stalls uncomfortably, sensing a stranger. I slip up next to the closest one and in between shakes of its head I manage to stroke its nose all the while talking in soft tones. I use all the old tricks I had used on Stahlhand, and they come back to me as effortlessly as it was yesterday. The giant Clydesdale senses I mean it no harm, and within five minutes allows me to stand next to it as I continue to whisper softly and stroke. The other horses take cue from this monster and resume munching on the hay in their stalls. A quick check reveals it's a female. *Hmmm,* I think, *what would be a fitting name?* I settle on Myrrh, one of the three gifts given to our Lord by the wise men. Three horses, three gifts. "Myrrh, I shall call you," I whisper into the horse's twitching ear for I feel a horse should always have a name if it were to serve a worthy man. "Myrrh, I will be back soon, and we will go for a ride," I whisper to it as I slowly leave the stall to continue my salvaging. On my way out of the stall, I notice I am sweating profusely. *I wouldn't have really harmed the family...would I?*

A great buckboard wagon sits smack in the middle of the barn, and I shuck off the rucksack and swing it up into the seat. I search high and low in the barn but can't find any wood. I even climb the rickety ladder to the hayloft in hopes of finding scrap wood, but to no avail. Not a single piece exists in the barn. *Damn!* I think, growing desperate. As a last-ditch effort I steal back outside the barn to look around. By God's good grace I find the farmer's pile of scrap wood at the rear of the barn! Silently rejoicing, I find exactly what I want. It appears that when the barn was built the leftover cuts of the great beams had been stacked in the rear of the barn. Most of them were great, long pieces of timber, but I get lucky and spy two pieces about eight feet long each. Even my supple frame has trouble pulling off the larger beams and random pieces of scrap wood above the pieces I desire. But after considerable exertion, I come to the pieces I want. I am a little disappointed after all my work digging through the pile, for the pieces are a little worse for wear after years and years of the bombarding elements, but they'll have to do. I duck back into the barn and hitch Myrrh to the buckboard and lead horse and wagon out of the barn with as little noise as possible. Once outside, I back the wagon to the woodpile and test the beams. They weigh roughly a hundred pounds. *This would've been no problem five years ago...* I think bleakly. Sighing, I heave one beam end into the back of the buckboard. The springs squeak and groan in protest and the wagon tilts crazily in the direction of all the weight. Myrrh twitches her ears and swats her tail. Getting behind the beam and using the edge of the buckboard as a fulcrum, I squat down and put my shoulder to the end of the beam. It slides with some hesitation into the back of the wagon, hanging off perhaps a foot. My legs feel on fire from pushing off them with such force, and I am forced to rest for a spell until the pain subsides a little. Then I repeat the process with beam number two, mount the wagon, and drive my rig off on down the road. As I cruise down the road away from the Jackson Farm I think, *I wouldn't have really harmed the family...would I?*

I had not bothered to find the way to the field via roadways, and get lost even though the field is only a half-mile or so from the farmhouse in a straight line. Finally, I figure I am going in the wrong direction, turn around and find the field. I curse myself for costing precious time, but my skills have decidedly softened a little from being up the river.

I drive the rig off the road and to the edge of the field where I eject the beams onto the earth. Then I drive the rig into the woods. Hopping out, I grab the rucksack, tie Myrrh to a sapling, where she happily commences to eat foliage, and head to my beams. I dump my collection of tools into the dewy wild grass. Selecting the saw, I saw three feet from one length of beam and work the five-foot and eight-foot sections in such a way that they are perpendicular. Sawing through the thick beam was strenuous work and my blouse is soaked with sweat. I wipe the sweat from my eyes, and in doing so; accidentally run my hand down my scar. It burns and throbs with usual fury tonight; pulsating with a life of its own, *Thu-thump, thu-thump, thu-thump!*

At one point flaming torches dance through the night in the distance. I know they can only mean one thing. I hastily extinguish the feeble flame from the lamp I am working from and duck down into the tall grass of the field. I peer through the weeds so I can see the roadway and see the silhouettes of men on horseback, muskets laid across the saddles. The horses dance and prance around as the men rear them up when they came to the town limits. Soldiers of Satan never looked so grim. They are close enough that I can hear snatches of their conversation.

"That son 'bitch took flight. No doubt 'bout it," I hear one man say to the other.

"…Kilt Bam-brey and took off like 'n Injun. He's runnin' scair't, no doubt 'bout it…"

Five men. Five muskets, five pistols. And I bet more were lurking around every corner. Undoubtedly, they were just country bumpkins, sworn in, their eyes gleaming with revenge and breath laced with booze, but I know they are crawling about Ossining like cockroaches, and I didn't want to disturb the nest. I have learned that trained soldiers are less dangerous than these types of men, for soldiers are at least predictable; these men are above the law and *literally* loose cannons. I sink back down into a prone position on the rich New York soil and wait until the flaming torches diminish back into the dark reaches of hell.

Things get a little more interesting, I muse to myself as I coax the feeble flame back to life.

Chapter 66

Sometimes I wonder what I'm thinking these days and curse myself yet again as I scrabble blindly in the dirt for the half penny nails that I dumped out not a half hour ago. My fingers finally locate a handful of nails covered in moist black earth, and I drive the three-inch nails into the perpendicular beams at an angle, effectively nailing the two sections of beam into a cross. Pleased at my impromptu handiwork, I dust my hands together to wipe off the earth and set about with the whetstone and awl. After forty-five minutes of vigorous work I have transformed the harmless borer into a makeshift stiletto, sharp enough to stab and ant in the ass with. I smile as I run my finger along the edge and it draws blood. "It is time!" I say aloud to the forest, but not too loud. It answers with a fury of thrashing branches.

Thankfully the foliage Myrrh was able to forage caused her to defecate, and I cover myself with the blanket like a shaw and smear feces all on it as well as on my face and hands until I effectively look and smell like a filthy beggar. Nobody gives a second glance to a person like that—they are an open sore on pristine American society. I clamber up onto Myrrh bareback and click the reigns. Myrrh dutifully sets off through the field to the road. I ride darkened streets past ghostly houses in the darkness before the dawn, the darkest part of the night. I head south through town until I come to Revolutionary Road where I turn left onto it. Ironically enough, the road overlooks Sing Sing. After I herd Myrrh into the brush, I sit on the side of the road and watch the sun rise over Sing Sing; my first time watching the sunrise over the prison as a free man instead of watching the sunrise from the perspective of Galileo.

The road is dotted with coniferous trees mainly and a smattering of hardwoods, still too early to see the first tiny buds on them.

Revolutionary Road is far enough from the town of Ossining that it's not kept up like the rest of the roads, and small gulches of erosion crisscross at various places, exposing the earth's core beneath them. Tiny puffs of measured breath work their way in front of my perspective. *Breathe in...breathe out...*

I glance up and calculate the sky with the eye of a seasoned professional. Judging by the slate grayness of the morning as the sun fights its way up, I figure Savage should be getting off night shift soon. My guess is correct, and within twenty minutes a figure staggers around a bend of pine trees further up the road. He is all decked out in his blue, woolen prison uniform, gay yellow string tassels from the shoulder pads swaying with his unsteady gait, and his shiny brass buttons and accessories glinting off the first rays of his last rising sun. Jack Savage still looks ugly and mean, not that I figured he'd change since I saw him last, his wide pitted face has the look of concentration that only a drunk has when they're trying to function normally. That look dissolves as his black boot catches a root and his thick Irish arms windmill forward trying to keep balance. The lunch pail in one hand is abandoned in his quest to stay afoot, all for naught. Savage collapses in a heap with a resounding, "Fo'ck!" I smile in spite of myself at this little private vaudeville act, and quickly catch myself, prison has softened my skills, never would I have allowed myself the luxury of a smile in Prussia during the hunt. I wait patiently for Savage to get up and come a little closer.

As Savage collects himself, a second blue uniformed form rounds the bend. *Dammit, Get outta here, boy!* I will. This kind of complication is not surprising, but it will probably just add another unnecessary causality. On second thought, this young man, whom I don't recognize, is a new addition to Savage's night crew, and therefore guilty of *some* offense to some poor bastard. In a movement imperceptible to anyone watching, I slip the makeshift stiletto from my sleeve and heft it just so in my left hand. In my other hand I lightly finger a rock about the size of a tomato I had selected earlier. My eyes never leave the two men. Savage slowly shakes his head as a dog does ridding itself of water and pulls himself onto all fours. The man behind him, also visibly intoxicated, staggers over and tugs at Savage's uniform. Savage shakes the man off his uniform and shouts some profanities. The guard shrugs and continues walking. As Savage rooted around amongst the tree line like a sow looking for food in a barnyard, the other guard passes me without a second glance. I can smell the whiskey oozing from his pores and surrounding him like a fog. I can smell it through the musky, rank smell of my feces-smeared body. The guard looks young, not more than seventeen, and certainly not over twenty. His watch cap is cocked crookedly over his closely shaved head, and not a single strand of facial hair sprouted over the smooth face. His blue eyes stare straight ahead, unfocused and watery as his feet feel their way to his bunk amongst the gulches and stones. I watch all this from deep within the folds of the blanket, keeping my other eye on my query.

Savage finally locates his lunch pail, gathers his bearings as best he can, and picks himself up. After dusting his hands off and brushing at his uniform half-heartedly, he resumes his drunken stumble. "Spare a penny?" I mumble in perfect English as he staggers by.

He turns to face me, his face contorted in the Jack Savage rage I knew all too well. "Why ya' filthy fo'ckin' begg'ar," he yells, arms gesticulating wildly. "Think I 's a gonna wor-aigh all night long 'n then give a basta'd the like's ah ya' a copp-aighr?" He stumbles over to me and viciously kicks me a few times. "Fo'ck ya' then!"

Out of the corner of my eye I can see the other guard has turned and is watching, not really processing what is taking place. It registers. He laughs. A line of saliva runs down his smooth face. Confident he poses no threat, I smash the rock held in my right hand into Savage's left knee with as much force as I can muster. A loud crack resounds, and Savage falls to the ground clutching his left leg and screaming in pain. The other guard drops his lunch pail without caution and foolishly runs to Savage's aid. As he leans down over Savage's body I deftly slip the long rusty knife between the clavicle and scapula and thrust dorsally. Metal easily slices cloth, skin, and tissue. The spinal cord cleanly severs about an inch below the base of the neck. The young boy feels no pain and just falls limp. The blood drains from Savage's usually ruddy face as he witnesses the other guard's demise through his own pain and tears. He knows. Deep down in his soul, he knows. I give him the gift of sweet blackness with a fierce blow to the base of his skull.

Both men lie inert now on the ground. I move quickly, dragging the boy as deep into the forest as I can before I am met with a large felled tree. The trunk of the tree lies slightly off the ground near the top where its thick branches have kept the trunk from touching. I stuff the body in the space made by the branches between the trunk and rich soil. After hastily covering the corpse with a thick layer of dirt and dead leaves I back sweep my way out of the area to make the boy's presence there is almost undetectable. The buzzards will soon give it away. An amateurish hiding place, but I am a hunted man and dare not waste precious time doing a thorough job.

Sweat beads on my brow as I emerge from the forest though my breath still ejaculates forth in little clouds of fog. The sun is well on its ascent and daylight not being an ally, I scramble to haul Myrrh from her hiding place and sling the inert Jack Savage across the great beast's rump. Having no hiding place for the body, I must ride back to my little camp by skirting the roadways and cutting through fields. My progress is retarded three times when I spot people on the roads. I use my concealment techniques and blend with my surroundings best I can. The gentleman on horseback just trots by me, noticing not a thing, but the two farmers, one on foot herding an ox, and another on a buckboard, laden with earthenware jars, sense me. They are men of the earth, wrought from what they can tease from soil, sun, and water. They know when something is not right. And while they can't not put their finger on my presence, just a mere stones throw away, I can tell by the way they look about they sense something to be amiss. For their lives' sake they pass without incident. Thankfully, Myrrh is content to just nibble on whatever roots may be while the people pass. She reminds me so much of Stahlhand I am sorry I am going to have to be abandoning her in the near future.

Morning birds still twitter when I finally reach my little encampment at the edge of the field. I have to wait for nightfall to complete my mission, so a long day stretches ahead of me. *Scheisse, I should've waited to catch him on his way to work, not home!* I curse myself, but there's nothing that can be about it now. I just hope Savage, like Bambury, is a lone bachelor and nobody will miss him. No use in worrying about it now. After tearing the blanket into strips and tightly binding and gagging Savage, I sit down to wait. Savage looks like a trussed up pig, ankles bound to wrists. He came around after a bit, eyes blinking wide with fear. "Well, well, well Mr. Savage, appears the fly is now the spider, eh?" I laughed. The irony seemed lost on Savage because he did not answer.

The hours drag by with agonizing slowness, even for one accustomed to the long hours of prison, and all the while thoughts swirl madly around inside my brain. What if the posse comes across me…the farmer will surely come looking for his delinquent horse…some children playing may discover me; will I kill them?

Softly, my lips form solace, "…which giveth us the victory through our Lord Jesus Christ. Therefore, my beloved brethren, be ye steadfast, unmoveable, always abounding in the work of the Lord…" The words of the Good Book bring comfort as I recite lines I learned in English during my days of incarceration. The Lord is my new king, a salve on my soul, and during this long day, the most trying of my life, I found comfort in the knowledge that I was not working alone in my quest against evil.

Chapter 67

Patti Savage was nearly sixty years old and looked every year of her life. The years had literally lain so heavily on her broad shoulders that she was shrinking year by year; she knew because she now had trouble reaching things she once could reach with no problem. Her smallish figure that had hopped a ship bound for America over thirty years ago was now rotund and heavy, and her flowing mane of brown hair had been replaced with a small, wispy, white bun of hair. She had become matronly in her old age, her former Irish spark beaten out of her by life and five kids.

Once again, Jack hadn't come home for breakfast, not that that was anything out of the ordinary. Sometimes he got drunk and passed out at work and other times he stopped at any number of haunts for a lip-full on his way home in the morning. The Savage's youngest, Riley, was the only Savage still living at home. The other boys were over the age of fourteen and out in the world working or serving apprenticeships. But Riley was eight, and if you asked Patti they had had him way too late, but Catholicism didn't care if one was too old or too tired. Patti was just too tired to have a little ragamuffin tearing about the house. "Where's Papa?" the boy asked over a breakfast of gruel and bread.

"Aye, I dunno now. Held up at wor-aigh prob'bly," she told the lad while motioning for him to hurry up and eat.

"I can't wait to get home from school and show him the kite I built!" Riley cried with the unbridled enthusiasm youngsters have, even those beaten by alcoholic fathers. He gobbled down the last of the breakfast, picked up his tin lunch pail and ran out the door, late for his studies as usual. Patti just sighed and began clearing the dishes. She put Jack's breakfast off to the side and covered it with a piece of cheesecloth to keep off the flies. He'd be home eventually, too liquored up to even eat, fall into bed and spend the entire day in a drunken stupor then exercise his marital rights before staggering back to his beloved prison to start the cycle all over again.

Finally, Patti settled on the idea that he might actually have been held up at the prison doing something productive. Jack had told her there had been a breakout and small riot, three…four…five days ago? She finished up the dishes and headed out back to do the wash, thankful for the momentary peace. All morning as she scrubbed and pounded at the clothes in the tub of soapy water, she expected Jack to burst in but he never came. And all afternoon as she mended clothes and sewed seeds in the garden she watched for him but nor did he come then. As the sun fell from the sky Patti figured there had to be some sort of problem at the prison, and Jack had to stay right through, which was fine with her, for it meant a little more money next pay. She moved Riley's kite from on top of her sewing box, where he had stored it when he finished it the night before, and began the family mending. *I surely have a lot of mending to do*, she thought despondently.

Chapter 68

Darkness came about, as it inevitably does. Jack had been in and out of consciousness throughout the day. He would struggle until exhausted, and then pass out. I figure he had repeated his little cycle at least three, if not four times. Finally, he fought not, but merely lay, bound by his fears and chains. He knew.

I wait until the witching hour. No flaming torches…yet. By my best guess, if the two missing guards hadn't been discovered during the day, then surely when they fail to show up for work this evening their absence will be suspect. I know when that happens more men will be hastily deputized. And more men will swing by the general store for a pint of amber liquid to fortify themselves against another chilly, long night. So I wait patiently for the flaming torches to come. They never do. When they fail to appear and the world is cloaked in inky blackness I *know* the time is now.

I tie my wooden contraption to Myrrh by a harness I had fashioned during the day using a length of rope. She dutifully drags the big wooden cross across the field, bumping and jarring rocks loose, catching on depressions, but never falling apart. At the edge of the field, near a low stone fence, and under a great tree, its low branches spreading out over the roadway leading into Ossining, I untie it. Myrrh happily trots back across the field with me to collect Savage. We find him straining against his bindings once again, thick ropey veins standing out from his neck; his one last ditch effort. I shake my head. "Your time has come," I plainly tell him, reaching down and slinging him up onto my gaunt frame. A grunt is my only reply. I throw him over the broad back of Myrrh and collect my tools. Together, we walk languorously toward the tree; I wanted to savor the moment. An owl hoots in the distance. I see the silhouette in the sky and know a mouse will be a mouse and the owl will be itself, and come morning, the mouse will be no more.

Once under the tree, I work like a possessed man, only pausing to step back and admire my handiwork. I hitch Myrrh up, and she strains under the weight, but never falters. My master plan complete, I step close to my quarry and proclaim loudly, "Denn also hat Gott die Welt geliebt, da? Er seinen eingebornen Sohn gab, auf da? alle, die an ihn glauben, nicht verloren werden, sondern das ewige Leben haben." I pause, then spit out, "Here is *your* everlasting life you piece of shit! Let the world witness your black soul!" I launch a large glob of spittle right onto Savage's cheek. He doesn't flinch. I climb upon Myrrh and ride south leaving the wind to whisper, "'For God so loved the world...'"

Chapter 69

Tommy Montgomery lived in a log cabin two and a half miles north of Ossining. He was a fair-haired boy, slender, and short for being ten years of age. In fact, he was short enough to pass for an eight-year-old. Tommy dreamed of one day becoming a soldier. He would secretly study the soldiers that came into the store he worked in to buy chocolates, licorice roots, quarts of beer, and other treats. Soldiers were constantly coming into the store, for the store was very near the train station, and the soldiers had it timed just so that they could disembark and load up at the store while the train was changing passengers. Tommy's general store did quite a brisk business from train passengers, most of them soldiers. And while Tommy measured out candies into small paper sacks he drank in every detail of their eloquent uniforms and professional demeanor. Most days on his way to work, Tommy would march like he envisioned a soldier would. Tommy liked to shoulder big sticks, the size of muskets, and whistle marching music to and from the general store. One of these days, maybe when he was twelve or thirteen, he reckoned he would run away and join the army. He would make his mother proud when he came home sporting his fancy new uniform, complete with tall black boots, shiny medals, a macaroni hat, and his pocket overflowing with money. He imagined his dear mother kissing him, and thanking him for finally getting enough money necessary to get Papa better.

His father, a farmer, had been kicked in the head by a mule eleven months ago and had lain in bed every day since. Dr. Warren, had done everything he could to make his Papa right, or so Mama said. But Papa still lay in bed groaning, sometimes screaming in the night. Tommy could imagine the pillowcases, hanging to dry in the yard of their log cabin, large brown spots on them from the holes Dr. Warren had to cut in Papa's head to, "relief the pressure," as he had put it…or that's what Tommy thought he said. Dr. Warren was really nice to Tommy and he liked him. Dr. Warren would always bring his brother and sisters and him beautiful chocolates, and sometimes, if he wasn't in a hurry would tell the boys fantastic stories about pirates and soldiers and battles. Dr. Warren didn't charge much either, Mama had told him. "He does it 'cause Papa used to supply him with medicine, and he wants him to get better so he can keep making it," is what Mama said. Tommy figured she was referring to those bottles in the barn Papa filled with a medicine he made in the woods from his leftover corn crops. But the bottles were long gone, all given to Dr. Warren in payment, and Tommy hoped he would cure his father soon.

Since that fateful day, Tommy, along with his older brother, Abraham, had to get jobs in order to keep the family from starving to death. Tommy and Abraham hardly made enough money to feed themselves, their mother and father, and three sisters. So Mama and his sisters tended a small vegetable patch to supplement their meager earnings. And, combined with the boys' meager wages, the family held on by a thread.

Tommy found work as a clerk for the cranky Mr. Leon Collier at the only general store in Ossining. It was a grand old store, holding much wonder for a small boy like Tommy. He was proud to work in such a place, even if Mr. Collier did cuff him once in a while for the various distractions a small boy in a place of magic can endeavor upon. For the most part, Tommy was an honest, hard worker, and bustled about the place from six in the morning until six in the evening. Tommy had to make sure everything in the store was stocked: from the great kegs of nails, to the bolts of colorful cloths imported from England, to the sides of hams hanging form the rafters in burlap, to the great glass candy jars lining the sagging wooden shelving, to the boxes and boxes of colored tallow candles. In addition to stocking items, Tommy had to wait on every customer that walked through the door. Mr. Collier just sat in a rocker, smoking his clay pipe, and making sure nobody, including Tommy, stole anything. Occasionally, Mr. Collier would greet an acquaintance, but he mainly sat and rocked.

On this crisp, early spring morning, as Tommy jubilantly marched to work, excited that it was Saturday, and therefore, he had the morrow off. Under his left arm was tucked a greasy paper sack with his dinner, a slab of ham between two pieces of thick homemade bread, and nestled in his right arm was a four-foot stick. The stick was almost as large as Tommy, but he had it balanced perfectly in his cupped hand. Tommy usually didn't pass anyone on his way to work at five o'clock in the morning, and today was no exception. As he crested the hill that led into Ossining a strange sight greeted him. At first Tommy was puzzled by what appeared to be an apparition in front of him, but as he drew closer his horror grew. Tommy's fear crescendoed.

The dinner and stick fell to the ground as the small boy fled past the horrific sight. Mr. Collier found him some time later, around six, crouched, shivering at the general store's front door. After some coaxing, he was able to learn what frightened the boy so much. By the time Mr. Collier had rounded up the sheriff and a handful of deputies, other people had stumbled across the gruesome sight.

Chapter 70

Mr. Collier and his posse found Jack Savage suspended from the large willow tree, nailed naked to a crucifix, slowly twisting in the wind. The sharpened wooden pegs, usually used in building houses, were nailed through each wrist and both feet. A large stain of black-colored blood had formed under the roughly hewn crucifix and had soaked into the dusty dirt. Most of the men present, about twelve now, with more men arriving, were seasoned outdoorsmen, used to scratching a living from the earth, but more than one could be heard in the bushes puking his innards out. "What in the hell is that on his head?" the sheriff exclaimed loudly as he arrived, reining his horse in. He was referring to a strange symbol carved into Savage's forehead. The symbol consisted of two line segments. Each line made a right angle and then another right angle in the opposite direction with the two line segments imposed upon each other. None of the men present answered for none knew. The sheriff spoke up again, not getting an answer, "Who the hell could've done something like this?"

It was a rhetorical question, but one of the sheriff's lean grizzled deputies quietly said, "I think we know who don' this. That same son'bitch that tortured poor Bam-brey." The man, seemingly unperturbed by the gruesome sight leaned over the back of his horse and expelled a large stream of brown tobacco juice and continued, "Seem to me, he got it out for guards. They best be more careful 'lest they end up like this poo' basta'd." With that, Savage let out a low moan and lolled his head to one side.

"Holy Mother!" the sheriff proclaimed. "Why he's…he's still alive! Cut him down boys!" His deputies, with the help of Mr. Collier and a few other men quickly got to work cutting the thick piece of rope that suspended the cross in the air. The cross fell with a mighty thud. "For Christsakes, boys, carefully, lets not kill him then!" the sheriff shouted excitedly. The men swarmed around the inert Savage and tugged fiercely at the wooden pegs, finally removing them with much difficulty. They stemmed the blood flow by tying makeshift scarves, pieces of filthy shirt, and other random pieces of cloth around the wounds. The men boosted Savage up and threw him over the back of the soft-spoken deputy's horse. The soft-spoken deputy hopped on the back of one of his contemporaries' horses and off the posse galloped to the center of town, to the office of Dr. Kerouak.

Chapter 71

Dr. Kerouak answered the door in his nightshirt looking confused and a little worse for wear. In fact, he felt like a piece of the horse manure located in the filthy quagmire Ossining called its road system. Dr. Kerouak spent most of his evenings in the local saloon, fortifying himself with whiskey, women, and playing the occasional card game, and therefore he usually didn't go to bed until the sun rose. Dr. Kerouak figured he didn't need to schedule any teeth pullings until the afternoon, that way, once the depression set in that *was* his profession it was time to head to the saloon. Nice little arrangement, or so Dr. Kerouak thought.

On this particular morning, Dr. Kerouak's head had just hit the pillow not twenty-seven minutes earlier when a violent pounding on his door woke him up to the most gruesome spectacle of his life. "Shit!" is all the good doctor said. Then, recovering somewhat, "Bring him on in." The men dragged the unconscious man in.

As the sheriff brushed passed he patted Jack on the shoulder and chuckled, "Ya' know we normally wouldn't call on you, but with Dr. Warren and all…Well, you know…" The sheriff trailed off before heading on into Dr. Kerouak's office to inspect his men's work. The doctor could hear the sheriff in his office congratulating the men on their fine work.

Mr. Collier, having come back with the posse, poked his head in to investigate. He was unusually animated today and with good reason; nothing this exciting had happened in Ossining since he could remember and he had lived in Ossining all his life. "Come with me," Mr. Collier said wearily to Dr. Kerouak and he motioned with his head. The doctor followed Mr. Collier three shops down the wooden sidewalk until they came to Mr. Collier's general store. He fumbled with the keys and unlocked the door. Once inside, Mr. Collier retrieved an earthenware jug from under the counter, produced two cut glass tumblers and poured a healthy slog into each glass. "To steady nerves," the owner said. They clinked glasses.

"Thanks, Leon," Dr. Kerouak said to Mr. Collier, addressing him by his first name for the first time in his life.

"You'll need it," was the only reply he got. "That monster made a mess of that man."

Chapter 72

Jack Savage lingered. The wounds turned gangrenous, and even the nurses with the stoutest stomachs wouldn't go near him, for the stench of the festering wounds was nearly unbearable. His pain was so excruciating he had to be restrained else he hurt himself with one of his fits. In his fevered state, Savage lay in sweat soaked sheets, screaming at hallucinations brought about by the fever. He'd sit up; yellow eyes wide, making wild proclamations about a man with the strength of an ogre, the speed of lightning, and reflexes of a bobcat. "Lock ya'r doors! He's coming to get me! He'll kill us all!"

By the fourth day, the violence had gotten so bad that Dr. Kerouak took to administering extreme amounts of opium to settle him. He had done all he could, he figured. After all, he was just a dentist not a medical doctor. Even if Savage broke the fever he would be severely crippled for life, for the spikes had done irreversible damage to the hands and feet by severing blood vessels and turning the extremities necrotic. By the fifth day Dr. Kerouak performed his first amputations, removing the black and shriveled appendages, but not before tying one on with Mr. Collier over at the general store. "Sure is a shame, 'bout the boy; he ain't been right since," Mr. Collier said in his usual even manner, referring to Tommy. "Mother said he just hides in his bed all day, won't speak, hardly eats, and shivers like he's cold."

"Shame, cryin' shame," Dr. Kerouak said belting down the whiskey and slamming his tumbler down on the counter for Mr. Collier to refill it. "One more, then I gotta go take of Savage. His hands an' feet went rotten."

"Here, take some of this," Mr. Collier said adding hastily, "on the house, of course. Dr. Warren is always coming to get it. I suppose it

269

helps out you medical men." He reached behind him and put a tin of *Dr. Swügechewnz's* on the counter.

"Thanks. Never tried the stuff before," Dr. Kerouak said, pocketing the tin.

Part V: Clarity

Chapter 73

My new cell is much nicer than my previous one at Sing Sing. It is made not of the dreadful white marble, but rather thick wooden timbers. Escape is not an option, at least not while the door is bolted, for I have inspected every inch of the rather spacious cell and the timbers are bolted together snugly, no Achilles tendon. Hay is heaped in one corner and a commode in another. The commode, essentially a wooden seat with a tiny hole for waste to go down, is real step up from the slop buckets at Sing Sing. *Scheisse*, I can almost *see* Sing Sing. Hay dust, suspended in the air, swirls about me in little violent whirlpools and eddies in the sunshine shining through the small barred window as I pace around with the ferocity of a caged lion. The newfound time on my hands gives me ample time to think, and so I work on wearing a path in the jail cell.

My life finally made sense February 23, 1840. God's plan, the course of my life, was revealed to me then. Wilhelm Oister, my old society buddy, that I had not seen since he had graduated over a year before showed up at my doorstep at number eight Alb-Ueberla Street. "Wilhelm, so good to see you!" I cried upon opening the door, "What brings you here?" I asked innocently, figuring he was back in town as a visiting alumnus.

"Gregor, it has been…a long time. What are you doing?" he asked mysteriously

"Well, I was just brushing up on some applied mathematic theory for our exit exams, why?"

"The time has come. Pack your things for an overnight trip."

"Where the hell are we going?" I demanded, noting the lateness of the hour. "It's dark, for Christ's sake!"

"I'll wait on the walk," he simply said, turned, and walked to two magnificent black stallions standing on the street, pawing and snorting. I ran upstairs and threw some things together in a small grip before calling to Frau Grüner and bounding out the door. We rode hard. The roads became more and more familiar.

At one point I pulled my trotting stallion up even with Wilhelm's and called, "Where are we going?"

"We'll be there soon," he replied back. As we neared the town of my birth I felt as if I had been suddenly pulled from a smoke filled room and led out into the fresh air and sunshine. *Of course! The mysterious donors to Neue Dämmerung, the unidentified riders from my childhood, the "abandoned castle."*

Sure enough, just below the town of St. Goar, we branched off on a trail overgrown with weeds and brush. In another mile or so, we stopped short at the gates of Schloss Rheinfels. Wilhelm emitted a sharp whistle and a small door set in the great gate opened. We rode through. I had the feeling that eyes were watching me even though I couldn't see a soul. In the empty castle yard we gave the reigns of our lathered stallions to a man about our age with a two wicked-looking scars crossing his face. One of them merged with the left corner of his lip and left him with a lopsided looking, perpetual grin. I absentmindedly fingered the right side of my face. We didn't speak to the man; Wilhelm motioned me to follow him. Wilhelm led me to a grand banquet hall with a long wooden table set under Prussian military banners and rich tapestries. I sat next to a roaring fire in the six by ten foot fireplace and ate cold game pie with Wilhelm. We ate in silence, though I was brimming with questions. After we ate Wilhelm simply said, "Get some sleep. I'll come for you early in the morning."

"Is this?" I asked motioning toward his right arm while I spoke. He nodded and walked out of the long hall, his footfalls enveloped by the massive bearskins rugs. I stretched out on a rug near the fire and soon was fast asleep.

Wilhelm shook me awake. "Here, drink this," he said and handed me a steaming mug. I had just enough time to down the bitter, unsweetened tea before Wilhelm consulted his watch. "Come on; we have to go. We have a six o'clock appointment." I followed Wilhelm through a twisting maze of hallways, empty rooms, up unlit stone staircases until we finally came to a heavy wooden door. Wilhelm knocked loudly and a muffled sound replied from within. We entered, and I was greeted by a peculiar little man seated at a desk amongst stacks of paper. His office was large, probably the former lord's stateroom. It commanded a breathtaking view of St. Goar, I could see as I snatched a quick peek out the narrow windows at the gray dawn. The little man, lord of the room, had tufts of white hair surrounding his baldhead and wore simple canvas pants with suspenders off his shoulders, hanging down around his knees. When he got up, his cotton undershirt was unbuttoned halfway down his chest and marked with numerous stains of past meals. His barrel chest was covered in a thick mat of hair that protruded from the unbuttoned shirt. Wilhelm offered him a smart salute; the man saluted back and offered me his hand. I shook it.

"Gregor, I would like to introduce you to Commander Otto Werschulz. Commander, Gregor Opfer."

"Please, sit," the man said, his tone cool; the voice of someone that was used to being obeyed. We sat in the wooden chairs in front of Commander Weschulz's desk. He raised an eyebrow, "So, Herr Opfer, I guess you have many questions about why you are here." He paused.

"Yes," I replied dutifully.

"Well, Herr Opfer, due to your intellect and other connections," he motioned with his hand in a vague manner, I assumed he was referring the Neue Dämmerung, "you have been selected to join an elite governmental organization run by the *kaiser* himself." He stopped to let that sink in before continuing, "We are the Friedrich Wilhelm's police force. We keep the peace within the borders, and eliminate and threats to the crown—in Prussia or abroad."

"Are you military?" I interjected.

"Sort of; we technically draw funding the same as the military, and many soldiers here go on to other branches of the military, in high-ranking positions of course, but we are more informal around here. We prefer to think of ourselves as…above the military. And by that I mean we have greater freedoms, and more liberties…more room to maneuver, unofficially. Which," his voice went up a decibel, "we do! Around here our soldiers, or agents as well call them, operate independently most the time. We find it more effective not to be fettered by the same laws of combat the traditional military is chained to."

Weschulz continued, "Our agents draw a salary of seven hundred marks a year in addition to anything confiscated from an enemy agent, are issued a private horse, and are guaranteed any job in the government they wish after they have served…What do you say, my boy?" I sat thinking, not wanting to make a rash decision. "Herr Opfer, this is the opportunity of a lifetime, a man with your skills could get you far…I don't think you have anything better on your plate right now." He leaned forward and his gray eyes pierced me to my soul.

"All right, I'll do it," I said, realizing I had *no* other choice, these people basically owned me.

"Good, good." The Commander grinned the grin of a cat after swallowing a bird.

"So, how does this all work?" I asked. "What do I do now?"

The Commander smoothed his white hair and toyed with a pair of specs on his desk. "It's really quite simple really. The kaiser issues orders through the general of his armies, Kapoc. And if General Kapoc decides the mission is unsuitable for the standard military, he gives them directly to me. I, in turn, assign them to specific men or teams of men. Simple, very simple," he said furiously stroking his fringe of hair. "We also gather intelligence and give it back to the kaiser."

I interrupted the commander. "Does this organization have a name?"

He chuckled, "Sure, Die Sonneleute. The kaiser himself came up with the name because coincides with the strength and omnipotence of the organization." He consulted a pocket watch, "I must be going. Nice to meet you, Opfer, I shall see you, and will be looking in on your progress. Oister will see that you get everything you need." I guessed the meeting was over. Wilhelm saluted, and we left.

"What now?" I asked, a million questions swirling around in my brain. I felt sick in my stomach, almost like I had signed my soul over, but there was nothing I could about it now. I had unwittingly become obligated when I joined Neue Dämmerung

"Nothing. You go back to Heidelberg, finish school and report back to Schloss Rheinfels when you get out in three weeks. But before that…" He led me to the stables where the perpetual smile man met us, the same one that took the horses last night. "He needs a tattoo," Wilhelm told the man, and jerked his head in my direction.

"Surely," he said issuing me a full grin.

While the perpetual smile man cut at my arm with peculiar tiny knives and poured black ink into the wounds, Wilhelm talked at me to take my mind off the pain. I could hardly answer, for a wooden dowel was inserted between my teeth. Wilhelm prattled on like nothing was out of the ordinary, "…it's an eastern technique called tattooing. It's a permanent badge, so to speak. It identifies members of Die Sonneleute. This," he said pointing at his own tattoo, "is called a swastika. It comes from the Middle Eastern countries, specifically Egypt. The pharaohs devised it as a symbol of the sun, a symbol of purity, power and beauty…essentially a reflection of the power of themselves and their empire. Hence the name, People of the Sun."

"It's an interesting symbol, for sure," I grind out through clenched jaws, inspecting Wilhelm's tattoo through painful tears. "You will be glad to be living back in the town of your birth, no?" Wilhelm asked, almost nonchalantly. I let out a groan as one of the tiny knives cut too deeply.

"But, how do you know…" I trailed off, and let out another groan.

Wilhelm's face blossomed into a smirk, "Wait, wait, until this is over. All will be revealed, my friend," is all he enigmatically said.

Chapter 74

I rode hard back to Heidelberg on my new horse with my shirt sleeve wet with fresh blood oozing slowly from the freshly inked badge on my arm. My horse was a great black stallion named Demmerhung. However ancient he was, he still had a few good rides left in him. I finished out the year at the University of Heidelberg, graduating at the top of my class at the tender age of twenty. Two days after commencement I had packed all my belongings, and how painfully few I had, save my father's clock and my cherished Duellgesellschaft uniform. I kissed a tearful Frau Grüner goodbye, promised to keep in touch then cantered away on Demmerhung, my footlocker tied over his massive back.

Training started immediately. Phase one consisted of physical training. Myself and twenty other agents from across the German states, other members of Neue Dämmerung, subjected our bodies to rigorous physical activities in order to condition and tune them. The weights, combat training, calisthenics took place inside the castle while the runs and swims took place in the surrounding countryside of my boyhood. Phase two consisted of classroom training with practical applications. The courses covered such subjects as camouflage concealment, language—in which I knew more than the instructor, infiltration tactics, and information gathering and dissemination. Phase three consisted of going on tactical operations with operatives or teams of operatives and applying the classroom knowledge. A year after beginning the program, I was a full-fledged operative of Die Sonneleute along with twelve other young men that completed the class.

The guard's baton smacking the bars set in the heavy wooden door snaps me from my meditational state and back to reality. I hear a jingling key ring and the heavy wooden door swings slowly open. "Time to go," he says with a jerk of his head. I know what the jerk signifies, but somehow I am not afraid. Behind the guard stands the sheriff of Ossining, four deputies, as well as an additional guard from the Ossining county jail.

"I won't give you any trouble; no need for all the men," I calmly state to the assembled group of men.

"All the same," the sheriff replies pulling at his handlebar mustache, "you have a history of violence, so don't try anything funny." I shrug and step out of the cell and into the dusty courtyard beside the courthouse, jail, and sheriff's office combination building.

Not a cloud in the sky, I note. The guards grab each of my arms and march me toward the town square; my crippled gait slowing their pace to a crawl. The deputies follow behind, hands nervously gripping their muskets. A large crowd has gathered in the town square of Ossining to see the only hanging on the docket today, and as I enter the town square a hush falls over the crowd.

The guards march me up the stairs and bind my hands and feet. The last guard off the platform whispers in my ear, "Hey, Opfer, hangin' ain't so bad once you get the swing of things." He laughs to himself and steps off the platform.

Chapter 75

The authorities caught me when I tried to hop a freight ship bound for England. It is hard to conceal so many of my features, so the American authorities had little trouble putting out a wanted poster for a man with, "a jagged scar on face…cripple…design on right arm." I had secured passage on the packet ship using money I had stolen from a house I broke into in lower Manhattan. I should've known better than to return to the city to make my escape, but maybe deep down I was tired of running, tired of fighting, just plain…tired. The captain of the vessel, a decidedly American fellow, sailing under an Argentinean flag, took my money then contacted the metropolitan police. The night before the ship was scheduled to set sail a detachment of soldiers and policemen stormed the ship and snatched me from my bunk. I was extradited back to Ossining in very short order, where my latest crimes were committed, stood trial, and was condemned to death. June 29 was the exact date of my sentencing. After the quick trial and sentencing, I was put inside a hot, but spacious cell to await my date with the hangman: a glorious end to an illustrious career.

Chapter 76

The crowd remains silent as the local circuit judge mounts the steps just after the last deputy steps off. He pulls out a paper and reads the sentence, "Gregor Opfer, you have been convicted of murder as per New York State law. A panel of your peers found you guilty. You are to be hanged by the neck until you are dead." He continues with a little moral monologue. The crowd waits with bated breath. "We thought prison might rehabilitate you and save you." He pauses as if awaiting an answer.

I decide to give him one. Little beads of perspiration to run down my face, not from fear but from the hot sun high overhead; I wipe at my face with my shoulder and look the white wigged judge in the face and reply, "Prison made me an animal. But that is of little matter; I was saved years ago."

The judge's eyes widened a bit at my answer, then he turned to the crowd and says mockingly, "Really? He is obviously confused!" With a contemptuous snort, he asks, "When might that be *Mr.* Opfer?"

Not playing for the crowd, I stare him straight in the eye, "On the original good Friday, sometime between noon and three in the afternoon." Not expecting my answer, the judge stops showboating for the audience and nods to the executioner. The trap snaps. The rope snaps. And thus my neck snaps.

As the final brain waves sound through my brain, I think of the most peculiar thing. When I later questioned Wilhelm on the day of my tattooing how he had known I was from St. Goar he had only answered then in his usual doublespeak, "Die Sonneleute knows everything. We *always* knew, even when you were a second-year student, hell, even before. You were chosen. You *are* one of the chosen. In time you will figure it out…" It finally made sense, and I'm glad I figured it out while I still had time.

Epilogue:
Freedom at Last

Night fell over Ossining slowly, the way it always does in the early summertime. Clouds gathered and the town square emptied to escape the drizzle of rain. The people of Ossining moved the festivities to the local saloon. The corpse of Gregor Opfer slowly twisted in the slight breeze, the hemp rope making a lonely creaking sound in the silent square. The fine rain saturated the filthy rags that passed as clothes, and washed the dirt and grime from Gregor's body. Emerging from the muted background of laughter, but not from the saloon, a lone figure shakily hobbled to the gallows using two crutches secured to his upper arms by leather straps, for he had no hands. The man walked very rigidly, almost as if he had no shins. He turned his face upwards, a face hideously disfigured from a peculiar symbol etched in his face, and spit onto the suspended corpse with as much contempt as he could muster. The sheriff, standing in the shadows keeping the peace, heard the man spew forth, "Jesus Christ was the fir'st non-violent rev'lut'nary, ya' fo'ck! I hope ya' buh'rn in hell fa'hr eter'nity!"

Printed in the United States
58884LVS00003B/103-105

9 781424 123537